ASHRAM ASSASSIN

The Paperback Sleuth

Also by Andrew Cartmel and available from Titan Books

THE PAPERBACK SLEUTH
Death in Fine Condition

THE VINYL DETECTIVE
Written in Dead Wax
The Run-Out Groove
Victory Disc
Flip Back
Low Action
Attack and Decay
Noise Floor

The Paperback Sleuth

ASHRAM ASSASSIN

Andrew Cartmel

TITAN BOOKS

The Paperback Sleuth: Ashram Assassin
Print edition ISBN: 9781803367927
E-book edition ISBN: 9781803367934

Published by Titan Books
A division of Titan Publishing Group Ltd
144 Southwark Street, London SE1 0UP
www.titanbooks.com

First edition: June 2024
10 9 8 7 6 5 4 3 2 1

This is a work of fiction. All of the characters, organisations, and events portrayed in this novel are either products of the author's imagination or are used fictitiously. Any resemblance to actual persons, living or dead (except for satirical purposes), is entirely coincidental.

A CIP catalogue record for this title is available from the British Library.

Printed and bound by CPI Group (UK) Ltd, Croydon, CR0 4YY

For Kelsey Short,
superb actor and steadfast ally.

"Resentment is like drinking poison
and waiting for the other person to die."

—St Augustine

1: AT LEAST ONE

You might have thought Cordelia would have become accustomed, perhaps even acclimatised, to being confronted with sudden death.

After all, in the course of her young life she had already seen two men die in front of her.

(And at least one of those she had killed herself.)

But none of this did anything to lessen the abrupt, deep thrill of horror she felt when she stepped out of the gentle autumn sunlight into the cool shadows of the trees and saw the body lying there on the ground in front of her.

Admittedly, she did also think, *Oh shit. Here we go again.*

That was on the Saturday.

2: SET A THIEF

On the preceding Wednesday, Cordelia was thinking, *Set a thief to catch a thief.*

It was a cliché, all right, but an apt one.

And it amused her to reflect on it. Not least because the people who wanted to hire her didn't realise this was exactly what they were proposing.

Edwin did, though.

Edwin was Cordelia's landlord. And he'd lined up this job for her—potentially a juicy lucrative job, thank you very much, Edwin—through one of his girlfriends. Although "one of his girlfriends" made Edwin sound considerably more exciting than he actually was; perhaps "latest girlfriend" would be more accurate.

But even that made him sound undeservedly exciting. Edwin was pretty much dullsville... except in one spectacular regard.

And it was that aspect of him which guaranteed Cordelia made damned sure she paid her rent on time every month.

Anyway, Edwin's latest dreary girlfriend was into yoga. His paramours were always into something like that—growing biodynamic vegetables in their gardens, performing Tai Chi as the sun rose over the village green, going on long boring bicycle rides (Edwin's own special passion) or, in this case, doing lots of yoga.

Lorna, for that was the girlfriend's name, was a regular attendee at the local ashram or, as Cordelia preferred to think of it, mantra-chanting clipjoint. To wit, the Silverlight Yoga Centre on Abbey Avenue.

Cordelia knew it well because she had once been a regular attendee there herself, before being booted out for dealing weed—an activity that had not amused the ashram fascists. As soon as they'd found out about it, they'd summoned Cordelia upstairs to the meeting room for a thorough scolding before drumming her out of the place for good.

As they warmed up to her ejection they'd taken pains to explain it wasn't the fact that she'd been dealing weed per se that they found so objectionable. Oh no, they were far too hip for that. What they really couldn't tolerate was the degrading exploitation of their premises for purposes of rapacious money-grubbing capitalist transactions.

The fact that the meeting room in which they reprimanded Cordelia was situated above the ashram's *gift shop*, where you could buy yourself sustainably farmed hemp yoga mats in a variety of attractive colours for—wait for it—300 quid a pop did not escape Cordelia, and she didn't scruple to point this out to the admonitory morons, along with a few other home truths along similar lines.

This drove them batshit crazy with rage because, of course, Cordelia was right and they knew it. But hell hath no fury like a hypocritical yoga capitalist in loose-fitting orange pyjamas when you call him out. And, as satisfying as Cordelia's tirade had been (delivered at volume and well spiced with profanity), it didn't prevent her from being booted out.

Ever since then, she had nursed a grudge against the Silverlight Yoga Centre. It wasn't so much that she missed the opportunity to deal weed there—she'd phased that out anyway, as she was earning enough from her vintage paperback hustle—but she missed the yoga itself, not to mention the regular festive feasts provided at the ashram. These were really spectacular curry banquets that caused her mouth to water even now.

How dare the orange-pyjama-wearing bastards tell her to leave and never come back?

Well, as luck would have it, Cordelia now had a chance to make them eat humble pie. To eat crow. To eat humble crow pie. Possibly curried.

Because Edwin's girlfriend, the aforementioned Lorna, had told him about a robbery at the yoga centre. A robbery of, wait for it, books. And not just books—*paperbacks*.

Who would steal paperbacks? you might well ask. And the answer would be Cordelia, for a start.

Not that she'd robbed the yoga centre. Indeed, she'd known nothing about the heist until Edwin told her about it. But she had, once upon a time, stolen some paperbacks herself. Rather a lot of rather rare and valuable paperbacks.

That theft had landed her in a good deal of trouble. Potentially terminal trouble. But good old Edwin had helped her get out of that trouble. Thank you, Edwin. And because he'd provided this assistance, it had been unavoidable that he should learn all about the cause of the trouble: Cordelia's bijou book burglary.

So when Edwin heard through Lorna that the Silverlight Yoga Centre had suffered a break-in and were desperate to get the books back—were, in fact, willing to pay a tidy sum to get them back— he'd thought...

Set a thief to catch a thief.

"You didn't think I might have done the robbery myself?" said Cordelia when he told her about it.

"Of course not," said Edwin. He spun the wheel of the bicycle he was repairing, or maintaining, or something, and smiled at Cordelia through the spinning spokes.

Edwin was a tall, lean bloke with untidy sandy hair. He was almost good-looking… if you liked goofy types who did the *Guardian* crossword puzzle with the tip of the tongue slightly protruding from the corner of the mouth in concentration, and whose idea of a good time was listening to the opera on Saturday night on Radio 3.

"I know there's no love lost between you and the Silverlight Yoga people," said Edwin. "But they weren't your sort of books. The sort of books you were likely to pinch, anyway."

The two of them were standing outside the house they shared in the leafy London suburb of Barnes—Edwin ensconced in the flat at the back of the ground floor, Cordelia in the attic room at the very top of the house—accompanied by Rainbottle, Edwin's dog.

Cordelia had become Edwin's lodger soon after she left university, when she was starting her vintage paperback business. Edwin seemed suitably gratified to have a gorgeous (in all modesty) young babe in his attic room—though, very much to his credit, he'd never have dreamed of hitting on her. Which was just as well, because Cordelia couldn't see herself accompanying him on long bicycle rides or helping ponder the *Guardian* crossword.

Rainbottle was sprawled on the grass beside Edwin's beloved bicycle, which was upside down, resting on its saddle and handlebars while Edwin crouched over it and worked on the wheels. He had a specially designed contraption he could have used that would have held the bike handily in place while he ministered to it but, as was the way with these things, it was too much trouble to set it up and he generally ended up doing his bicycle work in a manner similar to this. (It really was remarkable how little trouble something had to be to be too much trouble.)

"They weren't crime novels," continued Edwin, pausing to wipe the sweat of honest labour from his brow. Rainbottle whined in agreement and gave his tail a few experimental whacks against the lawn.

It was true, crime fiction was Cordelia's forte. Or was it her métier? Anyway, it was her thing. "Any idea what sort of books they were?" she asked. "Yoga stuff, I suppose?"

"They said they'd provide a list. They'll email you to arrange a meeting and then they'll give you all the details."

But the thing was, Cordelia wasn't hurting for money and she didn't especially need the work. And, that being the case, it was just too tempting to get her own back on the ashram idiots by bluntly telling them "no" and leaving them in the lurch. After all, who else could they turn to?

So, with cool cordiality and consummate professionalism, she turned the job down flat. She pushed send on the email politely rebuffing them, with a wonderful sense of satisfaction and old wrongs finally righted. Take that, you orange-pyjama-clad fuckers.

And that was that.

Or, at least, that would have been that if fate hadn't then taken a hand.

And shown a considerable dry sense of humour into the bargain.

Because, within minutes of her emailing the ashram and telling them to get lost, a message pinged into her inbox from Murder Silhouette Books.

Murder Silhouette Books was an elegant and well-stocked shop located above a trendy café in Soho. And, as their name suggested, they specialised in crime fiction.

It should have been just the sort of place for Cordelia, except for two factors...

Firstly, their prices were astronomical. True, they had a splendid vintage paperback section that often featured rare titles, in exemplary condition, but they expected you to pay through the nose for them. And if, like Cordelia, you were operating on a margin—attempting to buy low to sell high, hopefully very low and very high—there was no chance of turning a profit on anything purchased there. In fact, their prices were so extortionate that she even hesitated to buy stuff for her own collection.

The other factor that militated against Murder Silhouette Books, in Cordelia's view, was the shop's owner, Duncan Fairwell. A short, hairy, bearded man with an unfortunate passion for argyle tank tops, Fairwell had earned Cordelia's enduring enmity one murky winter afternoon of smoky skies and intermittent rain, several years ago, on her very first visit to the shop.

She had found Fairwell himself sitting behind the counter and manning the till (she would later learn this was a task more usually delegated to a series of vacuously comely young bimbos). Cordelia, excited to have discovered this very promising new bookshop that specialised in her favourite genre, eagerly asked the owner if he had any British Sleuth Hound paperbacks in stock. These vintage beauties were a veritable passion of hers and, at the time, she'd only managed to collect a handful of them. Duncan Fairwell had looked up from his reading matter—a glossy brochure for the estimable Hard Case Crime imprint—and had snapped the single abrupt and very final syllable, "*No.*"

He'd then returned to checking out the Hard Case goodies.

Chastened and disappointed, Cordelia had also been a little angered by his rudeness. But not nearly as angry as she was a couple of minutes later when, feeling it was too much of a defeat to just slink back out of the shop, she'd been half-heartedly poking around, wandering among the rows of bookshelves, and had turned a corner to find herself face to face with an *entire section* labelled in big and highly legible sans-serif letters: British Sleuth Hounds.

It was too implausible to suggest that Fairwell didn't know his own stock. No, he was perfectly aware this rack of books was here.

He had just, for some inexplicable hairy, tank-topped reason of his own, taken one look at Cordelia and instantly conceived a dislike of her, such a dislike that he didn't even want to sell her any of his overpriced books.

Baffled, offended and above all pissed off, Cordelia had then and there conceived her own profound and permanent distaste for Duncan Fairwell, esquire.

Hence it was with somewhat mixed emotions that she now read the email that had just arrived.

It was addressed to all previous customers of Murder Silhouette Books (despite herself, Cordelia had been compelled to buy the occasional, irresistible, item from them over the years) and signed by Betty Fairwell, wife of you-know-who.

It began:

Due to the recent loss of my husband, Duncan, I am now contacting you to let you know...

Given how much she'd hated his (argyle-clad) guts, Cordelia now felt a little bad and retroactively guilty about the dear departed Dunc. She realised she might even miss his hairy, bearded little face frowning at her whenever she dared enter his shop.

But there were no mixed emotions whatsoever when she read further down the email and learned why his widow was contacting all former customers.

As you won't be surprised to learn, Duncan has a huge library of crime fiction, including many very rare and valuable collector's items, at our house in Richmond. Since he no longer has any need for these books, and since I have no interest in them, I will be selling them, on a first come, first served basis, here at our home...

Cordelia had barely read these words before she was out the door.

First come, first served.

Despite racing straight to Richmond as fast as she could, Cordelia wasn't the first to arrive at Betty Fairwell's very large and luxurious house.

It was just over half an hour from the moment Cordelia had received the email to when she hurried through its street entrance, a solid black steel gate set in a white stucco wall, normally designed to keep people firmly out, but currently invitingly wide open.

She went up the winding driveway, trotting along the band of decorative grey-blue gravel, between neatly manicured swathes of lawn, up gleaming black steps through the front door (also invitingly wide open) and into the softly carpeted Georgian splendour of the house itself, only to discover there were several people from the trade already there, including her nemesis, the Mole.

The Mole, not actually his real name, which was Bertrand Huckvale—so it was hardly surprising that Cordelia stuck with "the Mole"—was a myopic, pot-bellied, secondhand book dealer, always clad in the same stultifying ensemble of grubby jeans, green waxed-cotton jacket and Coke-bottle-bottom glasses. Despite his bumbling appearance, he had a ruthless knack of getting to the bargains just before Cordelia and stuffing them into his omnipresent rucksack. This was currently a pink-and-white-checked Powerpuff Girls rucksack. But if you were to assume, on the basis of this, that he was either a harmless idiot or possessed a sense of humour, you'd be sadly wrong on both counts.

Right now, the Mole and the rest of the book-buying buzzards were to be seen through a doorway to the left of the high-ceilinged entrance hall in which Cordelia had paused.

The buzzards were in what was clearly the dining room, jostling each other as they moved around a large, highly polished antique walnut table on which was spread a vast array of books. Cordelia didn't even bother going into the room, because she could see that all the books on that table were hardback editions.

Unlike Cordelia, the Mole didn't specialise in paperbacks. Which was good news for her. It meant that while he was happily hoovering up the hardbacks, she could be profitably plundering the paperbacks.

But before she did that, there was one piece of protocol to be attended to.

Through another doorway, on the opposite side of the entrance hall, in a sparsely elegant sitting room, was a woman, standing all alone. Cordelia surmised this person to be Betty Fairwell. The widow was a petite, stylish woman. Her face had a distinctive catlike beauty which was yielding somewhat to the relentless erosion of the years, but still possessed a saucy, benevolent allure.

She was wearing a lavender cashmere sweater, black jodhpurs and lavender Doc Marten boots with black laces. Around her neck was a string of pearls, softly and expensively luminous against the cashmere. It looked as though her bottom half was dressed to go out into the country for a sporty weekend while her top half was planning to stay in town and drink cocktails.

She wasn't drinking a cocktail now, though. She was holding a chic tubular glass that looked as though it might have come from a mad scientist's laboratory, and contained what was, or had been, a half pint of lager, which she was sipping at frequent intervals with evident pleasure.

Cordelia went in and introduced herself, confirming that this was indeed the bereaved Betty. "I'm so sorry to hear about your husband," she told her, not entirely insincerely as, since learning of his departure from this mortal coil, the deceased Duncan had lost his place in Cordelia's personal black museum of shit-heels and time wasters, and begun to seem a little less disagreeable. Not least because his demise had opened up the possibility of a jackpot for Cordelia.

The widow Fairwell took these condolences with equanimity. "Oh, please…" she said, and began to make an expansive gesture of dismissal with her right hand. But then, realising this was the hand that held her lager and that she was likely to slop it all over her sparsely elegant sitting room, she lifted the other and made the gesture with that one instead. "I'm just pleased you could spare the time to come for a visit."

"My pleasure," said Cordelia, "So… where are the paperbacks?"

The paperbacks, it turned out, were up the thickly carpeted stairs and through a door to the left on the second floor, in what had once been the late Duncan's combined library and study, an impressively large room that ran the entire length of the back of the house and had tall windows that looked out on the river. Looking out there herself, Cordelia realised she was in a riverside house and there was even what looked like a dock and some kind of a houseboat moored to it down at the far end of the lawn.

She only wasted a fraction of a second registering this (though she did mentally add a couple of million to her estimate of what the Fairwell family home was worth) and then focused on the books. Which pretty much filled the room.

The wall space between the windows, and the entire wall on the other side of the room, had fitted bookshelves. A number of these were now empty, with books dispersed to other rooms for viewing by prospective customers, like the mob in the dining room downstairs.

But the paperbacks were all still in situ.

Cordelia didn't waste any time; she knew exactly what she wanted. The late lamented Duncan had been much given to bloated blog posts, some of which had contained the occasional useful nugget of information. For example, Cordelia had learned that—like herself—Duncan was a massive fan of John D. MacDonald.

Largely forgotten these days, except perhaps as the author of the novel *The Executioners*, which went on to become the film *Cape Fear*, MacDonald had been a towering figure in his time. And, as far as Cordelia was concerned, he was the greatest American crime writer of them all. What's more, almost all his books had originally been published in paperback. It was a long-term aim of Cordelia's to obtain first, or early, printings of everything by John D.

And it just so happened that Duncan Fairwell had a library full of such items.

Aware of her heart beating rather quickly, she went straight to 'M' in the usefully and scrupulously alphabetically ordered bookshelves on the far wall and began to pull handfuls of books out immediately, which was just as well, because it felt like she'd hardly embarked on this enterprise when she heard the sound of someone padding along in a sinister fashion, approaching inexorably in the carpeted hall outside. And who should step through the door and violate her peace and privacy, but the Mole himself. How the hell had he got finished downstairs so quickly?

The Mole was now carrying, in addition to his pop art rucksack, two large Sainsbury's shopping bags with cartoon squirrels on them, all presumably full of loot. He looked at Cordelia—daylight from the high windows flashing across the lenses of his spectacles— and then, without bothering to utter a greeting, plunged right in to sacking the shelves. Cordelia accelerated her own pillage, snatching fat handfuls of books off the shelf in front of her.

She ignored all British editions (with a certain amount of regret because some of these, especially the Pan "handcuff" versions, were really quite nice) and anything printed later than about 1980—easily identifiable because the cover price went above two dollars. Even so, this left a hell of a lot of books since John D. MacDonald had been a prolific and hugely popular writer and his books had gone through many reprintings. And Duncan Fairwell, in true obsessive-collector fashion, had felt compelled to obtain not only every variant he came across but also was quite fond of out-and-out duplicates.

All of which meant that, by the time Cordelia had strip-mined the John D. MacDonald section, even though she'd done her best to restrict her terms of reference, she had more books than she could carry.

It took several trips to transfer them from the carpet immediately beneath the bookshelf where she'd first deposited them to the floor on the opposite side of the room. She put them beside an armchair that was usefully positioned in front of one of the tall windows, with excellent daylight for reading.

In this case, for reading the fine print and other textual clues that allowed Cordelia to identify the earliest editions of all the books. Sometimes it was the cover price that was the clue—the lower the price, the earlier the date of printing. Obviously. But what to do when faced with several different variants, all with the same price?

Luckily, Cordelia had done her homework. All the books she'd chosen had been published by Gold Medal, the folks who had invented the paperback original, and ground zero for almost all of MacDonald's publications. Gold Medal had a number of eccentricities and oddities in its printing designations, and Cordelia knew them all.

She knew, for instance, that in 1964 and 1965 they had used the "bullet" system. This consisted of putting dots on the copyright page, so a second printing was identified by two so-called bullets, a third printing by three and so on.

Whereas, from 1965 to 1970, they'd used something called the End Print Number, whereby on the last page of the text there would be a string of numbers like this: "66-6-1" (a fairly devilish example, true) which meant the book was published in the year of 1966, in the month of June and that it was the first printing.

Using these and other criteria—always looking for copies in fine condition, favouring those with cover art by the likes of the redoubtable Robert McGinnis—she went through the stacks of books like an expert casino dealer distributing cards, selecting some, discarding others, and had soon reduced the pile of books from enormous to merely mammoth.

She left the ones she'd spurned on the floor by the chair instead of putting them back on the shelf. This was simple pragmatism rather than bad manners because, as she'd predicted, as soon as she got up and headed for the door with as many books as she could carry, the Mole immediately pounced on the ones she'd left behind. He knew Cordelia's taste in paperbacks was so exemplary that, even among her rejects, there would be some choice items.

Cordelia headed downstairs, treading carefully, hardly able to see over the pile of books she was carrying.

They say that a successful transaction is the one in which both parties think they've swindled the other. This was more or less true of Cordelia's negotiation with the cashmere-clad, lager-sipping, pearl-bedecked widow. While it was true that Betty Fairwell didn't want any of her late husband's books for herself and was eager to clear the house of them, that didn't mean she was going to let them go for a pittance. On the other hand, she wasn't an expert in evaluating old paperbacks and probably ultimately didn't give a damn. And although she ended up asking a great deal of money for

Cordelia's books (as Cordelia had already begun to think of them), it was vastly less than they were actually worth.

Cash talked in situations like these, and Cordelia had paused on the way to Richmond to visit a bank machine and effectively empty her account. This stake wasn't remotely enough to pay for all the books, but it would cover a decent deposit so that Betty would hold them for Cordelia and no one else, especially the Mole, would be able to get his grubby mitts on them.

Once they'd struck their bargain, shaking hands on it (the widow's palm cool from the glass of chilled lager she'd been holding), Cordelia forked out the cash and they carefully wrapped her purchases. She was ecstatic about these. They included a complete set of MacDonald's Travis McGee series, plus key standalone novels, among them *The Drowner*, *Clemmie* and *One Monday We Killed Them All*. Not to mention the amazingly rare *Weep for Me*, in both its 1951 and 1959 printings (Gold Medal 200 and Gold Medal 884).

Together they sealed these wonderful items in bags, affixed Post-it notes with Cordelia's name on them and stored them in a cupboard. Cordelia was sad to see the door close on her lovely bags of lovely books.

"When do you think you might be able to pay the rest?" asked Betty, all business despite her pearls.

"Not long at all," said Cordelia. "As it so happens, I've just had some paying work come in."

Then she rushed home. There was no way she could un-send the email she'd sent to the ashram, turning down the potentially lucrative job they'd offered her. But the situation might still be salvageable. It had better be, because she needed that money now. Badly.

When Cordelia explained the situation to Edwin, he just smiled and said, "Leave it to me."

3: CHATTING SHIT

It turned out that the folks at the ashram were as desperate to give Cordelia another chance as she was to be given one.

She was swiftly booked for a meeting with the yoga centre's big kahunas as soon as the place opened the following morning. And it opened early, both because—obviously—it was essential to greet the beginning of each new day with appropriate meditation, breathing exercises and yoga practice to guarantee suitable spiritual harmony and balance, and so the ashram could do a lucrative and booming trade in people on their way to work. Cue the sound of cash registers.

But, even though the ashram opened early, Cordelia made sure she arrived a good half an hour earlier, while the centre was still silent and dark and empty, and proceeded to perform certain measures.

When the staff did eventually turn up, along with zealous early-bird customers, Cordelia was first in line, waiting at the door to be let in like an eager mutt. The door had a wide glass panel in it—quite easy to smash through if you wanted to break in, Cordelia reflected, though clearly no one had done so because it was untouched.

The view of the interior was obscured by an orange blind with a dark red Om symbol on it. This disappeared from view as the blind was rolled up and a vaguely visible figure in orange unlocked the door then hurried away as if fearing the flood of humanity that was about to pour through the entrance.

Cordelia was the first of the flood. She stepped into the shop (of course you had to enter the ashram, and leave it too, through the gift shop) and went up to the counter.

The girl behind the counter said, "Namaste." She looked familiar to Cordelia; a mousy little thing… her name was Jan or Jane or Jenny or something. "Welcome to the Silverlight Yoga Centre."

Cordelia wasn't surprised to see the girl working in the shop. She'd been a student here at the same time as Cordelia, but unlike Cordelia, she had always been sucking up to the staff and volunteering to do things. Now here she was, having graduated to orange pyjamas.

"Your first lesson is free," said Jan or Jane or Jenny or something. Then her face fell. She'd recognised Cordelia. "You," she said, managing to pack a fair amount of accusation into that single syllable.

"Yup."

"You're banned from the Silverlight Centre."

"*Was* banned," corrected Cordelia. Though she might still be as far as lessons were concerned. She'd have to check on that. Why not insist on reinstatement of her yoga privileges as part of her deal? In fact, how about a year of free lessons? Or even two years? So long as the bastards were willing to throw them in as a bonus that didn't in any way erode her fee.

"I'm here for a meeting in the meeting room," she said. "Right about now." She glanced pointedly up at the clock high on the wall behind the till. It was fashioned from a smiling bronze sun face, was emphatically ethnic and, like everything else in here, was for sale for a hefty price.

"A meeting?"

"Yes. In the meeting room," said Cordelia, starting to get fed up with the tautological nature of this utterance. "Now."

"I will just confirm that," said Jan or Jane or Jenny or something with a prim pursing of her lips. She picked up the phone beside the till—which, disappointingly, wasn't emphatically ethnic or apparently for sale, though Cordelia was sure they'd be open to offers—and dialled a number.

"It's Joni in the shop," she said as someone answered at the other end.

So, it was Joni, not Jan or Jane or Jenny.

Joni turned away and made a big thing of talking in an undetectable whisper with her back to Cordelia.

While she was waiting for her bona fides to be confirmed, Cordelia had a quick snoop around the gift shop. Mostly she wanted to check on the hemp yoga mats. Did they really cost so much or had she dreamed it? No dream at all. Indeed, they now were priced considerably north of their old price.

"Watch out," said a voice behind her.

It was a cheery voice and Cordelia turned around to see a cheery face—red cheeks, blue eyes, red-lipped mouth shyly revealed in a large white beard.

The man was big in both senses, tall as well as fat, and was dressed in a blue-and-green Black Watch tartan shirt, yellow silk neckerchief and faded jeans secured with a broad brown leather belt that had a large bronze peace symbol for a buckle. He was shod in shabby pink espadrilles and was sockless, revealing bony, blue-veined ankles.

Altogether, he looked like a bohemian lumberjack gone badly to seed. Alternatively, if you dressed him in a hooded red garment trimmed with white, he might have made a very useful department-store Santa Claus.

"Those things aren't cheap," he said, nodding at the exorbitant yoga mats.

"I'd noticed," said Cordelia.

The man grinned at her and Cordelia found herself grinning back at him as if they shared an amusing secret. Perhaps the secret of the idiots who might actually spend that much money on a yoga mat, sustainable hemp or no.

"My name's Alfie," said the man.

"Nice to meet you, Alfie," said Cordelia. "I'm Cordelia."

Alfie took her hand and, for a foolish but not entirely unpleasant instant, Cordelia thought he might be about to kiss it. But instead he just shook it. "And nice to meet you, Cordelia," he said.

"*You can go upstairs now*," said Joni from across the room. Actually, she shouted. In fact, you might almost have said she screamed the words, but that would have been a weird thing to do. Scream, that is.

"It was an inside job," said the Silver Shrew.

Cordelia was sitting with the Shrew and Howdy Doody. The latter was the head honcho of the ashram, the former was in charge of its finances. They were in the meeting room, a long rectangular space mostly filled with a long rectangular table. There were also fitted shelves, including bookshelves, wall hangings (orange), wood panelling, lots of framed photos and thick but worn carpeting (also orange).

The Silver Shrew was known at the ashram by the Sanskrit name of Gunadya, which meant "full of virtues" (her real name was probably Gwendolyn Blort). She was a small, pinch-faced woman of at least middle age (it was sometimes hard to judge with yoga devotees, it certainly did seem to keep them young—young-*looking*, that is—as advertised). She possessed beady dark eyes, a long, pointed nose and short, cropped hair that had gone quite silver, all of which made Cordelia feel she had come up with an excellently accurate nickname for her.

Howdy Doody, officially Harshavardhana—"creator of joy", real name unknown and Cordelia didn't care to hazard a guess—was a big guy, well over six foot tall. Slim, rangy and probably quite muscular under all that orange cotton (yoga was also surprisingly good for building useful muscle), he towered over the Shrew. He had a jug-eared, goofy, freckled face and short ginger hair, which was why Cordelia had given him the name of a puppet in a wildly popular American children's TV show of the 1950s. Cordelia had never seen this, but she'd read a parody of it in the comic book *Mad*, as reprinted in paperback form (Ballantine Books U2103, 1955).

"An inside job," repeated the Shrew.

It was a decisive declaration that brooked no disagreement. So Cordelia set about disagreeing. "What makes you say that?"

"All major crime is. All major crime is an inside job."

"True enough," said Cordelia. "But this is minor crime."

The Silver Shrew's face darkened agreeably and Howdy Doody didn't look too pleased, either.

"This is a *serious* crime," said the Shrew.

"These are *immensely valuable* books," said Howdy.

They'd apparently picked up the habit of emphasising certain words through years of giving yoga instruction to dullards.

"How valuable?" said Cordelia.

"In terms of their sentimental, emotional and historical value, they're priceless," snapped the Shrew.

"How about in terms of money?"

"We are still making an assessment."

"Well, when you've made an assessment, let me know," said Cordelia.

"Why?" said the Shrew, instantly suspicious. "Why do you need to know how much the books are worth?"

Cordelia smiled. "Well, for a start, so I know how much to bill you when I recover them."

She could see Howdy and the Shrew were torn between being offended by her greed and impressed by her confidence.

"I still maintain it was an inside job," said the Silver Shrew. She seemed to have latched on to the term "inside job" and wouldn't let go of it.

"But that would imply it's someone associated with the ashram," said Howdy.

"Yes," said the Shrew, rolling her eyes. "That's what 'inside' means."

"Surely no one who comes here would do such a thing."

"Comes here or *works* here," said the Shrew.

Now Howdy looked genuinely shocked. "Why would any of our people do something like that?"

"Who else could it be?" said the Shrew, looking him in the eye. "How else could they get inside without leaving any signs of breaking in?"

Cordelia cleared her throat to remind them she was there. "You feel confident this place is totally secure?"

"Total…" began the Shrew and then, not wanting to echo Cordelia, changed it to, "Absolutely secure."

"Absolutely," said Howdy.

"There's no way anyone could just come in off the street?" said Cordelia.

"Not without leaving clear signs of a break-in," said the Shrew.

"And there were no such signs," said Howdy.

"They couldn't just… climb in through an open window?" suggested Cordelia.

"Absolutely not," said the Shrew.

"No way," said Howdy.

Cordelia took out her phone and showed them the photo she'd taken outside the centre before it had opened this morning. It showed an upstairs window, quite clearly ajar. It was a long window, about two metres wide and half a metre high. Large enough for a person to climb through. Large enough for any number of people to climb through.

Howdy and the Shrew stared at it with matched expressions of disgust, as though she was showing them some vile porn on her phone. "That's an open window," said Cordelia, not scrupling to point out the obvious.

"When did you take that photo?" said the Shrew.

"This morning, just before I came in to see you," said Cordelia. "The point is, someone could easily have got in through that."

"Nonsense," said the Shrew. "It's far too high off the ground."

Howdy nodded in agreement.

"There's a tree growing beside it," said Cordelia.

"Nobody could climb that tree," said the Shrew.

Howdy nodded again.

Cordelia showed them another photo, this time a close-up shot of the open window, with her hand in fact touching it. Taken when she'd climbed the tree.

Howdy and the Shrew looked at it and looked at each other, then fell gratifyingly silent.

Cordelia wished she could have got someone, perhaps a helpful passer-by, to have taken a photo of her up in the tree, cheerily waving, after she'd climbed it. But you couldn't have everything.

While Howdy and the Shrew were digesting this titbit, Cordelia went and inspected the actual scene of the crime. One wall of the room consisted of bookshelves that went all the way from the ceiling down to waist height. Below that it was just attractive wood panelling. Presumably because it was too uncomfortable to bend down and get at books situated any lower. A damning indictment of the efficacy of yoga, perhaps.

The bookshelves weren't evenly spaced. Instead, they were set at varying heights, to accommodate books of different sizes. Cordelia appreciated the good sense of this. It maximised how many volumes you could pack in and, as someone who was always trying to find enough room for her own books, she thoroughly approved.

There was only one shelf designed for paperbacks—a shallow space because proper classic, pocket-sized paperbacks weren't at all tall—and it was now completely empty, a narrow blank band of pale wood in the wall of books, like an archaeological stratum in a bank of sediment that indicated some primordial catastrophe.

Interestingly, the shelf was just below shoulder height. The most comfortable shelf to get at. Which led Cordelia to speculate that perhaps the thief hadn't specifically targeted paperbacks but had simply gone after the books that were most easy to access.

She turned to Howdy Doody and the Silver Shrew. "Can I have a list of the missing books?"

"Stolen books," Howdy corrected her.

"We have a list for you," said the Shrew, somewhat grudgingly. She made no move to produce it, though.

Cordelia felt the Shrew was still reluctant to hire her, even though she and Howdy had summoned Cordelia here urgently and had now reached the point of actually briefing her for the job.

"The books we're most anxious to retrieve are those by Avram Silverlight," said Howdy Doody.

"Avram Silverlight?" said Cordelia.

"Yes. They are signed by Avram Silverlight himself."

"Avram Silverlight?" persisted Cordelia. The more often the name was repeated, the more preposterous it sounded. "That's a person?"

"Yes," said Howdy Doody and the Silver Shrew simultaneously in identical tones of contemptuous sarcasm.

"The Silverlight Yoga Centre is named after a person?"

"Yes." More synchronised sarcasm.

"Of course it is," added the Shrew. She marched over to a framed photograph that hung on the wall and tapped it, as if to wake up the people depicted in it.

Cordelia went and looked at the picture. It was in black and white, and showed a group of young men and women standing in front of what was recognisably the ashram. The photo had evidently been taken at least half a century ago, judging by the clothes and other accoutrements the people were wearing (bell-bottom jeans and beads were the least of it).

In the centre of the group was an imposing, powerfully built young man with shoulder-length hair. He was bare chested, and across that chest was a large lotus flower tattoo. It was distinctive and would have been even more so at the time, in the late 1960s, when only sailors and nutcases got tattooed. And this guy didn't look like a sailor.

"*That* is Avram Silverlight," declared the Shrew, peering at Cordelia beadily.

"Good grief," said Cordelia.

"Where did you think the name came from?" asked Howdy.

Cordelia turned away from the photo and looked at him. "I just thought it was some kind of fatuous reference to a mystical yogic thing. Now, is there anything else you can tell me about the burglary?"

This question had an odd effect. Both Howdy Doody and the Silver Shrew fell profoundly silent. They looked at each other, then looked away and remained silent some more. Cordelia decided to remain silent herself and see who would give way first. Clearly she was on to something here, though she had no earthly idea what it might be.

Finally, Howdy Doody and the Silver Shrew broke the silence as a kind of double act.

"The thief didn't just steal some books," said the Shrew.

"They defaced the room," said Howdy.

"Defaced it?" Cordelia looked around. There was no sign of anything like that now.

"Using a very particular material," said the Shrew.

"What material?" said Cordelia, her interest now well and truly piqued.

More silence.

"Their own excrement," said Howdy Doody, finally and abruptly.

"We assume it was their own excrement," said the Silver Shrew.

Howdy gave her a look of annoyance. "What are you suggesting? That the thief came equipped with *someone else's*? With a bag of human faeces?"

"I'm not suggesting anything…"

"As a bonus accessory for their break-in?" persisted Howdy. "Along with their bag of burglary tools?"

Cordelia, who knew a thing or two about burglary tools (she still possessed a useful set of her own), did some breaking in herself now and interrupted the bickering.

"Are you sure it was human faeces?" she asked.

"We have no idea," said the Silver Shrew tersely.

"You didn't have it analysed?" said Cordelia. "Because, if it was human, you could…"

"Yes, yes, DNA, identify the culprit, et cetera et cetera," said Howdy Doody. He really did have some annoying conversational habits.

"So?" said Cordelia.

"We did not have it analysed," said the Silver Shrew curtly. "We cleaned it up."

"You didn't think to retain a sample?" said Cordelia, with a hint of condescending reprimand. She was rather enjoying this little chat. Chatting shit, so to speak.

"No, we didn't," snapped the Silver Shrew.

"With hindsight, we realise that was something of a mistake," said Howdy Doody. "We should have retained a sample, instead of scouring the whole place with bleach and removing any possible trace of evidence. That was a somewhat foolhardy course of action."

"Well, if it was foolhardy, who was the fool who issued the orders?" The Shrew was glaring at Howdy now. "You demanded we clean it up immediately." She turned to Cordelia. "You should have heard him shriek when he saw it."

"I smelled it before I saw it," said Howdy diffidently, lost in reminiscence. "Perhaps I should have been more measured in my response. You're quite right. But in the heat of the moment…"

"Of course," said the Shrew, conciliatory now. "It was only natural to respond the way you did."

"Perhaps, but still, I should have thought…"

"No one can think of everything," said the Silver Shrew comfortingly.

"Still, it's a pity," said Cordelia.

The Shrew turned to her, becoming combative again. "Well, it's a moot point. There's nothing we can do about it now."

"Yes," said Howdy. "No point crying over spilt—"

"Poo," said Cordelia helpfully.

"—milk," concluded Howdy, wrinkling his nose. Speaking of noses, Cordelia couldn't help giving the place a surreptitious sniff with her own, but all she could detect was the smoky, spicy perfumed hint of old incense.

"Is there anything else you want to tell me before I get started?" she said.

"I think that's all you need to know," said Howdy Doody.

"I think it's more than she needs to know," said the Silver Shrew, turning towards Howdy. "I still say we shouldn't have told anyone about the… dirty protest."

"There was no way we could keep it quiet," said Howdy. "It was the day after our anniversary celebration, which made it so much worse. Everyone in the ashram knew what happened. Half of them helped clean it up."

"I still think it's bad for our reputation."

"I won't tell anyone," said Cordelia with magnificent insincerity. She literally couldn't wait to get home and tell Edwin. Odd that Lorna hadn't already told him. But maybe she didn't know. But wasn't that odd, too?

"When are you going to start your investigation?" asked the Shrew, with heavy quotation marks around the word *investigation*.

"As soon as you give me that list of the missing books," said Cordelia. "And pay me a hundred-pound advance on my fee." This last bit she just threw in for the hell of it. It would be fun to see their response.

"A hundred pounds?" said the Shrew.

"In cash," said Cordelia.

"But you haven't done anything yet," said Howdy Doody, a plaintive note creeping into his voice.

"And I'm not likely to if I don't get an advance." Cordelia, who hadn't even thought of asking for an advance until a few seconds ago, now found herself prepared to stubbornly defend the principle.

"Oh, let her have it," said the Shrew, surprisingly. She gave Cordelia a sharp look. "This will be deducted from any eventual fee."

"Hence the term 'advance'," said Cordelia.

"I suppose you want it now," said the Shrew, sighing heavily.

"Yes, please," said Cordelia, suddenly all cordiality. The thought of money always cheered her up.

The Shrew took a laptop out of a drawer in the side of the table and opened it, then began to type briefly onto what Cordelia assumed was a spreadsheet, and then type at greater length into what Cordelia assumed was some sort of memorandum ("Paid the evil bitch one hundred pounds at her insistence"). When she finished, she closed the laptop and left it out on the table.

"Now, you'll get started right away?" said Howdy Doody.

"Right away," said Cordelia.

"And you'll report back as soon as you make any progress," said Howdy.

He certainly sounded anxious.

"Yes," said Cordelia. "In the meantime, might I suggest you start keeping your windows shut and locked?"

"We need the windows open when we use the *shala*," snapped the Shrew. The shala was the studio or "yoga space" where lessons took place. "We need to have access to a constant flow of fresh air for our students during their instruction, for their breathing exercises."

"Do you need to have access to a constant flow of fresh air during the night when they're not here?" said Cordelia, making no effort not to be snotty. "If not, then close the windows and lock them after the last lesson of the day or before the last member of staff goes home."

"Thank you for the benefit of your expert advice," said Howdy Doody, also not sparing the snottiness.

"You need to take your security a lot more seriously around here," said Cordelia.

"We do take our security seriously."

"Really? By just leaving stuff lying around?"

"We don't just leave stuff lying around," said the Shrew. "Anything valuable is locked in the safe."

The safe? What safe? thought Cordelia.

As if in answer to her unspoken question, the Silver Shrew went to the wall hangings. These consisted of two large pieces of saffron silk with Sanskrit words embroidered on them. On the left-hand side, previously unnoticed by Cordelia, a gold-braided cord hung half-concealed. The Shrew pulled on this and the pieces of silk swept apart like curtains to reveal a cylindrical metal safe recessed in the middle of the wall, like the third eye in the unwrinkled brow of an enlightened yogi.

Having opened the curtains, the Shrew scurried to a corner of the room and came back with a folding set of bright purple plastic steps with pink polka dots on them. Nice steps. She opened these with a clack and climbed up towards the safe. Then she turned and stared at Cordelia. "Look the other way," she said. "Make sure she looks the other way, Harshavardhana."

"Oh, for Christ's sake," murmured Cordelia. But she looked the other way, out the window, which provided a view of the peace garden below. It was set in a kind of courtyard with the walls of the building surrounding it. To the right were the kitchen and dining area, scene of many happy curry banquets, to the left were some boring storerooms and stuff, and directly ahead were the changing rooms and shala. Unseen, because it was directly beneath them, was the gift shop.

Cordelia heard the Shrew spin the dial on the safe and click it open, rifle in it briefly, then thud it shut again, spinning the dial once more so no prospective thief—i.e., Cordelia—would have any clues about the last digit of the combination. Then she heard the curtains swishing shut again.

"Can I look now?" asked Cordelia with exaggerated courtesy.

"Here's your money," said the Shrew by way of reply.

Cordelia turned and gratefully accepted a thin sheaf of ten-pound notes. "Thank you. And about that list of the books…"

"Oh, yes," said Howdy Doody. He opened another drawer in the table and took out a sheet of paper, which he handed to Cordelia. Neatly printed in one of the over-elaborate fonts favoured by the ashram, it consisted of a list of titles and authors. Mostly one author, the aforementioned Avram Silverlight. Cordelia folded it and put it in her pocket along with the cash.

"And you reckon that most of the books are on it?" she said.

"We *know* that *all* of the books are on it," said the Shrew.

Suddenly Cordelia smelled a rat. A very large, very odorous rodent.

How did they just happen to have a complete list of the missing books on hand? It wasn't as though they were jewellery or something else you might keep routinely listed for insurance purposes. These were paperback books. Treasured items to someone like Cordelia, but otherwise widely regarded as worthless.

All at once an inside job began to seem likely. Very likely indeed.

Was the robbery a set-up? But, if so, to set up what? An insurance scam?

Cordelia kept her voice carefully casual. "How can you be sure it's complete?"

"We use this room for award ceremonies," said Howdy Doody. "We take photographs in here, lots of photographs."

Well, all right, now things were beginning to sound a mite more plausible.

"And you had the bookshelves in the background?" said Cordelia.

"Yes. And, from scrutinising various photos from various angles, we were able to compile a full list of the missing titles."

"I didn't need the photos," said the Silver Shrew. "I could have listed them all from memory."

"Yes, I'm sure you could, Gunadya," said Howdy Doody, in a tone of voice that suggested placation was the better part of valour. Or, more simply put, it wasn't worth contradicting a Shrew.

"Now," said Cordelia, in full business mode, "just to be clear, I am being hired to restore the books you've lost. By which I mean that, if I can't, despite my best efforts, actually locate and retrieve the stolen merchandise, I will replace them with equivalent copies. Alternate copies of the same books, in equally good condition."

"They were all pristine," snapped the Shrew. "Not just good. Pristine."

"Then I'll have to find copies that are pristine," said Cordelia, unruffled. "Now, we're agreed that's acceptable?"

Cordelia could see that Howdy Doody and the Silver Shrew were a little disappointed at the notion they might not get back the exact books that had been stolen. But common sense prevailed. After all, they wanted the books, and if Cordelia could come up with copies that were indistinguishable from the ones that had gone missing it became a philosophical question what the difference was—very appropriate for an ashram, with it being such a philosophical place.

The pair nodded. "Yes, that's all right," said Howdy.

"I suppose so," said the Shrew grudgingly.

"Now, if I do find alternative copies," said Cordelia, "will they need to be signed?"

This would present no problem for Cordelia, since she had a knack for forging authors' signatures in rare books. She just needed a specimen to work from.

But her question had an odd effect on Howdy Doody and the Silver Shrew. They looked at each other quizzically for a moment, then Howdy said, "We'll have to get back to you on that."

This was interesting because Cordelia had assumed these two were the top dogs at the ashram. But, clearly, they needed to consult with someone higher up the food chain.

Very interesting.

4: BAD PENNY

Their little meeting obviously took longer than Cordelia thought because, when she came downstairs, she saw that the first yoga class of the morning had concluded and the students were exiting through the peace garden.

Among them was Cordelia's favourite teacher, a small man with a neat little white moustache and a carefully trimmed tonsure of white hair on his otherwise bald skull. His name was Mr Thirunavukkarasu. But he was better known by an abbreviated name, as evidenced by a couple of teenage girls who said, "Goodbye, Mr T," and fluttered away, giggling.

Cordelia was pleased and rather proud that people were still referring him as Mr T. The idiots had apparently forgotten, or perhaps never known, that it was Cordelia who'd invented this name for him in the first place, a name that had clearly stuck because it was so cool and compact. (Especially compact, compared to Thirunavukkarasu.)

They also probably didn't realise it was a reference to a TV show called *The A-Team*, from some bygone era before Cordelia had been born. She only knew about it herself because of her father's passion for pulp television. Passion was not too strong a description.

Indeed, Cordelia been named, at her father's suggestion (actually, "insistence" might be more accurate), after one of the characters in *Buffy the Vampire Slayer*, Cordelia Chase, as played by Charisma Carpenter.

Cordelia didn't particularly object to her name. In fact, she considered it a lucky escape she hadn't been called Charisma.

"Good morning, Cordelia," said Mr T, looking at her with a sly smile. "So, you are back again?"

"It looks like it."

"I never doubted it," he said, nodding sagely. "They say that the bad penny always turns up. Therefore I never doubted it."

"I did," said Cordelia. "I doubted it." But she felt warmed and cheered by his remarks. She'd always liked Mr T. He was an excellent teacher—knowledgeable, patient and so serene you could never imagine him losing his temper.

"Will you be coming to classes again?" asked Mr T.

"It certainly looks that way," said Cordelia. She'd haggled with Howdy Doody and the Shrew and they'd reluctantly agreed to the reinstatement of her yoga privileges at the ashram. They had drawn the line at free lessons, though, the penny-pinching bastards.

"Do come along to one of my sessions, if you like," said Mr T.

It was a casual, off-hand invitation, but it meant a lot to Cordelia.

He opened the sliding glass doors at the side of the peace garden and then, as if struck by an idea, turned and beckoned to her. "Come inside, if you like. It's entirely up to you."

Despite the Dracula-like nature of this invitation, Cordelia followed him—Mr T politely holding the door open and sliding it shut behind her.

The two of them were now alone in the ashram's dining hall, a long, thin space flooded with daylight thanks to the big glass doors that faced onto the peace garden. The hall contained stripped-pine tables and chairs scattered with ethnic cushions, and a glass-fronted serving counter that was lined with shelves on which the various dishes of the day were displayed. Other than on festival days, this was a fairly sparse selection, and, at the moment, there were only half a dozen items on offer.

Behind the counter there was a circular serving hatch, ringed with glazed orange tiles, which provided access to the kitchen area. A figure now loomed up in there. "We're not open yet," she said, or perhaps more accurately snarled.

"Good morning, Carrie," said Mr T.

There was silence behind the serving hatch and then the figure briefly disappeared from sight. A door opened in the far left of the wall to reveal a glimpse of a brightly lit kitchen beyond, and a tall middle-aged woman emerged dressed in a chef's white tunic and apron, and baggy black-and-white check trousers. She wore a kind of white turban over her hair, which was thick and curly and, for her age, suspiciously black. Her wary blue eyes were emphasised with striking black eyeliner that made her look like Cleopatra, or at least like Elizabeth Taylor in the movie *Cleopatra*.

She was holding a large, gleaming knife.

Cordelia's heart raced at the sight of her, and not because of the knife. She immediately moved to the counter and began to pay close attention to the food displayed behind the glass. There was also a certain amount of salivation going on, because this woman was Carrie Quinn, a professional chef who had a longstanding association with the ashram. She was known, perhaps inevitably, as the Curry Queen, both because of her name and her speciality.

A one-time restaurant owner, she had long ago abandoned that as a bad job and now did catering for events. Whenever she had any leftovers from one of these, which was often, she brought them to the ashram. It was an arrangement that meant the

Silverlight people got a great price on their (great-tasting) food while Carrie squeezed a bit of extra profit out of it. And since curry kept well—indeed, was actually tastier the following day—everyone was a winner.

Including Cordelia, who had been deprived of Carrie's spectacular cooking for so long. She now gazed excitedly at the food on offer and saw, *yes*, there was a bowl of saag bhaji, her favourite, nestling green and golden and tawny on a bed of saffron rice. Behind her Mr T and Carrie were talking and, with the segment of her attention which wasn't hypnotised by the spicy chow, Cordelia registered their conversation.

"I hope that nasty big knife isn't for me, Carrie."

"It should be, T. You know we're not open for business yet."

"Not even for me, Carrie?"

"You're not alone, though, are you?"

Cordelia now had to choose between pretending she wasn't aware they were talking about her or looking at them. She looked at them.

Carrie Quinn the Curry Queen met her gaze. She had a surly expression. "This one isn't even supposed to be allowed in the ashram," she said.

"Haven't you heard?" said Mr T. "She's helping us with our little incident."

"Helping how?" Carrie kept staring steadily at Cordelia, surliness now compounded with suspicion.

Cordelia didn't mind. She was willing to forgive any amount of bad attitude in someone who could cook like Carrie could.

"Helping recover the books," said Cordelia.

"They're thinking of asking you to do that?"

"They've asked me."

"And why would you want to help that lot?" Carrie wasn't a member of the ashram hierarchy and had no great respect for them.

"Because they're paying me," said Cordelia, simply. She didn't need to add that this was the same reason Carrie was involved with the ashram.

"They must be out of their minds," concluded Carrie. But she set her knife down with a clank on top of the counter and moved into the space behind it. "Mind you," she said, "I thought it was bang out of order what they did, banning you for life like that. And all for a little weed." She leaned on top of the counter, chin on her folded hands, and studied them both. In case what she'd just said seemed like too much of a softening of her attitude, she now shifted her sceptical gaze to Cordelia then back to Mr T and said, "She still can't eat here, you know. Only members can buy food."

"Well then, I shall buy some for her," said Mr T. "For I am a member, am I not?"

"Oh, I give up," said Carrie.

Cordelia's heart leapt.

"Just don't sit where anyone can see you," said Carrie. "I don't want them all wanting to be fed. We're not—"

"Open for business yet," said Mr T. He chuckled. And instead of erupting in fury at his mockery of her, Carrie just smiled. She had a soft spot for Mr T.

"What are you going to have?" She straightened up, wiping her hands in a businesslike fashion on her white apron that, despite frequent washing, bore the ineradicable ghostly golden traces of turmeric from meals of days gone by. It was as close as Carrie ever got to wearing orange, which was another reason Cordelia liked her.

Mr T turned to Cordelia. "What would you like? My treat."

"The saag bhaji, please," said Cordelia, just about being able to make her words comprehensible despite the saliva that flooded her mouth.

"I'll have the same," said Mr T. He fetched cutlery and napkins and set them down on one of the tables at the far end of the room, near the door to the kitchen, where they were unlikely to be seen by anyone passing in the peace garden.

Cordelia sat down opposite him while Carrie made wonderfully promising clattering sounds, putting the curry onto plates for them.

"You haven't abandoned us for your cookery school yet, then, Carrie?" said Mr T. He winked at Cordelia. "Carrie is threatening to move to Marrakech."

"Marrakech or Algiers," said Carrie. "I haven't made up my mind yet. And it's not a threat, it's a promise."

"Well, I am hoping you will change your mind," said Mr T.

So too was Cordelia, whose heart had instantly sunk at hearing that Carrie and her stellar culinary skills might be exiting her life.

"Well, it's one step closer," said Carrie with satisfaction. "I've got a new partner to help me set up the school."

"And who is that?" asked Mr T.

"Not you," said Carrie in a manner that closed the discussion.

Cordelia, sitting with her back to the counter, could smell the curry before she saw it. And then, gloriously, Carrie was leaning over her shoulder and setting the plate down in front of her. She also put a plate down in front of Mr T, but that hardly registered. Cordelia gazed down at the saag bhaji—fat chunks of mushroom, amber with aromatic oil, translucent golden slices of onion, bright green twists of spinach—and inhaled the heavenly smell.

She reflected that anyone who came to the Silverlight Yoga Centre in search of a spiritual experience need look no further than the dining hall.

Cordelia picked up her fork and was just pondering—gloating, actually—over what to taste first when she heard a door open. Not the door to the kitchen, which was still standing ajar, but the door at the other end of the room that led to the gift shop.

Cordelia's heart sank even before she turned to see Joni slithering through the door, arms wildly semaphoring. "No," said

Joni, in a very loud, very flat voice. "No, she can't eat in here." She hurried over to the table.

Mr T and Carrie looked at her.

"I purchased her meal for her," said Mr T, in a soft, reasonable voice.

Softness and reason cut no ice with Joni. "I rang upstairs. I asked. They told me. She can't eat in here."

Carrie shrugged. "Sorry, love," she said under her breath as she took Cordelia's plate away.

Mr T didn't say anything. He just gave Cordelia a sad, soulful look as she shoved her chair back and got up from the table. Joni stood watching, arms folded, a triumphant smile on her face, as Cordelia struggled with the sliding glass door, feeling the sweat of humiliation begin to lubricate her limbs, and finally wrenched it open.

Even as she was struggling with the door, she wondered how Joni could have possibly known that she was in here. Then, as the door opened and let in a fresh, fragrant wash of air, scented with the herbs from the peace garden, she glanced back into the room and saw the camera mounted high in one corner of the ceiling.

As she closed the door behind her, the portion of Cordelia's mind that wasn't preoccupied with a vengeful fantasy of seizing the big kitchen knife and cutting off Joni's head with it wondered why no one had mentioned the security cameras when they'd discussed the robbery with her.

Odd.

Cordelia's chain of thought was interrupted by the sight of the Silver Shrew emerging from the gift shop and heading for the dining hall. Any hopes that the Shrew would be booted out too were cruelly dashed when she saw Carrie greet her, if not with open arms, then at least with a big, friendly smile. It looked as though Carrie actually liked the Shrew. How could anyone actually like the Shrew?

Oh well.

Maybe the Shrew would end up eating Cordelia's saag bhaji.

Cordelia stood in the peace garden and realised that she was going to have to face Joni, the triumphantly grinning little shit, again when she went out through the gift shop. She was seriously considering going upstairs instead and clambering out that window she'd photographed and climbing down the handy adjacent tree, when she was distracted by another group of yoga students emerging from the direction of the shala.

Among them was none other than Lorna, who—via Edwin—had been responsible for Cordelia being here in the first place.

Lorna was a brisk, well-scrubbed redhead who looked dismayingly wholesome. That was the way Edwin liked them. Apparently.

She saw Cordelia and hurried over, bright-eyed and smiling. She glowed pink from her recent yogic exertions. Her hair was tied back in a bun and she wore a grey tracksuit and black-and-orange Converse high tops that squeaked on the irregularly shaped zen-garden flagstones as she trotted over to Cordelia.

"Have you had a word with them?" she said.

"Yes."

"Brilliant! And they're going to hire you?"

"Yep."

"Brilliant! I am so pleased for you."

To her credit, Lorna did appear genuinely pleased. But then she seemed to be the easily pleased type. Which was just as well if she was going out with Edwin.

At that moment Cordelia happened to glance back at the dining hall. Through the glass she could see Carrie smiling and chatting with the Silver Shrew. Then Carrie looked over the Shrew's shoulder and suddenly the expression on her face changed, quite dramatically.

If looks could kill might have been an old cliché but, as old and clichéd as it was, it accurately described Carrie as she stared out the window. Cordelia turned to see who Carrie was looking at.

It was Alfie, the bohemian lumberjack.

"Ladies," boomed Alfie as he lumbered towards Cordelia and Lorna. He was fastening his peace-sign belt buckle and hitching up his jeans. This behaviour wasn't quite as odious as it might seem, since the changing rooms were just behind him, between the peace garden and the yoga studio, and Alfie had just emerged from them. Now he began adjusting the knot on his yellow silk neckerchief. He'd obviously raced out of the changing room in a hurry.

Because he wanted to catch up with Lorna?

"I'm so glad to see you, see you both." Alfie beamed at them. "I'm having a few folk over for a picnic. A curry picnic. Folk from the centre, and a few others. On Saturday. We'll go out on the common to a little spot I know. I might even fire up the hibachi since it's forecast to be beautiful weather, so we can combine some barbecue with the assorted curries, which incidentally will be provided by Carrie—catered by Carrie, ha-ha—so you know they'll be good. Please do join us." He beamed some more at Lorna. "Lorna, I've got you on my socials, so I'll send you the details." He now beamed at Cordelia. "I don't have any way of contacting you, though, love. Which is heartbreaking."

"Well, we can't have any broken hearts," said Cordelia and handed him her business card. As she did so, she reflected that Alfie's cheerful boast about Carrie catering his picnic sat very oddly with the filthy look she'd just given him.

Alfie, blissfully unaware of this enigma, was scrutinising the business card. On one side it read *Cordelia Stanmer, Paperback Sleuth* and gave her contact details. On the other side was the cover of a vintage paperback reproduced in miniature. In this case *The Living Shadow* with art by Sanford Kossin, Bantam H4463. Alfie studied the image—a toothy maniac with blazing pistols—with obvious approval.

"I'll save this," he said. "It's much too nice to use as a roach."

"Don't talk to that man!"

They all turned to see a tall, skinny, elderly gent ambling towards them from the gift shop. He was wearing a strikingly unusual outfit—not necessarily an easy thing to achieve in a yoga centre. What at first appeared to be black Lycra cycle leggings turned out to be attached to a sort of bib top, to form a garment like tight, black Lycra dungarees. He was bare chested underneath the bib, revealing grey chest hair and a peace-sign tattoo that looked faded with age. Draped across his shoulders was a jeans jacket, but not as we know it. In fact, it was made of white denim decorated with little yellow-and-green daisies. Yes, daisies.

The man's face had clearly once been very pretty, with perfectly shaped and symmetrical features, rosebud lips and liquid, beguiling eyes of a dark brown hue. But the ravages of time and, Cordelia strongly suspected, a heroic intake of recreational chemicals had taken their toll and he now had a raddled, wrinkled, simian countenance.

His hair, presumably dyed, was the same colour as his eyes and was worn in a long ponytail that draped over his right shoulder and hung down, fastened with a hair clip in the shape of a fiercely fanged skull, made of what looked like real silver.

"Oh my god," said Alfie, with a good-natured groan. "How the hell did you manage to get them to let you into the ashram? Don't you know this is a sacred place?"

"I just told 'em I was here to take you off their hands and they couldn't get me in fast enough." The skinny apparition grinned—actually, leered would be a better word—at Cordelia and Lorna. "Looks like I was just in time to stop you preying on these tender young things."

"Cordelia, Lorna," said Alfie. "This is Hank Honeywell. Don't bother trying to remember the name because it really isn't worth the effort."

"He's just jealous because it's such a great name," said Hank diffidently.

"Hank and I go way back," said Alfie.

"Don't believe him," said Hank. "We met for the first time last week in a knocking shop. He was working there. Emptying chamber pots. I asked him what the money was like and he said, 'Fifty quid a week.' 'That's not much,' I said. 'I know,' he said, 'but it's all I can afford to pay 'em.'"

Alfie sighed. "Can you believe this man is my oldest and dearest friend? Come on, you reprobate." He draped his arm over Hank's shoulder and steered him towards the gift shop and the exit beyond. "Let's get you out of here before you get into trouble. Any *more* trouble."

As they made their way out, Alfie glanced back and called, "See you ladies later. On Saturday, I hope."

The two strange old men took their leave while the "ladies" stared after them. "I quite like that jeans jacket," said Lorna. "I wonder where he got it?"

Then, perhaps because she was in no hurry, or perhaps because she was particularly in no hurry to run into that pair again, Lorna sat down on one of the three weathered wooden benches positioned in the courtyard. Cordelia sat with her, quite content to linger and ponder the peace garden for a while.

It was a pleasant space that consisted of pebbled tiers set at different levels, edged with cylindrical wooden stakes driven into the ground. Flagstones meandered through flower beds, wooden planters contained flowering herbs—lavender was the only one Cordelia could identify—and there was a murmuring water feature and an elaborate set of wind chimes made from chromed pipes of various lengths that hung on metal cables from a wooden frame (it looked a bit like a mass execution of badly behaved chrome pipes on a miniature gallows).

Cordelia and Lorna watched Alfie open the door to the gift shop and usher his friend out. "He's an amusing old rogue," said Lorna.

"Which one?"

"I've never met the other one before. I meant Alfie."

"Can he actually *do* any yoga?" said Cordelia, watching Alfie trying to manoeuvre his ageing bulk through the doorway.

"Are you kidding?" said Lorna. "He's one of the best in the class. He's an adept."

"Really?" Cordelia was reluctantly impressed. "Are you thinking of going to his 'picnic'?"

"I don't see why not," said Lorna. "The food will be great. You heard him saying that Carrie will be doing the curries."

Cordelia remembered the saag bhaji of which she had been so recently and cruelly deprived and heard her stomach gurgle regretfully. Lorna heard too, and laughed.

"I guess that's a yes, then," she said.

"It's definitely a maybe," said Cordelia, although truth to tell she was increasingly inclined to attend the picnic. Alfie's remark about a roach suggested he knew one end of a spliff from the other, so maybe it wouldn't be a boring afternoon. "I do appreciate the work of the Curry Queen."

"Alfie used to date Carrie," said Lorna. "They were an item back in the day, apparently. And he's still a bit of ladies' man."

"In his own mind," said Cordelia, thinking this might explain Carrie's attitude to Alfie.

"There and elsewhere. He and Joni were caught in flagrante, you know."

Cordelia stared at her, then glanced in the direction of the gift shop. "What? *That* Joni?"

Lorna grinned. "Yes. That Joni. During the Christmas party. Up in the meeting room."

"No." Cordelia was genuinely taken aback.

"Yes. She was giving him a blowie."

"You're kidding." Cordelia was now not only genuinely taken aback but also a little scandalised. Who would have thought colourless, sexless Joni was capable of such behaviour? Perpetrating an oral outrage on Father Christmas in a lumberjack shirt?

"That's why she's working in the shop," said Lorna. "And still called Joni. She was supposed to have been promoted to giving lessons by now, and renamed Devika. But she's been demoted. For conduct unbecoming. I'm glad. I don't think she would be much of a yoga instructor. I don't like her voice. I think you have to have a good voice if you're going to instruct people. Mr T has a lovely voice, don't you think? He's brilliant."

Cordelia nodded absently. She was mostly preoccupied with contemplating Alfie, who very clearly was a dark horse. And something occurred to her. "Then why is he still allowed to come to lessons at the ashram? After the Christmas party incident? Why wasn't he kicked out for his transgressions, like me?"

Lorna gave a helpless shrug. "I don't know."

Now Cordelia shrugged; it was infectious. "Perhaps getting a blowjob wasn't regarded as quite so invidious as dealing weed."

"Perhaps," said Lorna. "You could ask him at the picnic on Saturday. If you come, I mean."

Cordelia nodded. She was indeed seriously considering attending.

"Do you think I should ask Alfie if I can bring Edwin along?" said Lorna.

"More importantly, will Joni be there?" said Cordelia. "Or do you think she's already dined?"

Lorna gave a naughty giggle.

Cordelia wondered fleetingly whether the festive fellatio in the meeting room could have had any bearing on the missing books. After all, it was the scene of the crime.

But it had taken place months before the robbery so, as much as she would have liked to implicate Joni, Cordelia set this theory aside.

5: AVRAM SILVERLIGHT

Cordelia trotted back to the house she shared with Edwin in leafy Barnes. And, as soon as she got home, she sent some emails and set about researching the stolen books, using the list provided. Some of these were straight-up yoga texts—*Be Young with Yoga* by Richard L. Hittleman, published by Paperback Library with some nice typography but a shitty cover photo; *Renew Your Life Through Yoga* by Indra Devi, also Paperback Library, with a fetchingly indolent cat featured on the cover; *Yoga, Youth and Reincarnation* by Jesse Stearn, published by Bantam with quite a groovy cover illustration (was it by Kossin?), to name a few—but the bulk of the titles were by the eponymous Avram Silverlight.

A quick but thorough online search of the usual suspects (Advanced Book Exchange, Zardoz Books, Etsy) revealed that the straight-up yoga titles would be fairly easy to replace. It might be a bit of a struggle to find them in "pristine" condition (to quote the Shrew), but Cordelia should be able to locate acceptable copies.

The Avram Silverlight paperbacks, however, were quite a different matter.

Published by Mayflower Books in the 1960s, they had titles like *Heart Centre, Crown Chakra, Wheel of Fire* and, a little alarmingly, *The Corpse Position*, and featured truly, wondrously bizarre psychedelic cover art similar to that of the Michael Moorcock science-fantasy novels that Mayflower had also published at about the same time. But unlike the Moorcocks, which were easy enough to find, the Avram Silverlight books were as rare as an honest man.

And, of course, these weren't science-fantasy.

Nor were they straightforward yoga guides.

Silverlight's books were very much products of the Swinging Sixties. Partially memoirs, partially picaresque tales of spiritual self-discovery, they occupied an oddball niche. The closest comparison Cordelia could think of were the works of Lobsang Rampa and Carlos Castaneda.

Appearing in the 1950s, some years before Avram Silverlight's publishing spree, Rampa's books had titles like *The Third Eye*, *The Cave of the Ancients* and *Living with the Lama*. They nominally explored Tibetan Buddhism and were heavy on themes like reincarnation, astral travel and auras. And cats. They had been massively popular in their day.

Published a few years after Silverlight's books, Castaneda's series of bestsellers about Don Juan (no, not that one) told the story of a Yaqui sorcerer, the Yaqui being the indigenous people of a part of Mexico. The books were heavy on drugs and philosophy and became increasingly outlandish but continued to sell in vast quantities. Castaneda had been an anthropologist and his first publication—his doctoral thesis—had been a surprise hit, which rode the wave of hippiedom, psychedelic drug experimentation and the exploration of alternative lifestyles. Auras also featured in his extravaganzas. But no cats.

Avram Silverlight's books were sandwiched between the output of these quirky authors both chronologically and thematically. Silverlight was concerned not with Tibet or southwestern Mexico but rather India. And his main subject of interest was not Buddhism nor the shamanistic use of psychedelics but, of course, yoga.

That was as far as Cordelia got in her first burst of research before she felt in need of some therapeutic socialising with Rainbottle.

Visiting the dog also meant visiting her landlord in his flat downstairs, but this wasn't entirely a bad thing because Cordelia could cajole him (the landlord, not the dog) into making her a hot chocolate. Edwin, always an avid hot chocolate tippler himself, didn't take much cajoling and they were soon seated at his table, holding mugs of Tesco Finest Santo Domingo Single Estate while Rainbottle comfortably sprawled under the table, making a valiant effort to lie on both their feet—which was to say, all four of their feet—at the same time, and fall asleep.

When Cordelia told Edwin about what the Shrew had so primly described as the "dirty protest" that had accompanied the robbery, he said, "Good lord. Why would anyone do that?" Then he considered his own question for a moment and added, "But it does suggest a personal motive, doesn't it? Not just a straightforward theft for gain. It suggests, at least to me, someone who had a grudge."

Cordelia conceded he may well be right. But she went on to explain that shitting burglars weren't such a rare phenomenon. "Opinion is divided about whether they do it simply because they become overexcited," she said, "or whether it's a deliberate act of symbolic desecration, rather like the robbery itself."

"But why don't they just use the toilet?" said Edwin. "After all, it's a very rare occurrence when a place being burgled doesn't have a toilet somewhere on the premises."

"Well," said Cordelia, "in the first case, the urge comes on them so forcefully and swiftly they don't have a chance to get to the toilet. And in the second, they don't want to."

"I suppose so," said Edwin. He sounded a little dispirited by this whole line of enquiry.

"But that second case definitely overlaps with what you were talking about," said Cordelia.

"The personal grudge theory? I suppose it does. Which means it must be someone associated with the yoga centre. And didn't they manage to get in without leaving any signs of forced entry? That also suggests an—"

"Please don't say 'inside job'," said Cordelia.

"—suggests an individual who knows their way around the place," concluded Edwin.

"Not necessarily."

Cordelia told him about the open window and the easily climbable tree.

"It sounds like they need to take their security a little more seriously," said Edwin.

"Exactly what I told them. But even though the tree and the open window indicate that it could have been the work of a passing tramp…"

"*A passing tramp?*" said Edwin.

"Sorry," said Cordelia. "Agatha Christie gag. In her stories, before they get down to identifying the real culprit, they always consider the possibility that the crime might have been committed by…"

"Oh, I see."

"But just because a passing tramp, or anyone else with no connection to the ashram, could have easily got into the place and stolen the books…"

"How would they even know the books were there?" said Edwin.

"Precisely," said Cordelia. "And perhaps even more to the point, how would they know that those books were worth stealing?"

"Were they?" said Edwin. "Worth stealing?"

"If my initial research is anything to go by, yes, certainly. Especially if you are into that stuff." She told him about Avram

Silverlight. "His books are very rare, especially in good condition. And what's more, these copies were all signed by the author."

"And he's the chap the yoga centre is named after?" said Edwin.

"Yes, a local boy apparently, according to Wikipedia."

"Who was he?" said Edwin. "I mean, what did he do? Besides writing some very rare books."

"Well, apart from doing that and founding the yoga centre, not much, again according to Wikipedia. That's about all they have to say about him. Plus that he died in 1999."

"And how are you going to go about recovering the stolen books?" Edwin peered at her over his hot chocolate mug, eyes alert. He was genuinely interested. Anything involving potential skulduggery could be expected to command Edwin's full attention.

"Okay," said Cordelia. "I've agreed a two-pronged approach with the idiots at the ashram."

"You really should be a little more respectful of them, considering they're going to pay you a large sum of money. I assume you got them to agree to a large sum?"

"Absolutely," said Cordelia. "But they're only going to pay on results. Otherwise I'm investing my time for no reward. Although I did get them to give me a hundred-pound advance."

"Good for you."

Cordelia frowned, remembering the Silver Shrew scampering up her little set of polka-dot steps and spinning the dial of the safe. "I really only asked them for it to see if they'd give it to me."

"You mean, to assess how serious they are about this enterprise?"

"Right. And the answer turns out to be, very serious indeed. They really want these books back. I mean, want them badly."

"And why do you think that is?" said Edwin. "Why not just shrug and write off the loss? After all, they're just some books."

"I assume because they're treasured relics bequeathed to them by the revered, illustrious Avram Silverlight himself. By his own holy hands. But now you mention it, that's a very good question. They do seem strangely desperate to get them back."

"Anyway," said Edwin, picking up their mugs, which were now drained of hot chocolate, and carrying them to the sink. "You were going to tell me about your two-pronged approach." He ran water into the mugs to make them easier to wash later.

"Oh, right. Well, they've agreed I can either retrieve the stolen books for them, the exact ones that were taken. Or I can replace them with equivalent copies, suitably 'pristine'."

"But you said his books are very rare, especially in good condition," said Edwin.

"Right."

"So they'll be hard to find."

"Bloody hard to find. I just scoured the internet and only turned up one lonely example."

"So it won't be easy if you need to replace a full set of them."

"Damned difficult by the look of it," said Cordelia complacently. She wished she had some more hot chocolate to drink. Would Edwin be up for making another one so soon?

"You don't sound worried. Clearly you have a plan in mind."

"Yup."

"Care to share?" said Edwin, eyebrows angled upwards in polite enquiry.

Sensing something in the drift of the conversation, Rainbottle added an imploring little whine from beneath the table.

As it happened, Cordelia was more than happy to share. "Right, so I've drawn up a list of the dealers who are most likely to handle Avram Silverlight titles if they turn up on the rare book market, and I'm drafting an email that I'm going to send to all of them, personalised in each case so it doesn't seem like I'm spamming a whole bunch of people."

"Although that is exactly what you are doing."

"Although that is exactly what I am doing," conceded Cordelia.

"And I take it that this email isn't going to just ask them to keep an eye out for Avram Silverlight titles for you?"

"That would be very boring, wouldn't it?" said Cordelia. "No, I've also asked them if they'd kindly put me in touch with anyone else who is looking for his books. Any other customers who might have contacted them."

"Ah," said Edwin. "Sneaky." But he said it approvingly. "Do you think they will, though? Share the confidential details of other customers, I mean? Why would they?"

"I'll tell them that if any books change hands as a result of any contacts they give me, I'll pay them a commission."

"And do you think they'll fall for that?"

"I don't see why not, since it's true. Anyway, I'll also tell them I want to contact other Avram Silverlight fans because I'm writing an article about him. And when it's published, online of course, I'll offer lavish thanks to the book dealers who helped and include a link to send customers to their sites."

"And will you be writing an article about Avram Silverlight?"

"Not if I can help it," said Cordelia. "But if the idiots don't fall for one ploy—being paid a commission—they'll fall for the other, helping me write an article."

Edwin sighed. "You really must stop thinking of people as idiots and assuming you're cleverer than them. In many, perhaps even most, cases you will be correct. But now and then you will run up against someone who is at least as clever as you are. And that could prove quite dangerous. For you."

"Duly noted," said Cordelia, although she didn't really note it duly.

And she would have more than one occasion in the near future to look back ruefully on this warning.

Especially when people started getting killed.

"But you do see why I want them to put me in contact with anyone who's gagging to get hold of Avram Silverlight's books?" she said.

"Yes," said Edwin. "Because that might be the person who stole them from the ashram."

"Exactly," said Cordelia happily. "Full marks, Edwin. Now, is there any more of that hot chocolate?"

6: THE CORPSE POSITION

Fortified by the mugs of hot chocolate (she did indeed score a second one) and the fraternisation with Rainbottle and, in fairness, also with Edwin, Cordelia felt sufficiently energised to get back to work. She prepared the emails for the book dealers and sent them off with a sense of a job if not well done, then at least well begun.

And, as she'd told Edwin, she had found one of Avram Silverlight's books online.

Just one—they really were extremely scarce—but this "lonely example", as she'd called it, was for sale at an incredible bargain price on eBay. And, if the photo was to be trusted (which of course wasn't always the case), it was in fine condition.

No author's signature, but naturally Cordelia could provide that. If indeed she had to. She was still waiting to hear back from Howdy Doody and the Shrew about whether they needed signed copies—after they'd consulted the mysterious figure in the shadows who seemed to be pulling the strings on this whole project.

Cordelia was very interested indeed to discover who this might be.

In the meantime, she had instantly purchased the one book she'd found and paid a premium for next-day delivery. She retired to bed that night with a gratifyingly tingling sense of things moving forward.

But if she thought she'd made a start on assembling a set of replacement books for the ashram, she was cruelly disappointed. Because, when the eBay book arrived, it was not—as shown in the photo on the listing—pristine. In fact, it looked as though it had been savaged by a mad dog. No disrespect to Rainbottle.

Far from being, in professional book-grading terminology, in fine condition, it was, at best "acceptable".

Which actually meant quite unacceptable. At least to Cordelia.

She immediately contacted the eBay seller, sending a photo of the book she'd received, taken with her phone, along with a screenshot of the original listing, which featured, as was now clear, an image of the same book that had been found somewhere on the internet, rather than one of the actual item for sale.

Normally when somebody used such a picture for a listing, they made a point of declaring it was a "stock image". Which was exactly what the fool who'd sold this book to Cordelia had failed to do, as she pointed out to him at some length in her message.

Soon, indeed gratifyingly swiftly, she got a reply from the seller apologising fulsomely, giving her a full refund and telling Cordelia she could keep the beat-up copy.

Mollified, but no nearer her goal of retrieving any of the stolen books, Cordelia reflected that at least she now had an Avram Silverlight book she could read. (There were no e-books or pirated PDFs of his work online, which might help to account for the high prices the physical copies commanded.)

Breathing in the evocative scent of an old paperback, she flipped to the back of the book, where it gave a list of other titles by the same author, along with a brief synopsis of each. Reading this, Cordelia was surprised to discover that the scarily titled *The Corpse Position* was about a murder in an ashram in India.

All Avram Silverlight's stuff was supposedly non-fiction, true accounts of the author's own experiences. But this one sounded like a classic Agatha Christie-style murder mystery. In other words, pure fiction. Pure crime fiction.

Cordelia felt a little stirring of excitement.

Now, who did she know who was selling a huge collection of crime fiction in paperback?

Cordelia looked up the phone number of the widow Fairwell and dialled it.

"Hello, this is Betty," said a businesslike voice.

"Hello Betty, this is Cordelia. We met the other day, I—"

"Oh yes, the John D. MacDonald girl. Would you like to come and pick up your books?"

"If you don't mind, could you hang on to them for just a little longer?" said Cordelia, beginning to regret making this call. She didn't know when she'd have the rest of the money she owed on her purchases and perhaps by ringing Betty she'd awoken a sleeping beast, so to speak. The last thing she wanted was for Betty to become impatient.

She didn't sound impatient, though. "Oh, what can I do for you, then?" she said.

"I was wondering if you had a list of your husband's books?"

"Oh yes," said Betty. "Duncan kept everything exhaustively listed on the computer." She said "exhaustively" in the manner of someone who actually was quite exhausted.

"Would you mind terribly looking something up for me?" said Cordelia, her heart beginning to pound. She gave Betty the name Avram Silverlight and the title *The Corpse Position*.

There was a long pause at the other end, long enough for Cordelia to actually begin to miss the absence of waiting music, then Betty Fairwell came back and said, "Sorry."

Cordelia's heart sank.

"We only have the one book by him," said Betty.

"What?"

"Just *The Corpse Position*. Nothing else by that author."

"But you do have that book?" said Cordelia, almost dropping the phone. Of course, it made sense that the late Duncan Fairwell wouldn't own anything else by Avram Silverlight, because that was the only thing Silverlight had written which even vaguely resembled a crime novel.

But he did have this one.

Or at least he had once had it… "You haven't sold it?" said Cordelia.

"Nope," said Betty. "I'm scrupulously marking on the database each book once it's sold. Tedious, but useful." There was a brief silence on the line and then Betty came back. "Sorry, I was just rewarding myself by having a quick drink. I think I've earned it, don't you?"

"Oh yes," said Cordelia fervently.

"Now, would you like to buy this book?"

"Oh yes," said Cordelia again.

An hour later she was back in Richmond at the Fairwell house, in the sparsely furnished but elegant sitting room with the equally elegant widow. Betty was dressed all in black today (cashmere sweater and jodhpurs again), which was fitting enough for one signalling a bereavement, but she still had a string of pearls around her neck and a glass of lager in her hand, which was perhaps less so.

The copy of *The Corpse Position*—unbelievably, yes, it really existed and here it was—was resting on the arm of the sofa in which Betty had been sitting. She handed it to Cordelia as soon as they came in. "There you go."

Cordelia could hardly believe she was holding it in her hands. The book was immaculate. It was in fine condition. Or, as the Shrew might put it, pristine.

"Ah, how much would you like for it?" said Cordelia, trying to conceal her astonished delight at having found such a rare item in such perfect shape, and thereby keep the price down to something reasonable. Or just south of extortionate.

Betty waved a hand in the air, the one not holding her lager. "Oh, you can have it."

"Have it?"

"As part of your deal with the other books. I'll just throw it in."

"Just throw it in?" said Cordelia. She began to wonder if she was dreaming.

"Yes, you seem like a good customer. Do you want to take this one home with you today?"

"Yes, please," said Cordelia. "And I'd like to pay off another chunk of what I owe you."

"That'll be nice," said Betty. Cordelia handed over the hundred pounds she'd got from the comedy double act at the ashram and Betty counted it happily. This still left a considerable sum to pay, but Cordelia had a pleasant sense that it wouldn't be too long until she was able to do so.

Betty gave her a receipt and also a printed invitation on green paper. "Please come along. I'm having a party. On the houseboat." She nodded towards the river.

"A wake?"

Betty smiled. "If you like. In much the same way that I'm dispersing Duncan's books, I'm going to empty his wine cellar, and I'm going to be serving most of it up at the party. And it is very good wine indeed."

"Don't you want to save it to drink yourself?" said Cordelia.

Betty lifted her glass. "I'm a lager lady. Do come along. There'll be fireworks."

* * *

Cordelia had a quick look at *The Corpse Position* on the way back to Barnes. It was indeed a classic Christie set-up, a killing in an exotic location with a collection of intriguing suspects, in this case assorted Western hippie types who had come to India in search of enlightenment and also, for one of them at least, revenge.

When she got home, she set the book aside—it was in perfect condition and she intended to keep it that way—and picked up *Wheel of Fire*, the mutilated book she'd purchased on eBay. Books in bad condition like this were often advertised as "reading copies" and Cordelia had decided that was how she was going to make use of this one. By reading the fucker.

She settled into the cushioned seat in the window alcove, which provided daylight for her little attic room, and set about finding out what Avram Silverlight was all about.

Wheel of Fire was his first book and, like the others, was presented as an autobiographical account of his adventures. The story began as a classic example of British kitchen-sink social realism, in which Avram described—thankfully briefly— his working-class childhood and upbringing. Things really got started when, as a teenager, he embarked on a life of petty crime, eventually leading to his arrest for breaking into a shop to steal a Rolling Stones record.

Cordelia wondered why he hadn't just shoplifted it, like any normal teenager.

Anyhow, the burglary resulted in Avram being sent to borstal (a young offenders' institution) where the crucial and revelatory turning point of his life took place.

And no, it didn't involve a gangbang in the showers. It involved the borstal library.

This was a facility virtually devoid of reading matter and, compelled by the desperation of extreme boredom, Avram ended up borrowing a book about—you guessed it—yoga. From that moment on, the teenage tearaway was on a new, and indeed spiritual, path.

It turned out that good old Avram had a vigorous and compelling prose style, albeit with a rather clumsy approach to phraseology and a general tendency towards the pretentious. Plus, his characters inclined towards the cardboard, with stock descriptions—for example, eyes "twinkled" with emetic frequency.

But he could bring his scenes to life and get the reader to turn the pages. And as he sent his protagonist on a quest for enlightenment from suburban London (rather a good portrait of Putney in the 1960s) through Europe to India, he provided a constant stream of incident and interest. There was sex—the girl on the ferry, who was quite prepared to engage in knee-trembling naughtiness in a toilet cubicle. There was violence—the knife-wielding gang of Parisian urchins who robbed our hero of his money, his passport and even his sleeping bag. There were drugs—hashish, Benzedrine, LSD; the effects of all of which were described in such a way as to confirm to Cordelia that here, at least, the author was writing from real experience.

And, of course, there was yoga. The descriptions of yoga practice were so vivid and immediate and sensual in evoking the flow of energy in the body and the ensuing ease and relaxation of the muscles that they made Cordelia want to get her yoga mat out of the corner, unfurl it and do some postures right now.

But oddly enough, the most sensual and immediate sequences in the book were about food.

Kingsley Amis had once written (was it in his study of the James Bond novels?) that a vivid description of a meal was perhaps the best way to make a reader feel they were really present in a narrative. And Avram Silverlight's descriptions of assorted repasts certainly did the trick for Cordelia. They were mouth-wateringly fabulous, or fabulously mouth-watering, ranking right up there with that account of the Persian dinner in Joseph Wambaugh's cop novel *The Blue Knight* or any number of meals in George R.R. Martin's *A Song of Ice and Fire*.

Whether it was a hot, greasy clutch of fish and chips, laced with a tart, stinging splash of vinegar, wrapped in a screw of newspaper and eaten while heading for the docks in Dover; a baguette in Paris, hot and fresh from the boulangerie, torn open and with chunks of brie thrust into it to soften and melt into oozing, mushroom-y delight, washed down with a rough red wine; or a tagine of lemon, chicken and olives cooked in its eponymous earthenware pot in Morocco at the house of a hash seller, Avram was clearly excited and turned on by what he described, and Cordelia got excited and turned on (in a culinary sense) too.

His ultimate food porn, however, was reserved for the accounts of curries.

It was these passages in the book which really tipped Cordelia over the edge.

When she got to the last page, with Avram just arrived in India and walking up the pathway to the ashram of the yogi who would change his life, Cordelia had come to a firm decision.

She was going to go on Alfie's picnic.

7: BLUNT FORCE TRAUMA

It was a sunny autumn Saturday, the air rich with the drifting smell of wood smoke and reverberating with the evocative seasonal cry of the leaf blower, when Cordelia set off to attend Alfie's al fresco frolic. Or, to be more precise, to score a free meal provided by none other than Carrie Quinn, the Curry Queen.

Cordelia had been keenly looking forward to this ever since reading that damned book by Avram Silverlight. Her stomach had hardly stopped muttering with gastric anticipation.

Carrie's curries really were that good.

Cordelia left the house early, at noon, because she'd agreed to meet Lorna so they could help Alfie with picnic preparations. Edwin wasn't coming, or rather hadn't been invited. Lorna had chickened out of asking Alfie if she could bring her boyfriend.

This seemed a little strange to Cordelia but she was just as glad not to have her landlord attending, especially if, as she hoped, there would be scope for smoking dope and getting spectacularly ripped out on the tranquil autumnal common while contentedly digesting a fine lunch. It wasn't so much that Edwin would disapprove, it was just that his very presence, in his Rohan corduroy trousers with a copy of the *London Review of Books* rolled up in the back pocket, figuratively speaking, would be a bit of a downer and a dampener on the whole occasion.

Cordelia walked to Barnes Bridge station, pausing to watch the flash of oars on the sunlit Thames as a boat crew rowed past, then hopped a train to Putney where she alighted and walked the remaining distance to Alfie's house. This involved a stroll along Disraeli Road, then Oxford Road and finally down Winthorpe Road to the cul-de-sac where Alfie lived. This was a rather verdant residential lane near Wandsworth Park.

Alfie's house was a large, detached residence with an adjacent garage—a rare luxury in London and unique in the street; his neighbours probably hated him. Judging by the size of it and its slightly run-down look (the windows apparently hadn't been cleaned in recent years), the house must have been purchased decades ago. As she surveyed it, Cordelia reflected, not without envy, that in those days all you had to do was buy a house for a few (very few) tens of thousands of pounds and, eventually, pay off the mortgage to become a millionaire. Or, in this case, a multi-millionaire.

Before she could become too immersed in covetous bitterness, Cordelia was distracted by the front door opening and seeing none other than Mr T emerge. It was a little strange to encounter him wearing something other than the standard ashram uniform of orange pyjamas. As a matter of fact, he looked rather natty in his civilian garb—a houndstooth jacket and maroon trousers of a classy baggy cut that looked somehow Italian. Mr T was so small that Cordelia wondered fleetingly where he got his clothes. Perhaps a shop for exceptionally stylish Italian children.

He saw Cordelia as soon as soon as she saw him. "The bad penny," he said with apparent approval.

"Are you coming to the picnic?" said Cordelia.

"Certainly. I shall be along a little later. I will see you then."

"See you then," said Cordelia.

Mr T smiled and walked away, his highly polished leather shoes making a clipped and confident sound on the pavement.

Cordelia rang the doorbell and waited an unconscionable length of time for anything to happen. She might have been tempted to give up and assume the house was empty if she hadn't just seen Mr T emerge from it. Finally, she heard footsteps hurrying and the door was flung open to reveal a harassed-looking Lorna. "Thank god you're here. It's total chaos. Nothing's going to be ready in time."

"Is that Cordelia?" said an eager voice behind Lorna, and Alfie's grinning, bearded old face appeared over her shoulder. "Hello, Cordelia! Come in and let me show you around."

"We need to get things ready," wailed Lorna.

Alfie ignored her and affably ushered Cordelia in. "Let me give you a guided tour around the old homestead."

While Lorna wrung her hands in the background, both metaphorically and literally, and tried to remind them how much there was to do, and how little time to do it, Alfie did indeed give Cordelia a guided tour of his house. He was clearly proud of it while, paradoxically, clearly not being at all houseproud, judging by the general train-wreck appearance of the place.

It wasn't squalid or filthy, just utterly disorderly (in this regard it reminded Cordelia of her former playmate Jordon Tinkler's house, also in Putney). The sitting room, for example, might well have had the usual complement of furniture, but it was difficult to tell, shrouded as everything was by an impressive layer of books, magazines, clothes and records—vinyl LPs, many of them separated from their covers and looking somehow sinister in their glittering, circular blackness. There were also two huge wooden speakers that flanked the fireplace, each almost as tall as Cordelia. On top of one was an elaborate candelabra and several ashtrays.

On the other was a bong and, as if in hopeful compensation, a small statue of the Buddha.

The kitchen, by contrast, was clearly a serious working kitchen; many a meal had been prepared here and it contained not only an enormous refrigerator and a mass of professional-looking equipment—blender, juicer, pressure cooker, air fryer, myriad pots and pans of all shapes and sizes, and even a blow torch—but also an extravagant array of herbs, spices, condiments, pulses, grains, dried mushrooms, pickled mushrooms and other mysterious pickled things (all in glass jars), fresh mushrooms and fresh vegetables (including ropes of garlic and string bags of onions that hung from ceiling hooks) and fruit in a fruit bowl, none of which was rotten or going off. Other generalised foodstuffs included sacks of rice and boxes of breakfast cereal that appeared to have been chosen by a hyperactive child with a very sweet tooth.

On the walls in every room, including the downstairs bathroom, were framed paintings and photos of nudes—some of them pretty explicit (and explicitly pretty; quite alluring, in fact) Plus, posters of the Beatles, the Stones, Pink Floyd and the Who. Mostly the Who.

"This place is huge," said Cordelia as Alfie led her from room to room, pursued by Lorna, who wasn't getting any less anxious about the passing time. Indeed, she was now behaving like a cross between the white rabbit from *Alice in Wonderland* and the Ghost of Picnics Yet to Come.

"Isn't it just?" said Alfie. "Buying it was the smartest thing I ever did. Basically, I got it cheap, fixed it up to a very high standard and then let it get run down again." He looked around and laughed. "Now this is what I really wanted you to see…"

"Alfie, people will be arriving on the common soon," moaned Lorna.

"Hank will be here in a minute," said Alfie soothingly. "We'll set off as soon as he arrives."

This answer seemed to mollify Lorna. Maybe because it would afford her an opportunity to ask Hank where he'd got his daisy-decorated jeans jacket.

"Now, I was saving the best for last," said Alfie, looking at Cordelia with an expression of happy expectancy. He strode through a second sitting room at the rear of the house, adjacent to the kitchen, whose messiness was partly concealed by the low light conditions—all the windows had their curtains firmly closed.

Alfie opened a door in the far wall and they stepped through into a sort of solarium or greenhouse, which had clearly been attached as an afterthought to the back of the house. There were standard doors that led into the kitchen and sitting room and somewhere else, and, on the other side, French windows led out towards the garden. Furnished with wicker armchairs and a wicker sofa (pimped with spray paint to an unholy shade of purple that Prince himself would have approved of), the place had a red-tiled floor and a slanting roof that looked deplorably jerry-built, fashioned from corrugated transparent plastic that had become heavily stained with green growth, especially in the runnels where rainwater would flow down.

But all these details only gradually made themselves known to Cordelia, long after she had registered the main feature of interest in the annexe.

Which was to say, a fair-sized collection of the most enormous cannabis plants she had ever seen.

They filled the central area of the room, rising from a cluster of large and brightly coloured porcelain pots of indeterminate (Chilean? Peruvian? Welsh?) ethnic origin, the smallest of which was the size of a large bucket. These were filled with some kind of dark loam which looked moist and well-tended—a pink enamelled watering can with a spray nozzle stood vigilantly nearby and, judging by the small puddle of water spreading around it on the tiled floor, had been deployed very recently.

The plants themselves were vast, vibrant green entities, which stretched all the way to the plastic roof. Cordelia had never seen their like. A rich resinous scent, spicy with cannabinoids, twitched her nose. They were less like plants and more like trees, and the intensity of their green colour was such that she wondered if she had begun tripping already, just from being ushered into their noble presence and inhaling their intoxicating aroma.

She felt like falling on her knees before them and abasing herself in worship.

Behind her she heard Alfie chuckle, presumably in response to the look of adulatory astonishment on Cordelia's face. She also heard Lorna sigh, presumably in resigned resignation that there was going to be no way to convince either of them to speed their departure now.

But Lorna's worst fears and Cordelia's fondest hopes—which were very much the same thing and involved abandoning the whole notion of any picnic and instead sampling some of the resinous bounty of the cannabis canopies—transpired to be groundless. Because, once he'd shown the women the greenhouse and its contents, Alfie clearly felt his tour of the house had peaked and he abandoned it (Cordelia never got to see upstairs). Instead, he began to organise their departure to the picnic with an alacrity and an efficiency that was everything poor Lorna could have hoped for.

He started by herding them out to the garden and gathering furniture for the excursion. Perhaps furniture was too grand a word for the dozen or so folding canvas chairs in various states of rust, perforation and general disrepair which were arrayed out there, apparently since some none-too-recent party.

As they folded these up and leaned them against the garage, Cordelia had a chance to take in the garden. It consisted of lawns, flower beds and paved areas. Or rather, it had once consisted of these. But now it was so overgrown that the distinction between the three had all but vanished. The place had a wild, neglected look that was somehow perversely appealing. The local wildlife certainly appreciated it. Dragonflies hovered and darted over the pond and Rainbottle would have enjoyed chasing the frogs who lurched around in the long grass. Cordelia began to regret not making more of an effort to involve Edwin. Birds were hopping around the undergrowth and a squirrel or two were also on the prowl.

On the prowl as well was Alfie, not doing much to assist in their gathering of the garden furniture, but doing a lot of supervision—and fretting.

"Where the hell is Hank?" he muttered.

"He was supposed to be meeting you here?" said Cordelia as she tried to force a theoretically foldable but well-rusted chair to shut.

"He was supposed to be *staying* here. He spends half his life crashing at my place." Alfie took out his phone, selected a number and barked a message into it. "Hank, I've been trying to reach you. If you haven't listened to my other messages, we're having lunch on the common. The usual spot. On our way there now. Be there or be square."

On our way there now was a bit optimistic, reflected Cordelia. But they were making some progress.

"Lorna," said Alfie, putting his phone away, "could you help me with some stuff from the kitchen? Cordelia, love, do you know what a hibachi is?"

"Small Japanese barbecue," said Cordelia concisely.

"Basically, it looks like a big wooden box lined with metal. You can't miss it. Would you mind just sticking it in the back of the car? The garage is open, and so's the car."

As Lorna and Alfie went into the house, Cordelia entered the garage by its small back door and cursed Alfie for not telling her where the light switch was. A bad-tempered search in the petrol-scented darkness eventually proved successful, relatively speaking. A lone bulb on the ceiling came on and shed enough illumination for Cordelia to make an educated guess about her surroundings.

It was a large garage, easily big enough to accommodate two cars but, in what Cordelia already recognised as typical Alfie fashion, contained just one—an old silver Saab estate—with the rest of the space dedicated to the storage of junk.

There was actually a whole corner devoted to barbecue stuff, including several different designs of barbecues of varying sizes, with the hibachi being the smallest. Cordelia went over and, finding it was surprisingly light, picked it up and carried it towards the car.

As she did so, she noticed something out of the corner of her eye. Something among the barbecue paraphernalia she had just left. Before she could identify what it was, and why it had caught her eye—which would have involved going back and getting a proper look at it—Alfie and Lorna came through the door at the back of the garage laden with boxes of food. Cordelia put the hibachi in the car then went to help them.

They set off for Barnes Common with the car full of garden furniture, food and wine (bottles of rosé, cold from the big fridge) and cookery implements, and Cordelia, Lorna and Alfie squeezed in. Alfie drove along Montserrat Road towards the High Street, then turned right and then left onto the Lower Richmond Road, following this alongside the river.

Cordelia had to repress the urge to duck when they drove past the street in which Colin Cutterham lived. Guilty conscience. Cutterham was the wanker whose books she had burgled. A somewhat dangerous wanker, true, but luckily all that was history.

From the riverside road, they turned onto Mill Hill Road and headed into the bosky green heart of Barnes Common. As they drove, Cordelia asked Alfie about how he had come to know Carrie Quinn, the Curry Queen. Lorna had already intimated she was an old flame, but Cordelia wanted to hear Alfie's side of the story. "I understand you guys were an item," she said.

"We were an item all right. A top-drawer item, too." He sighed.

"Then what went wrong?" said Lorna. She was at least as interested, or, to be frank, as nosy, as Cordelia. But it wasn't a question Cordelia would have asked. It never surprised her that relationships concluded. Not living happily ever after (together) was, in Cordelia's books, the norm not the exception.

"Ah, it all came down to money," said Alfie. "Filthy lucre. Carrie was running her own restaurant at the time and she got into trouble. Financial trouble. And she wanted me to bail her out, because she knew I had a few quid."

Cordelia thought about his house, which was worth several million in the current market, and reflected that "a few quid" was an understatement.

"And she asked me for a loan," said Alfie. "And I said 'no way'."

"Why?" said Lorna. She sounded a little shocked. Lorna was the easily shockable sort.

"Because restaurants are money drains," said Alfie. "The only quicker way to lose money is to buy a boat. Anyway, I said no because I didn't see any point in throwing good money after bad. Carrie was inevitably going to lose the place and, if I'd given her the money, it would only have delayed the inevitable; made it slow and painful instead of being quick and painful. Consequently I didn't give her the dosh, the restaurant duly closed and she never forgave me."

"But she's still catering your picnic," said Cordelia.

Alfie smiled. "That's a business arrangement. I'm paying her. And Carrie never turns down business. She's all about the money."

"And the curry," said Cordelia.

Alfie's smile turned into a wolfish grin. "True. She's an artist in the kitchen all right. And pretty creative in the bedroom, too. But a gentleman never talks about that sort of thing."

"Fortunately," said Cordelia. She genuinely felt like they'd had a narrow escape. The last thing she and Lorna needed was an account of Alfie and Carrie's sexual history. The notion of those two old people thrashing around in a carnal frenzy, like a couple of dinosaurs writhing in a primordial swamp, was not to be borne.

"Fortunately indeed." Alfie chuckled.

"I understand Carrie's moving to Morocco," said Cordelia. Was it Morocco?

"Her cooking-school fantasy?" said Alfie.

"It doesn't sound like a fantasy," said Cordelia, a trifle glumly. "She says she's found a business partner."

"Not one with any money," said Alfie.

"How do you know?"

"Because if she had, she wouldn't still be hassling me for cash," said Alfie, squinting through the windscreen. "And she would have gone to Morocco. Here we are." He slowed the car down and found a place to park.

Carrie and Mr T and sundry hangers-on from the ashram and elsewhere—including, Cordelia was interested and a little annoyed to note, her nemesis Joni—were already waiting for them on the common. They had spread big, striped blankets on the grass and various containers of curry, rice and fruit were already arranged on them and opened. Joni had been assigned the duty of shooing away flies and any other interested insects, which Cordelia regarded as a task about commensurate with her pay grade and abilities. Perhaps a little above it.

Cordelia and Alfie and Lorna put down the hibachi and the food they'd brought from the car—bread and cheese and olives, and some interesting-looking salads Alfie had made, plus the bottles of rosé—then Lorna and Mr T went back to the car to get the folding chairs.

The site of the picnic was a patch of grass surrounded by trees, in handy proximity to a couple of benches. It was a pleasantly secluded, well-chosen spot. "Nice place," said Cordelia.

"An old favourite," said Alfie. "Hank and I have been coming here for years. A fair amount of cannabis resin has been smoked in this vicinity, it may not shock you to hear."

"I'll try not to be too shocked," said Cordelia, whose heart, as ever, lifted at the mention of drugs.

"Which reminds me," said Alfie. "Where is the old bugger? Hank, I mean." He took out his phone. "Not like him to miss a picnic." He punched in a number and put the phone to his ear, then suddenly lowered it again.

From the copse nearby there came a jaunty, jingling ringtone. Alfie switched his phone off and the ringing stopped.

Alfie looked at Cordelia, then put his phone away again, grinning. "The bastard's already here. Hiding and waiting to pounce." He moved towards the trees, calling out jovially. "We know you're there, you old bandit. Your cover's blown!" He hurried into the shadows of the trees, chuckling like a child playing a game.

There was a moment's silence and then a small cry—again, very like a child.

Somehow it pierced Cordelia and she froze.

Alfie came backing out of the trees, his face pale. He was breathing raggedly and loudly, as if he was about to have a stroke.

Cordelia hurried into the copse. There, on the ground, a man lay. If the white jeans jacket with the daisies on it hadn't been sufficient to identify him, the long dark ponytail with the silver hair clip would have done the trick.

If Alfie's face had been pale, it was nothing compared to Hank Honeywell's, which was as white as a mushroom. Dried blood was dark and clotted in a large patch on his pale forehead. And there was something misshapen about his skull.

Clearly Hank had been lying there for a while.

Equally clearly, he wasn't going to be able to join the picnic.

8: PIGEONHOLES

Not surprisingly, the discovery of a body—the body of Alfie's oldest, dearest friend—led to the cancellation of the picnic.

While Alfie waited for the police to arrive, accompanied by the ever-reliable and supportive Mr T, everyone else scattered to the four winds. "No point any of you having to be questioned by the filth," Alfie had told them. "It's not much fun. And it takes forever." He sounded like a man who knew what he was talking about.

"They'll want me here because I was the one who found... him," said Alfie, glancing back towards the trees where his friend lay out of sight. "And they'll want me to identify him."

All of this made sense. But Cordelia got the strong impression that Alfie would have stayed anyway, simply because he didn't want to leave his friend alone.

It wrung her heart to think about it, and she would have remained with Alfie to keep him company. But Mr T shooed her away. Alfie gave them the car keys and his house keys, and Cordelia and Lorna reloaded the car—it seemed particularly poignant that all this festive picnic stuff had hardly touched the ground before being returned—then drove back to Alfie's.

There they unloaded the garden chairs, leaving them folded in a corner of the garage, then Lorna started carrying the food and wine back into the kitchen. Cordelia helped her and, once everything was inside, she went back to get the last item, the hibachi, out of the car.

As she lifted it out of the back seat, she remembered that something had caught her eye earlier. Lorna was busy in the house, wrapping up food and putting it in the fridge, so Cordelia had the garage to herself for a useful few minutes. She had already switched on the lone ceiling bulb. It provided an uncertain yellow light, but it was more than adequate to confirm what she'd thought she'd seen earlier.

In the corner of the garage devoted to outdoor cookery equipment there was a large, bright red barbecue that consisted of a truncated cylinder the diameter of a bicycle tyre. It had four long black legs projecting from the base of the red cylinder, like an alien landing craft in a 1950s science fiction movie, with wheels on the two legs at the back.

Inside the red cylinder of the barbecue a circular metal grille was fitted. It was bright silver and had apparently never been used. It was immaculately clean. Which was just as well, because it had something stacked on it.

Books.

Paperbacks.

A lot of paperbacks. All of them published by Mayflower and written by a certain Avram Silverlight.

(And, as it turned out on inspection later, all of them signed.)

The books were tucked away out of sight inside the barbecue. Cordelia had only glimpsed them, peripherally, when she'd picked up the hibachi before.

Now she stood here, breathing in the garage smells of petrol and dust, with her heart pounding and she felt a strange, vertiginous sense of unreality. Cordelia reached out a hand and tentatively touched the books…

They were real, they were solid, they were genuinely there.

Just then, Lorna called from the house and Cordelia, startled as if caught in the commission of a crime (it was a little early for that sort of reaction just yet), quickly turned away, switched off the light and left the garage, shutting the door behind her. She went into the house to help Lorna, saying nothing, but with her mind whirling.

She'd only had a quick glance, but it was enough to suggest that all the stolen books were there.

The women finished putting the food away in the kitchen. Then, since one of the bottles of rosé had been opened anyway, they poured themselves a glass of wine each and drank it swiftly, like much-needed medicine. At that point, Lorna started doing some (also much-needed) tidying up around the place. But Cordelia pointed out that if they pursued this project they would be here for several weeks.

So they locked up the house and, as instructed, left the keys in a yellow smiley-face plant pot on the windowsill by the front door (Alfie's idea of high security), said their farewells and headed for their respective homes.

Here Cordelia gathered her burglary tools, an LED torch she could wear on her head and a medium-sized rucksack. She waited until nightfall then hurried back to Putney, ready to stage a full-scale break-in. But the garage, perhaps predictably, wasn't even locked and she was home again within the hour.

With the books.

"So, that's that," said Edwin.

"That's mostly that," said Cordelia. "I've got all the stolen books that were written by Avram Silverlight."

"And they're the ones that are hard to find, correct?"

Cordelia had cajoled Edwin into making them hot chocolate, as usual. But today they were drinking it in the garden, where Rainbottle was basking in the sun on Edwin's well-trimmed lawn. Cordelia reflected that this was the nearest she was going to get to having a picnic in the near future.

"Correct," said Cordelia.

"So, effectively that's job done."

"Effectively. But I'm not going to tell the clowns at the ashram."

"I wish you wouldn't call them clowns," said Edwin.

"I'm not going to tell them anything until I've got *all* the books," concluded Cordelia.

"Which should be straightforward, since all the others are fairly easy to find."

"Once again, correct," said Cordelia.

"Why are you waiting until you do that?" said Edwin.

"Because I don't want to give the estimable people at the ashram any excuse for paying me less than an extortionate fee for successfully completing my job. And the estimable people at the ashram might theoretically have grounds for that if I don't provide them with copies of every single book that was stolen."

"Thank you for not calling them clowns," said Edwin.

"No problem."

"So…" said Edwin, with elaborate casualness.

"Yes?"

"Are you going to tell the estimable people at the ashram that Alfie is the thief?"

"I haven't made up my mind yet," said Cordelia. "Poor Alfie."

"Yes, I understand he was close friends with the deceased chap."

"Very close. They were thick as—"

"Yes," said Edwin tactfully. "Any idea what actually happened to him? The friend, I mean?"

"Looked like his head was bashed in. There was a bottle of whisky lying beside him." This was one of the details that Cordelia had only taken in later. Along with the strong smell of whisky around the body. But, although Hank might have died while drinking, it was pretty clear he hadn't died of drink.

"Blunt force trauma," said Edwin knowledgeably.

"Anyway, in the situation, I really don't want to land Alfie in the shit." In fact, Cordelia wouldn't have wanted to turn Alfie in, even if he hadn't just lost his best friend.

"And therefore you'll say nothing."

"Providing the estimable people at the ashram don't insist on making that a condition of paying me. Telling them where I found the books, I mean."

"And if they do insist on making it a condition?" said Edwin.

"I'll tell them," said Cordelia simply.

"Fair enough. By the way, Lorna is very anxious to talk to you." Edwin picked up his mug and sipped his hot chocolate. He'd used the matching mugs from the Wetland Centre in Barnes. These were Cordelia's favourites, and featured drawings of long-billed water birds (the Eurasian curlew or Numenius arquata; Cordelia knew this thanks to the informative text on the mugs). "She said it's really quite important."

"Any idea what it's about?" said Cordelia.

"None at all. Drink your hot chocolate before it gets cold."

Despite being so wholesome it was boring, Lorna did have a certain taste for intrigue. For example, she wouldn't just chat to Cordelia on the phone about whatever was on her mind. Instead, she insisted that they meet in person. At the yoga centre.

Well, that was fine with Cordelia. She was still exulting in her newfound freedom to enter the place whenever she wanted to. There was nothing quite like being un-banned. It almost made it worth being banned in the first place.

Lorna had arranged for them to meet after her class on Monday morning.

Cordelia could have attended the class itself, since her yoga privileges had been restored. But it still rankled that she hadn't managed to wheedle freebie lessons out of Howdy Doody and the Silver Shrew, and she hadn't yet abandoned hope of achieving this. For instance, when they discovered how swiftly she'd fulfilled her mission and returned their stupid books, Cordelia might well be in a position to add free lessons to her payment, as a bonus. For a year. Or maybe two…

But until she'd proposed that, she was damned if she was going to pay.

So Cordelia waited on a bench out in the peace garden instead. She'd hardly sat down when people began to emerge from the direction of the changing rooms and the shala.

And among them was Alfie.

Cordelia went over and gave him a hug.

"Thank you, dear," he said.

"You look like you're coping all right," said Cordelia.

Alfie nodded towards the building he'd just appeared from. "Yoga helps with everything. Whatever ails you, it helps with it."

"Do the police…"

"Have any idea what happened to Hank?" said Alfie. "Not really. I mean, they know he was hit on the head with something, presumably that whisky bottle. Which incidentally was one of my prized single malts. It's Hank's favourite. *Was* his favourite. He must have borrowed it from my house. Anyway, the police think that might be the murder weapon. A deduction which didn't exactly require Sherlock Holmes. But that's about as far as they've got. They did ask me if Hank was gay. You know, because perhaps he'd picked up the wrong guy on the common and got gay-bashed." Alfie gave a thin chuckle. "Hard to know where to begin with how many things are wrong with that theory. Starting with Hank being the opposite of gay. He'd shag anything with a pulse, yes, but only if it was female. Age no object, though. He offered to take up with Carrie where I left off—and I wished him luck. He also said he'd taken a shine to Gunadya."

It took Cordelia a moment to remember that this was the Silver Shrew. *Yuck.*

"Could it have been robbery?" said Cordelia.

"If it was, they didn't rob anything. He had his cash, his cards, his phone, his jewellery…"

Cordelia remembered the silver hair clip.

"Speaking of theft," said Alfie, "how's your search for the stolen books going?"

Cordelia felt a sudden wild impulse and, without thinking, she yielded to it—like diving off the high board.

"I've found them," she said.

Whatever she'd expected from Alfie by way of a reaction, it hadn't been for his face to light up with pleasure. And for him to then seize her and give her a fierce, joyous hug. "Good girl!"

To say that Cordelia was bemused would be a considerable understatement. As Alfie hugged her—she noted with relief that he was wearing quite a nice eau de cologne—she wondered what the hell was going on.

Alfie released her from his hug and held her at arm's length. "You're not kidding?" he said, studying her.

"Nope. I found them. All the Avram Silverlight titles, that is."

"But the other ones don't matter," said Alfie, echoing what was apparently a universal opinion. "And you've got all of them?"

"That's right," said Cordelia. "And they're the same ones that were stolen." She kept a close eye on Alfie. Even closer than before. But if she'd been hoping to flush out some kind of guilty reaction—and she had—she was disappointed.

"That's great news," he said, beaming at her. "How did you find them? Where were they?"

Cordelia felt an instinctive wariness that stopped her answering this question. "I think that will have to remain confidential for a little while," she said. "A trade secret, as it were."

"The Paperback Sleuth!" enthused Alfie. "Well done, you."

"And could you do me a favour?" said Cordelia. "Don't tell anyone. Yet." More wariness.

"Of course not. But I'm very pleased. Chuffed to my bollocks," declared Alfie. "If you'll excuse the expression."

"I will," said Cordelia.

Alfie chuckled happily and threw his arms around her again. He was still embracing her when people started to emerge from the changing rooms. Alfie saw them and released Cordelia. "I'd better not compromise your reputation any more than it is already. See you soon."

"See you soon," said Cordelia.

"And well done! Oh, and by the way…"

"Yes?"

"There's a message for you in your pigeonhole."

"Is there?" said Cordelia. "I didn't even know I had a pigeonhole."

As Alfie left—through the gift shop—Cordelia went through the door on the opposite side of the peace garden. Here in the corridor that led from the changing rooms to the shala there was a wall with a noticeboard on it and, beside that, a bank of wooden shelves divided into a grid of small, square nooks in which members of the yoga centre could leave messages for each other, on slips of paper. Because email had never been invented. Or the telephone, for that matter.

There were names under each nook, written on removable strips of paper, and, sure enough, Alfie was right. One of these names was now Cordelia Stanmer.

And, again, sure enough, nestling in the nook was a folded piece of paper.

Cordelia reached in and took it out.

Before she could read it, someone called her name. She turned to see Lorna approaching.

"Alfie was just here," she said. "He did a lesson with us."

"I know, I saw him." Cordelia pocketed the note.

"Poor Alfie," said Lorna. Then, almost instantly, "He doesn't seem that upset. I mean, he seems upset, but not *that* upset."

"Grief affects people in different ways," said Cordelia, for lack of something even more banal to say.

"Anyway, thank you for coming to meet me," said Lorna, dropping her voice to a conspiratorial whisper.

"No problem," said Cordelia. "What's this all about?"

Lorna looked around and dropped her voice to an even lower and more conspiratorial whisper. "Let's not talk here."

Cordelia repressed a sigh at Lorna's secret agent shenanigans, but she was quite happy to follow her out of the ashram and talk with her as they headed down Abbey Avenue towards Vine Road; this was Cordelia's route home anyway.

"I'll tell you someone who really is upset about Hank," said Lorna. "Joni."

"Was she... involved with him?" said Cordelia. After the Xmas close encounter with Alfie in the meeting room, she was prepared to believe anything about Joni's sex life.

"Not as far as I know," said Lorna. "But she was involved with Alfie, and she knows how tight Alfie was with Hank. After we found his body on Saturday, she was really distraught and she needed to talk with someone. And she rang me."

"Why you?" said Cordelia.

"It had to be someone who wasn't part of the ashram staff."

"Why?" said Cordelia.

"Because it's about them. About the ashram."

Cordelia was all ears now. "Okay," she said.

"Do you remember you were wondering why Alfie wasn't banned from the ashram after they found him in that compromising position with her, at the Christmas party? I mean, considering that you were ejected instantly, admittedly for a different kind of offence…"

"I do remember," said Cordelia.

"And we thought maybe it was because they were more forgiving about sex than drugs? Well, they're not. Gunadya was absolutely furious when she discovered the incident and wanted Alfie excluded from the ashram for life."

Lorna turned and looked at Cordelia. They were just approaching the railway crossing on Vine Road and they paused some distance away, as a train hurtled past, so they could hear themselves talk.

"Then why didn't she exclude him?" said Cordelia.

Lorna leaned closer, and not just because of the train noise. "Harshavardhana wouldn't let her."

Harshavardhana was Howdy Doody. Cordelia wondered fleetingly if she could get everyone else to take up her nickname for him. It would make life so much simpler.

"Because earlier that day Alfie had made an arrangement with the ashram." Lorna paused dramatically.

Cordelia was so eager to know the answer that she didn't mind asking the obvious question. "What kind of arrangement?"

"He named them in his will. His entire estate will go to the ashram. And that's a lot of money."

"It is a lot of money," said Cordelia. "So, Alfie got blowjob immunity?"

"It looks like it."

"Do you think that's why he had that little fling there in the meeting room in the first place, because he knew he could get away with it?"

"Maybe," said Lorna. "But that's not all."

The train had passed now and the barriers at the level crossing creaked upwards. Cordelia and Lorna walked across the tracks. "What else?" said Cordelia.

"Joni said that when Alfie heard about the stolen books, he was furious."

"Why?" said Cordelia.

"I don't know," said Lorna. "But he was so angry that he told them if they didn't get the books back, the whole deal was off."

"The whole deal being…"

"Naming them in his will."

"Holy shit."

"Yes," said Lorna. "No wonder they were so eager to hire you."

The two women were approaching the little bridge at Beverley Brook. They crossed it and said their goodbyes, then took their separate routes across the village green. Cordelia was happy to be on her own. She had a lot to think about.

At least this now explained why Alfie had the books in his garage. He'd obviously stolen them himself to get out of having to give money to the ashram, as he'd promised. Steal them, then pretend to be enraged, and tell Howdy and the Shrew that because of the robbery the whole deal was off.

Of course, Cordelia had now decisively spoiled that plan, which she really couldn't bring herself to feel too bad about.

If he didn't want to give them the money, he could simply man up and tell them he'd changed his mind.

Yes, that all made sense.

But despite it making sense, Cordelia felt a deep uneasiness, like someone setting out across a frozen lake knowing the ice hadn't had time to grow very thick.

Because weighing against there now being a logical reason for Alfie to have stolen the books was Alfie's reaction when Cordelia had told him she'd found them.

He had seemed genuinely pleased.

Of course, he could have been pretending.

But Cordelia had felt, as she occasionally did while watching some porn star in the throes of apparently 24-carat ecstasy: *they simply couldn't be that good an actor*.

Yes, she really believed Alfie was glad she'd found the books.

And then there were other problems with the theory of Alfie as the book burglar. Why the dirty protest? Stealing the books made sense, some kind of sense. But why this other act? To throw people off the scent, so to speak? No olfactory joke intended.

And wasn't stealing the books a very weird and roundabout way of getting out of making the ashram a beneficiary in his will? What if they found the books—as indeed they had, thanks to Cordelia? And even if she hadn't found them, she, or someone else, could have sourced replacement copies.

More to the point, if he'd wanted the ashram out of his will, why not just do it? Alfie didn't strike Cordelia as the sort of person who would have a problem being blunt about his wants. And if he'd changed his mind about giving them the money, he could just say so, instead of embarking on this stratagem.

And *then* there was the matter of the manner in which Cordelia had found the books. She'd only spotted them because she'd been tasked with loading the hibachi into the car. Why would he have asked her to do that if he knew the stolen books were right there in the garage and she was likely to see them?

The most logical, if Machiavellian, explanation was that he'd *wanted* her to find them for some reason…

But the argument against this was, again, his surprise when she'd told him she'd found them, just now.

He simply couldn't be that good an actor.

Curiouser and curiouser.

9: CAT AND MOUSE

Cordelia walked across the village green towards the duck pond, deep in thought.

By the time she arrived home she had formulated an action plan. It involved borrowing Edwin's car, which effectively meant also borrowing Edwin. Although Cordelia did have a licence of her own, she wasn't a particularly confident driver, especially in London traffic. And, in any case, Edwin didn't like anyone else using his Volvo.

Edwin was with Rainbottle in his little flat at the back of the house listening to *Composer of the Week* on Radio 3 (Stravinsky). At first, he was a little reluctant to help, but as soon as Cordelia explained what her real—nefarious—purpose was, he agreed readily. Indeed, eagerly.

Always up for a little intrigue, Edwin.

They left Rainbottle lying lazily on his rug, listening to the details of the genesis of *The Firebird*, and got Edwin's yellow Volvo out of the garage where it spent most of its life dormant. Cordelia felt that, like Edwin, it would appreciate this little outing. Sitting in the passenger seat beside Edwin as he drove along Barnes High Street towards Church Road, she called Alfie's number.

To Cordelia's delight and relief, he didn't answer immediately. Perfect. She let it ring three times, praying all the while that he wouldn't pick up, then she hung up, praying he wouldn't ring back.

The traffic going from Barnes to Putney, a very modest distance, was terrible. Edwin, a local boy and a seasoned pro at this game, used every trick in the book, avoiding the main roads and turning off Rocks Lane onto Queen's Ride. But little good it did them. Cordelia calculated how much swifter and easier it would have been to catch the train or walk to their destination.

But she needed a car for what she had in mind.

After crawling through traffic, with Stravinsky on the car radio to keep Edwin mollified, they finally pulled into the cul-de-sac where Alfie resided. "That's his house there," said Cordelia.

"Nice big house," said Edwin with the complacency of a man who also had a nice big house, and in an even better part of town. He put the handbrake on.

Based on her last visit, Cordelia was expecting a lengthy wait when she rang the doorbell, but the door opened so swiftly, indeed instantly, that Cordelia and Edwin took a startled step backwards. Alfie stood there with his phone in one hand and a spliff in the other, as rock music blasted out of the house behind him. He looked as startled as they were.

"Cordelia," he said.

"Alfie, this is Edwin," she said. Immediately adding, "He's my landlord," so there was no danger of Alfie thinking he might be Cordelia's boyfriend. Even for an instant.

"Hello, Edwin," said Alfie, transferring his spliff to the hand that held his phone and shaking hands warmly with Edwin. "Is it Edwin or Ed?"

"Edwin, thanks."

"Come on in. What a surprise to see you again so soon, Cordelia."

"I tried to ring you," said Cordelia, establishing her cover story.

"Oh yeah," said Alfie, sticking the spliff in his gob so he could now use both hands on his phone. He scrutinised the screen. "I've got a missed call from you. Sorry, I didn't notice."

"You probably didn't hear it," said Edwin politely, but sufficiently loud to be heard over the music.

"Oh, sorry," said Alfie. He went into the sitting room and turned the music down. "Lowell George," he said, by way of explanation, when he came back. "Has to be played at volume."

"Well, we'll try not to interrupt your listening for long," said Edwin, turning to Cordelia with a look that said *this is your show*.

"Ah, so we're going to have a barbecue," said Cordelia. "At our place. And we were wondering if we could borrow some bits. From you."

"Sure," said Alfie.

"I saw some things in the garage the other day," said Cordelia. "You've got so much great stuff, ha ha. And I thought…"

"No problem," said Alfie.

"Then you don't mind if we go into the garage now?"

"I'll be right with you," said Alfie. He nudged his gnarled old feet into his pink espadrilles, which were stationed by the front door, and shambled out of the house accompanied by Cordelia and Edwin. As soon as they entered the garage, Cordelia, by now an old hand, switched on the light and went right to the barbecue accoutrements corner. Edwin and Alfie followed obediently.

"I'd like to borrow this one," she said, putting her hands on the cylindrical red alien-spacecraft barbecue in which she'd found the books.

"Fine," said Alfie, not batting an eyelash and as affable as ever.

Cordelia grunted and tugged it around so Alfie could see, if he'd known about the books, that they were no longer there. She showed him the silver grille on which the pile of books had been sitting, now bare except for the can of lighter fluid and the clicking-sparking device (in a matching shade of red) that had been keeping the books company. This was Alfie's cue to show some signs of guilt.

But he just said, "Let me help you with that." He stepped into the spot where she'd been standing and eased the barbecue from its resting place.

With Edwin's assistance, he got it out of the garage and rolled it along the pavement towards Edwin's car, with an occasional arbitrary erratic detour caused by its stiff wheels. "Unlike a cabinet minister," said Alfie by way of explanation, "this thing occasionally has a mind of its own."

Edwin laughed appreciatively and, when they got to the car, the three of them managed to wrestle it inside. Then they all sighed with relief.

"When's the barbecue, then?" said Alfie.

Cordelia said nothing.

Alfie was looking at her, but she still said nothing. She had fallen profoundly silent.

But that was better than what she'd almost said, which was, "What barbecue?"

Alfie was still looking at her, still smiling a good-natured and apparently unsuspecting smile. But for how long? Cordelia needed to say something, but her brain was frozen solid and she had quite lost the power of speech.

Luckily for her, good old Edwin, cool as a cucumber, immediately stepped into the breach and said, "Friday. But I wanted to borrow it a few days beforehand so I could do some trial runs. To get the hang of it. I hope you don't mind."

"Not at all," said Alfie. "Good thinking. Give me a ring if you need any advice."

"I will, thank you," said Edwin. And, still cucumber-cool, "And do come along if you like. To the barbecue. On Friday."

"I might well do that."

Then Edwin got into the car and Cordelia thanked Alfie profusely and got into the car herself, and they drove off, leaving Alfie standing in the street in his espadrilles, waving and smoking his spliff.

"Good save about when the barbecue is," said Cordelia.

"Thank you."

"No, thank *you*. My mind just went blank."

"No problem," said Edwin. "So... when you tried to phone him on the way here, that was for the sake of veracity?"

"Yes, because it would have been just too weird and/or suspicious to simply turn up out of the blue."

"It was still pretty weird," said Edwin. "But presumably you didn't want him to answer the phone?"

"No, because then he would have been forewarned. I wanted to see the expression on his face when we took him into the garage and he saw that barbecue without the books on it."

"What would you have done if he had answered the phone?" said Edwin.

"That was just a risk I had to take."

"Audacious," said Edwin. "And what did you make of the expression on his face?"

"I don't think he ever knew the books were there. What did you think?"

"Picture of innocence," said Edwin. "But some people are very good and very plausible at deceit."

"I don't think he's that good an actor."

"That's what you said before," said Edwin. Cordelia had told him about her encounter with Alfie at the yoga centre earlier. "And since you told him you'd found the books, he would have had plenty of time to get used to the notion they're gone. Indeed, he would have popped into the garage to check as soon as he got home, don't you think?"

"I just wanted to confront him on the spot," said Cordelia. "If he'd known something, I'm sure he would have given himself away."

"You like him, don't you?" said Edwin, casually.

"So what?"

"So nothing. I like him too, and I've only just met him. He's a likable chap. But even likable chaps can be very slippery characters. And if he did steal the books, he knows you're on to him and now he's playing cat-and-mouse games with you."

"I still don't think it was him," said Cordelia stubbornly.

"All right. Was there anyone else who could have put them there, in the garage? Does anyone else live in that house with him?"

"No one *lives* there. But he has a frequent houseguest. Or had. Hank Honeywell."

"Is he the poor dead chap on the common?"

"Yes."

"Do you think he could have stolen the books from the ashram?" said Edwin.

"Yes," said Cordelia. "Very much so." Somehow Hank Honeywell seemed just the sort to do something like that.

"Hmm," said Edwin, mulling as he drove, swiftly and expertly. The whimsical gods of London traffic were being kind to them now and they were sailing along. "And do you think Hank's death might have had something to do with him having stolen the books?"

"I don't know."

They reached the junction by Barnes Pond where a left turn would take them home, but Edwin turned right.

"Where are you going?" said Cordelia.

"To the Ginger Pig," said Edwin. This was the name of the local butcher's shop. "To pick up some stuff for our barbecue. We might as well go ahead and actually have one now."

"I suppose so," said Cordelia, feeling a little guilty about where her web of lies had led them.

"After all, Alfie might be coming," said Edwin. And then, "I'll get some of those sausages that Rainbottle likes."

After they got home, and she'd helped Edwin to take the barbecue out of the car and put it in the garage—it seemed it was the appliance's destiny to be forever resident in such a place—Cordelia went up to her room. It was when she was changing out of her street clothes into something more casual, for general moping-about purposes, that she happened to put her hand into her pocket and feel a piece of folded paper.

As she drew it out, she remembered what it was: the note from her pigeonhole. She unfolded it, fully expecting it to be a bit of ashram-spam about an upcoming event or a new and even more exorbitant price for the yoga mats.

It wasn't. It was a note for her personally. It had been printed on a laser printer and was formatted like a business letter, except without a salutation, signature or return address.

It read:

If you want the stolen books, I have them and I will sell them to you cheap. I just want to get rid of them. Meet me tonight and we can do a deal.

It then gave details of where and when to meet.

The final words were terse and unambiguous.

Come alone.

When she went downstairs, she thought Edwin might be fed up to see her again so soon. But, if he was, he disguised it gallantly. And, as soon as she showed him the note, she had his full attention.

"Well, well, well," he said. "Now what do we make of this?"

"Maybe the books I found in the garage weren't the stolen ones," said Cordelia.

"But you said they were signed."

"That doesn't really mean anything," said Cordelia. No one knew better than her how little credence you should put in a signature in a book. "But, in any case, that's just one of several possible scenarios."

"Indeed it is," said Edwin, holding the note and examining it thoughtfully. "There's only one thing we know for certain."

"That whoever wrote this doesn't know I already have the books."

"Or *didn't* know," said Edwin. "If Alfie is the thief, he could have written this and left it in your pigeonhole before he saw you this morning."

"In which case, he won't turn up for the rendezvous," said Cordelia.

"Then you're thinking of going?" said Edwin.

"Of course. If someone really does have another set of books and wants to sell them cheap, I'd be crazy not to take advantage of the offer. I'll be able to resell them at a healthy profit."

"But if something sounds too good to be true…" said Edwin.

"I know," said Cordelia.

Edwin studied the final words at the bottom of the sheet of paper.

"So are you planning to go alone?" he said.

"Not on your nelly."

10: HOSPITAL VISIT

The site of the rendezvous specified by the enigmatic note-leaver wasn't far from the location where Hank Honeywell's body had been found, a fact which understandably gave Cordelia pause.

But at least the mysterious meeting place wasn't actually on Barnes Common. Instead, it was on a wide patch of waste ground known as Lower Common, facing Putney Common and, just for good measure, situated beside a street called Commondale. It was located adjacent to the Lower Richmond Road, opposite the bit with the church where the buses turn around.

This stretch of waste ground had once been the site of a hospital, and the building was still there, though now abandoned and derelict and invariably deserted.

All of which made it a good place for a secret meeting, though it was pretty high on the creepiness scale.

And the latter factor wasn't at all diminished by the fact it was now late in the afternoon, and what had been a bright and breezy autumn day was transforming into a moody, murky autumn evening. Somewhere a crow was making bloodcurdling cries, just to add to the fun.

Silhouetted against the darkening sky, the old hospital was a conglomeration of rectangular red-brick boxes with white stone strips outlining its windows. Some of the red-brick structures were low-lying and horizontal, forming the various wings of the building; some were vertical, rising in short, stubby towers.

All had seen better days, considerably better days, and were now a mess. The windows were in long rows, many of them boarded up, others broken by vandals. Here and there, between the rows of windows, were sections of smooth, grey panelling, presumably intended as an exciting decorative feature.

The place had been empty for years and the site was now overgrown and heading back to the wild—a fair chunk of the second floor of the main building was concealed by the dark, spreading branches of a large tree that grew close beside it.

It was all very quiet and there wasn't a soul in sight.

Cordelia realised she was deliberately delaying the inevitable, so she forced herself to cross the road and walk through the gap between a length of wire-mesh fence on one side and a high, blank section of wooden fence on the other, entering what had once been the hospital grounds.

She skirted a pool of rainwater, her reflection caught for an instant in it then erased as the surface of the water was ruffled by a sudden breeze. Cordelia kept moving, heading for the front of the building, the bit which had been the main entrance. Hard to imagine that, once upon a time, this had been a place of hectic activity with ambulances pulling up and patients being rushed inside to their fate.

As she drew close, Cordelia saw that one of the white strips on the red-brick wall had lettering on it—the name of the hospital. Not too unexpectedly, it was called Putney Hospital. Her speculations as to why the place had shut down were interrupted by an odd sound.

Pausing for a moment, Cordelia tried to identify it. It was a repetitive knocking sound, faint and somehow nerve-jangling in that, despite its persistence, there was no clear pattern or regularity to it. It came and went, apparently emanating from somewhere high above her.

She decided it was a loose section of plywood on one of the boarded-up windows, stirring in the strengthening wind. A plastic bottle and other random bits of rubbish—crisp bag, cigarette packet—came skittering along the ground like small creatures following at her heels as she approached the hospital, blown by the breeze.

She was nearing her destination now. What had once been the front doors of the hospital were sealed off behind a tall barrier of wire-mesh screens, chained together. Just in front of this rather uninviting security measure was the exact spot that had been specified in the note for the rendezvous. A green wooden bench.

There was no one waiting for her, which wasn't much of a surprise. The whole place had felt deserted as soon as she'd entered the hospital grounds and Cordelia's instincts told her she was quite alone here.

So either she was going to have wait around until her mystery correspondent deigned to arrive, or she was going to have to wait around until it became obvious they weren't going to arrive and that the whole thing was a mischievous hoax, or a deliberate and malicious waste of her time. Cordelia sighed, put her hands in her pockets and hunched her shoulders against the wind. She decided it would be best to keep walking, in circles if necessary, to keep warm.

But then she saw something.

There on the bench. A small patch of bright red.

Moving closer, she saw it was an envelope.

Cordelia went over and sat down on the bench to inspect it. It was intended for her, all right.

The red envelope had a small white rectangle of paper stuck to its front with Cordelia's name printed on it in capital letters. It was in the same font as the note from the pigeonhole and had presumably been printed on the same printer. Cordelia tore the envelope open.

Inside was a greeting card with a bug-eyed cartoon rabbit grinning at her and the word *Surprise!* in large and embossed bright rainbow colours. She opened the card. The pre-printed legend inside said, *I hope you like your present!* There was no handwritten message or signature.

"Cordelia!" It was Edwin's shout, loud and urgent. "Move!"

The imperative note in his voice—he sounded *scared*—galvanised Cordelia and she sprang from the bench, the card and envelope falling from her hand, and began to run.

She was just trying to work out what the hell direction she should be running in when, behind her, she heard a thunderous and rather sickening crunching sound.

Cordelia turned to see that a large, dirty-white shape was now occupying the bench where she had been sitting, with a cloud of dust rising from it. For a crazed moment it looked like the effigy of a person sitting there, with a bulky, pale grey body and thin, twisted brown limbs, and then her mind made sense of it.

It was a block of concrete with steel reinforcing rods jutting out of it, reddish brown with rust. The weight of it had smashed through the wooden slats of the bench and it was stuck, hanging just above the ground, like a fat man embarrassingly suspended after his seat had collapsed under him.

Right where Cordelia had been sitting.

Her eyes travelled up to the roof above, some three storeys up, a sharper edge of darkness against the darkening sky. The piece of concrete had fallen from there.

Although maybe "fallen" wasn't really the word...

There were footsteps behind her and she turned to see Edwin running out of the shadows. He stopped beside her and put his hand on her shoulder. "Are you all right?"

"Yes." Cordelia was surprised by her own calm, conversational tone. This didn't last long. "Fuck me," she said, her voice beginning to quaver. "I was sitting right there…"

"Yes," said Edwin. He wasn't looking at her. He was looking up at the roof. "You're quite sure you're all right?"

"Yes—"

But Edwin was already gone, running towards the building. Cordelia was putting everything together in her head now. Blindingly obvious, yes, but then she'd had a bit of a shock, so maybe she was justified in taking a few seconds to catch up.

Someone up on the roof had dropped that thing on her. On the spot where she'd been sitting, where she'd been lured by the envelope. What could have been more natural than to pick up the card from the bench and then sit down to read it?

Which was exactly what someone had wanted her to do.

Someone waiting up there on the roof with this massive chunk of rubble all prepared and good to go, poised on the edge, sighted on the bench, ready to tip over and drop from high above, out of the deepening evening sky, just at the right moment, right on top of her…

And now Edwin had gone after them, after her assailant. The fucker who had dropped this concrete payload so neatly on the spot where she was supposed to be sitting. *Would* have been sitting if not for Edwin.

Cordelia was fully up to speed now.

Edwin had just run around the left side of the building.

Cordelia ran around the right.

Between them, they would intercept the fucker.

As she ran, it occurred to Cordelia that her assailant might be armed. Oh well, Edwin would be armed too.

She ran along the side of the building, past smashed and boarded windows and graffiti-sprayed walls and doors. Her reflection ran beside her, flashes of it in the occasional surviving pane of glass, and her footsteps slapped and echoed. She reached the corner and sprinted around it to the back of the hospital, to what had once been a parking lot, the tarmac now cracked and pitted with clumps of weeds sprouting through it, growing as high as the top of her head and interspersed with shining depressions in the ground, full of oily rainwater, as big as ponds, with splashes of reflected light in them.

It was silent and still. There was no one there.

Cordelia heard a faint clanking sound high above her and looked up to see Edwin. He was scrambling up a fire escape, a big zigzag structure of black iron fixed to the back of the building, and he had almost reached the roof. Cordelia didn't try to wave to him or shout. He was clearly engrossed in the chase and she didn't want to distract him. As she watched, he reached the lip of the roof, climbed over and disappeared from sight.

She continued in the direction she'd been moving, no longer running now, and completed a circuit of the building, ending up back where she'd started—at the bench with that fat, jagged concrete effigy stuck on it, as though it was sitting waiting for her.

Cordelia paused, feeling a strange and disturbing sense of wrongness.

And not just the strange and disturbing wrongness of someone having just tried to kill her...

Something was *different* here.

Something had changed from the way it was, only a minute or two ago, when she had left it. What was different? Then Cordelia realised.

The card and the envelope were gone. She had dropped them on the ground when she'd jumped off the bench and they'd still been there when she'd left a moment ago. She was sure of that.

Now they were gone.

While she was on the other side of the building, someone had snuck around here and scooped them up.

Then, as if in ironic counterpoint to this realisation, she heard a whispering, whirring sound from somewhere out on the dark road. A bicycle. Being pedalled away at speed. She started to run towards the road, then stopped. It was much too late. Whoever it was would have long vanished from sight by now. Cordelia's shoulders slumped in defeat.

A moment later Edwin came out of the shadows at the side of the hospital, moving quietly. He walked over and stood beside her, towering over her protectively.

"No one on the roof," he said. "Not anymore."

"I went around the other side of the building," said Cordelia, "in case they went that way."

"Good idea. I don't suppose you saw anyone?"

"No, but while I was doing that, they came around here and took the card and the envelope they'd left for me." *The bait*, she thought. *And I took it like a good little fish.*

Edwin gave a disgusted snort. "The one piece of evidence which we might have wanted to give to the police."

"I'm sorry," said Cordelia.

"It's hardly your fault."

"And I just heard someone on a bicycle, hurrying away. I don't know for sure it was them, but…"

"A bicycle would have been a good choice," said Edwin. There was a note of reluctant admiration in his voice, and not just because he was a biking nut. "Fast and quiet for a getaway. And, as escape vehicles go, easy to leave in concealment, out of sight, and easy to access in a hurry." He sighed. "These bastards have been one step ahead of us all the way."

"No," said Cordelia. "If they'd been one step ahead of us, I'd be sitting there with a concrete block on top of me."

Edwin smiled a toothy smile.

"Good point. Let's look on the bright side."

"Thank you for saving my life," said Cordelia.

"Always a pleasure."

11: STALIN

You might think that it was somewhat foolish of Cordelia to accept another invitation to the abandoned hospital—a note provided via the ashram pigeonholes again—and to go back *without Edwin* this time.

When Cordelia turned up for this second rendezvous, the place was completely dark, the crow was screeching even more loudly than before and the repetitive thudding of the loose board, or whatever it was, was even more pronounced.

And it was indubitably even more foolish of her to sit back down on the bench—miraculously repaired—in exactly the same place, just because another bright red envelope was waiting for her, with her name on it.

And sure enough, inside red the envelope was the same greeting card. With the crazed cartoon rabbit, looking even more crazed now—there was something positively disturbing about his huge, manic cartoon eyes (did they actually *move*? This was a very deluxe greeting card)—and the big, bright, jolly word *Surprise!*

And, inside the card, the cheerful caption *I hope you like your present!*

Of course, by now Cordelia knew exactly what that "present" was, and she looked up to see the giant, jagged chunk of concrete plunging towards her out of the night sky, a darker shadow coming from darkness. And, above that, just visible over the lip of the roof, a triumphant figure, sadly not recognisable but waving cheerily at her, a cheerful farewell.

Yup, very foolish indeed, as Cordelia herself reflected regretfully, as the mass of concrete whistled towards her…

And then she woke up, tangled in her duvet, in a terrified sweat, with her heart hammering.

Post-traumatic stress. What a bummer.

To his credit, Edwin seemed to realise that she might be going through something like this (after all, he'd had experience of some extreme situations himself) and, when he heard her coming down the stairs—tipped off by Rainbottle—he came out of his flat and asked how she was doing. He then ignored her reply (a brave lie) and asked her a follow-up question about *what* she was doing. "How are you going to spend your day?"

"Well, I thought I'd just chill out," said Cordelia. "You know, not do anything ashram-related for a while."

"Very sensible," said Edwin. "Well, if there's anything I can do to help, don't hesitate…"

"Thanks," said Cordelia. But her landlord was already heading back into his flat, from which came the smell of bacon frying and the sound of an excited dog (the two phenomena were probably not entirely unrelated).

Cordelia let herself out of the house and walked through the bright morning, fragrant with recent rain, to the railway station. Not Barnes Bridge this time, but Barnes, which was further away but was a nicer walk, and she needed a nice, long walk.

Unfortunately, certain sections of that walk—the duck pond, for instance—brought back memories of a previous assassin (how dreadful to realise she'd acquired an assassin *again*; it was actually quite embarrassing, like the recurrence of a sexually transmitted infection).

But she was soon past the duck pond and walking through the village green, past the arts centre (no traumatic memories there), across Beverley Brook (ditto) and towards the station. There, after an unconscionable wait, she finally caught a train to Putney—she could have walked it in the time that had elapsed—and then set off down the High Street on a charity shop rampage. It was to be a fairly truncated rampage since Putney only had three charity shops at the moment. The situation constantly changed as legit shops went bust and their premises became available for charity shop occupancy.

Cordelia planned to start at Oxfam and work her way down the hill towards the river.

As soon as she began looking through the secondhand books, she realised what a smart decision it had been to do this today, instead of moping around her room and fretting about things. All her professional instincts and responses rose up in her afresh and she stopped dwelling on the nastiness of last night. Indeed, as soon as she made the first decent find, she forgot all about that, caught up as she was in the thrill of the chase.

The first decent find was a set of World War Two novels by Sven Hassel, including *Legion of the Damned*, *Liquidate Paris* and *SS General*. War novels were not Cordelia's cup of tea, but she knew she could always sell copies of these—there was a thriving market among devotees of mass annihilation in uniform. Speaking of uniforms, Hassel's books featured a cat in uniform. Yes, really—the hard-bitten members of the penal Panzer battalion who fought their way across Europe in his books had a pet cat for whom they'd sewn an official Panzer battalion uniform. He was called Stalin. The cat. Yes, again, really.

Stalin the uniformed cat (he also had an official paybook) was perhaps an early sign that Hassel's books were not entirely, as claimed, based on hard documentary fact and firsthand experience. But that hadn't stopped them selling well over ten million copies in the UK, and they remained popular. What's more, the set Cordelia had picked up were all early printings and were in beautiful condition.

She happily stashed them in her rucksack, calculating she could sell them for approximately five times what she'd just paid for them. She had a regular customer who would probably leap at the opportunity to pay a premium for these little beauties and whom she would email as soon as she got home.

In fact, why wait until she got home?

Cordelia went into the Sainsbury's car park to look for a car that was clean and the right colour (a neutral shade to provide an attractive background for the covers), and ended up spreading the books out on the bonnet of a gleaming black BMW and snapping a photo of them with her phone. It couldn't have turned out better if she'd shot it in a studio with a professional photographic backdrop. Glowing with triumph, she packed the books back in her rucksack again and hurried off before an irate BMW owner could come out of the shop and shout at her.

As she strolled down the High Street, she attached the pic to an email containing an excited message describing how she'd just found the books—all true, actually, including the excitement—and quoting the bargain price she was willing to part with them for. That bit was less true, at least the part about a bargain, as Cordelia had decided to ask for *ten* times what she'd spent on the books. After all, you never knew your luck, and they did look good against that gleaming black background.

She pressed send and went into the next charity shop. This proved to be a complete bust book-wise, which would have lowered her spirits if she hadn't started the day with a thrilling victory (the war rhetoric was infectious). Now she turned her attention to the clothes, which were particularly good in this shop, and ended up buying a couple of rather nice items.

What's more, while she was in the changing room, trying things on, she got a reply to her email from the war-book nut, enthusiastically agreeing to pay the extravagant price she'd quoted and begging her not to sell them to anyone else. (Yes, she had hinted she'd be offering the books to some other eager buyers, which was a lie.) In fact, he ended his message by imploring her to notify him that she hadn't already sold them elsewhere.

Cordelia put him out of his misery, letting him know the books were his. And, while she paid at the charity shop till for her garments, her phone alerted her that the funds had arrived from him in her own account.

She was so charmed by the swiftness of this transaction—from discovery of the books to a fully paid sale in less than 15 minutes—that she decided to maintain the bracing pace. She went back up the hill to the local post office, where she bought packing materials (she could have got them cheaper elsewhere, but she didn't need to watch her margins since she'd just made a killing), packed the books, addressed them and paid for postage. The customer lived in Barnes—near her own house, in fact—and Cordelia could have delivered them in person and saved some shekels. But mailing them seemed more professional.

So she handed them over the counter at the post office.

All done in less than half an hour and the war nut would have them tomorrow.

She then went back to the High Street and headed downhill towards the river and the final charity shop. She really didn't expect to make any more terrific finds today. One couldn't ask too much of the gods of paperback serendipity. But still, she felt a little lift of excitement, as she always did, when she pushed open the door, with its jingling set of miniature brass bells hanging from it, and stepped into the smell of old clothes and carpet cleaner and (the best part) old books.

Cordelia was alone in the shop except for a big, beefy woman sitting behind the till and a tall thin man with greasy grey hair dressed all in black, who was looking through the women's clothes with great care and attention. Obviously a pervert of some stripe, but live and let live. That was Cordelia's motto. Just so long as he wasn't competing with her for the books.

These were housed in the sort of freestanding racks known as spinners, for obvious reasons. Cordelia stood in front of one of them and spun it slowly. The good thing about the spinners was that half the books could be spun at such an angle that you could read the spines, which sped up the process compared to going through them by hand. The bad thing about spinners was that you couldn't read the spines on the other half of the books, and you had to go through them by one by one.

It looked like Cordelia had been right when she'd suspected there wouldn't be any further terrific finds today. Almost all of the books in the spinner were torrid romances. Dross, and not in particularly great condition. A lot of Mills & Boon stuff. It was hard to believe that, at the beginning of the previous century, the Mills & Boon imprint had actually published some ground-breaking feminist titles. These days the nearest they got to that was *The Scandalous Suffragette* by Eliza Redgold ("When chocolate heiress Charlotte Coombes is caught hanging her banner in a *most* shocking place...").

Cordelia was about to pack it in and go home to hang her own banner in a shocking place when she spotted the spine of a book at the very bottom of the spinner. Amid all the modern junk, the vintage appearance of it stood out instantly. Cordelia crouched down on the floor to get a better look and then excitedly extracted the book from the spinner.

It was Indra Devi's *Renew Your Life Through Yoga*: one of the titles on the ashram list—Cordelia immediately recognised the lazy cat lounging on the cover. (Along with Stalin in his adorable little SS uniform, this was turning into a sort of cat-themed day.)

Bingo.

Cordelia had taken another step towards having a complete set of the missing books to hand back to the jokers at the ashram.

Of course, the downside of this win was that she now had to look through every other book in the spinners, just at the point when she'd been ready to quit. Because if there was one worthwhile item among this garbage, there might be more.

And there was. As Cordelia painstakingly went through all the books in the halves of the spinners where their spines weren't immediately visible, she found *Yoga for You*, also by Indra Devi ("Complete Six Weeks' Course for Home Practice"). Again, this was on the ashram's want-list and, like the book with the cat on the cover, it was in immaculate condition. A warm glow of triumph began to settle over Cordelia.

And then she found another one: *Executive Yoga* by Archie J. Bahm, with its hilarious cover photo of an executive-type guy stripped for yoga but with his business suit hanging in the background. Again, ashram-wanted; again, in perfect nick. As Cordelia excitedly extracted it from the spinner, she suddenly experienced a powerful conviction that raised the hair on the back of her neck...

These weren't just *like* the books that had been stolen.

These were the very books that had been stolen.

12: LIKE THE COMPUTER

Cordelia searched, meticulously, through every book in the shop. Then she went through them again. In the end she came up with one more (*Yoga for Women* by Nancy Phelan and Michael Volin, a British Arrow edition with rather nice use of graphics on the cover) for a total of four.

But the question you had to ask yourself, or at least that Cordelia had to ask herself, was that if someone had possession of the books stolen from the ashram—excepting the Avram Silverlight titles, of course, which was another question entirely—and decided to get rid of them at a charity shop, indeed at *this* charity shop, why only four? Why not all of them?

Or, to put it differently, Cordelia had a strong feeling there were more books to be had here.

Just because they weren't on display and for sale didn't mean they didn't have them stacked somewhere out of sight in the back. That's what charity shops did. They kept their stock in the back room until it was sorted and priced, and they were ready to put it out. Which in this case meant when they sold enough dreck romance novels to make room for it.

Cordelia resolved to charm the woman behind the counter into letting her have a look in the back of the shop. Or, worst case, for the woman to go and have a look for her. But Cordelia would much rather look herself.

Despite being big and beefy, the woman behind the counter was rather girly. At least, she was wearing a beribboned dress with a peculiar orange-and-green pattern that looked as though it had been made from a pair of curtains that had gone out of fashion 50 years ago. She had a round face with soft, somewhat tentative features, covered with various kinds of makeup that had been applied with more enthusiasm than skill. She had, for example, lipstick on her teeth.

Although her features may have been soft and tentative, they hardened perceptibly and became quite definite when she caught sight of Cordelia.

Cordelia had no idea why this happened, but it did happen sometimes (c.f. the late Duncan Fairwell at his bookshop)—someone just took one look at her and decided for no apparent reason they didn't like her. At least, for no reason that was apparent to Cordelia.

Anyway, Lipstick Teeth had taken an instant dislike to her, and Cordelia knew it.

Her heart sank.

This was a massive pain in the ass. True, there was a limited amount that Lipstick Teeth could do to spoil things for Cordelia. She was hardly likely to refuse money for the books Cordelia had already found, which Cordelia quickly handed over now, in cash to prevent any possibility of complications. Lipstick Teeth grudgingly accepted the money and even, when asked, deigned to ring up and hand over a receipt (for tax purposes), although she did sigh heavily all the while.

She didn't offer Cordelia a carrier bag, though, which was fine because she had a rucksack, into which the yoga books were quickly and safely sequestered.

What wasn't fine was that Cordelia now needed to ask a favour and Lipstick Teeth, she knew instantly and without question, would be the last person to do her one. But she had to try. So Cordelia did a little sighing of her own, trying to keep it inwards and silent so as not to queer the pitch, and then smiled and said, in her most polite and friendly voice, "I was wondering if you might have any more books about yoga?"

"More books about yoga?"

"Yes. You see, I've just started doing it and I'm really keen." She smiled and tried to look like an eager yoga novice instead of a mendacious book dealer.

"If they're not there we don't have them." This was accompanied by an almost imperceptible movement of Lipstick Teeth's head in the direction of the spinners full of paperbacks. You couldn't glorify it with the term "nod".

"I've had a really good look," said Cordelia, still striving for a polite and cheerful note. "But I only found these."

"Then they're all we've got."

"Of course," said Cordelia in her most diplomatic manner. "They are all the ones you've got out on display."

"Out on display?"

"I mean, you might have some more in the back."

"In the back?"

"In the back of the shop," said Cordelia, the smile on her face beginning to feel distinctly strained. In fact, the whole conversation was feeling strained. It didn't help that the pervert who was looking through the women's clothes had stopped looking through the women's clothes and was now clearly listening to them.

There was such a long, tense silence that Cordelia felt she had to add, "In the back of the shop, where you keep the stuff that you haven't put out yet." As if what she'd already said hadn't been supremely clear.

"What we have in the back of the shop is none of your business," said Lipstick Teeth.

Cordelia repressed her swelling rage, forced a ghastly fake smile back on her lips and made herself speak in a slow, civil voice of sweet reason. "It's just that if you do have any more yoga books back there, then I'd like to buy them."

"If they're in the back of the shop, you can't buy them."

"But you're just going to put them out anyway..." said Cordelia, every civil syllable an immense effort of self-control.

"They're not out yet."

"I know, but if you're going to put them out anyway..."

"Maybe we're not going to put them out," said Lipstick Teeth.

"It's just that if you are going to sell them..."

"Maybe we're not going to sell them."

Cordelia forced herself not to ask Lipstick Teeth what, if they were not going to sell them, they were going to do with them, and to also provide a number of obscene and anatomically implausible suggestions. Instead she compelled herself to say, "Well, if you *are* going to sell them I'd really like to buy them."

"They're not for sale," said Lipstick Teeth, which was such a surprising escalation of rhetoric that even the pervert seemed startled.

"All I want to do..." said Cordelia, still trying to cling to her temper before it slipped out of her control, like the string of a savagely tugging kite from a child's fingers, "all I'm trying to do is give some more money to your charity..."

"You can make a donation in that box there if you like."

"... while also buying some books about yoga," concluded Cordelia.

"You've bought some books about yoga."

"I'd like some more."

"You've got enough."

Cordelia's heart was now beating furiously in her chest and she was looking around for something to hit Lipstick Teeth with. She kept telling herself that she mustn't lose her temper, but it was far from certain she was going to listen to herself, and she had just spotted a rather nice ship in a bottle that someone had donated. And this, if smashed over Lipstick Teeth's head, would have the twin virtues of liberating the intricate miniature sailing ship from its vitreous prison while also providing the satisfaction of smashing a bottle over Lipstick Teeth's head.

Perhaps it was just as well that at that moment the pervert cleared his throat and spoke up. "We could have a look in the back, Bea."

So he worked here, realised Cordelia with surprise. Which was why he'd been pawing through the women's clothing. He wasn't a pervert after all. Or, alternatively, he was a pervert who'd found the ideal day job.

"No, we can't," snarled Lipstick Teeth.

"I could have a look in the back," offered the pervert.

"No one is looking in the back. The manager isn't in today. No one is looking in the back unless the manager is in the shop."

There were now a whole range of questions which, under normal circumstances and in a civilised context, it would have made sense for Cordelia to ask. For example, when would the manager next be in the shop, and would it be possible to come back then?

But things had clearly escalated beyond the point of sensible questions and civilised contexts, so Cordelia just turned and walked out of the shop, through the jangling belled door, and back into the for-once-welcome traffic fumes and vehicle noise of Putney High Street. She forced her jaws to unclench with rage and wondered how long it would take her heart rate to return to normal.

She turned and started back up the hill towards the station, rucksack on her back with the four yoga paperbacks, forcing herself to count her blessings. Which right now stood at four previously stolen yoga paperbacks, safely recovered, and a profitable coup in selling Nazi war porn, plus the fact that she wasn't, at this moment, being marched into a police station to be charged with assault, and having a small sailing ship and various fragments of glass neatly bagged and tagged as evidence against her.

The count-your-blessings strategy worked for about a second and a half before she became absorbed in a fantasy in which she was saying, "Oh look, you've got some lipstick on your teeth, let me help you get it off." And then helpfully swinging a sledgehammer...

Just at that point, behind her, she heard the faint jingling of small brass bells.

She turned to see the pervert emerging from the charity shop and hurrying up the pavement after her. Cordelia stopped and waited for him. He began to talk before he even reached her. "Sorry about that," he said, or perhaps called.

Cordelia, not without some regret, set aside her vivid revery of sledgehammer dental-lipstick removal and made herself listen to what he was saying, or calling.

"You have to make allowances for Beatrice."

No, I don't, thought Cordelia.

"She's had a rough time lately."

Pleased to hear it, thought Cordelia.

"But listen," said the pervert, who had now reached her and was holding out a piece of paper, "why don't you ring the shop? Not today, though. And when you do, ask for Mac. Like the computer. That's me."

The pervert smiled, a rather charmingly shy and self-effacing smile for a pervert who was named after a computer, and waved at Cordelia, even though she was standing right in front of him. He went back to the shop. She looked at the piece of paper. It was a blank price tag with the shop's logo on it, designed to be attached to an item of clothing (in this case, probably women's clothing). There was a phone number scribbled on it. Cordelia put it in her pocket.

13: KILLER DILDO

Edwin inspected the phone number.

He had come to visit Cordelia's attic room—a rare event—knocking tentatively and politely on the door and bringing an eager Rainbottle in with him. Cordelia knew he was checking on her because he was worried about her, and she appreciated the gesture. Rainbottle had hurried into the room and established himself under the big square table where Cordelia kept her stock of books stacked in neat piles. Edwin sat down at the table and Cordelia joined him. She was pleased to see them. The only downside of the two of them visiting her instead of vice versa was that there was no hot chocolate involved. (She could have offered Edwin some cannabis edibles, but that wasn't really his thing.)

"That was lucky," said Edwin, handing the piece of paper back to her.

"It was for them," said Cordelia. She began to transfer the number into the address book of her phone under first name Mac, last name Pervert. "If he hadn't given it to me, I was going to go back there tonight and break in." Her burglary tools were still ready to go, nestled in a rucksack, from the nocturnal visit to Alfie's garage when she hadn't needed them.

"That wouldn't have been sensible." Edwin was big on sensible. "They have burglar alarms, even in charity shops, sometimes even quite elaborate ones. You're lucky this chap came after you." He watched her finish entering the number on her phone. "You don't sense an ulterior motive?" he added. Edwin was also big on ulterior motives.

"Hard to say," said Cordelia. "I got the feeling from the way he was fondling the women's clothing that the last thing he was interested in was a real, live girl."

"You felt he was…"

"A pervert."

"I see."

"But maybe he competes in more than one event in the pervert Olympics," said Cordelia. "So to speak."

Edwin chuckled. He looked at the four newly acquired yoga paperbacks, spread out on the table. "And you reckon these books were also part of the ashram robbery?"

"It just seems too much of a coincidence that they'd have all these weird old yoga paperbacks. And in such great condition."

"But coincidences do happen."

"Well, let's see how far we can push this one," said Cordelia.

"And now you'll get in touch with this chap…"

"Mac the Pervert."

"Good old Mac. You'll get in touch with him and arrange to purchase the other books?"

"If they have any." But Cordelia was quietly confident that they would.

"And if they do," said Edwin, "I must admit it makes it seem all the more likely that you're right and these must be the stolen books."

"There is one thing that could rule that out," said Cordelia.

Edwin fell silent and thought for a moment. As he did so, Rainbottle, who was cosily curled up at their feet, made an empathetic ruminating noise. Then Edwin said, "You mean if you find there are other yoga books there that *weren't* stolen from the ashram."

"Full marks, Edwin," said Cordelia. "If they had some other vintage yoga paperbacks in perfect condition which didn't come from the ashram then that would indicate they came from some other collection. Some other yoga pervert's collection."

"You've got perverts on the brain," said Edwin, and Rainbottle murmured in agreement. "Now, there's something else we must discuss…"

"You mean, we need to talk about last night," said Cordelia. And, as soon as she said it, she realised it sounded embarrassingly like they were a couple who were about to discuss some nuance of their relationship. Which, excuse us while we suppress a gag reflex, couldn't be further from the truth.

Perhaps Edwin thought it sounded the same way, because he added for clarification in his most businesslike manner, "We have to discuss your would-be assailant."

"There was nothing would-be about him," said Cordelia. "He was my assailant, big time."

"I suppose so."

"And the only thing that made him a would-be assassin, instead of a big-time successful assassin, was *you*." Cordelia was entirely sincere about this and wasn't buttering up Edwin at all; credit where it was due.

"I only wish I'd gone there earlier," said Edwin.

"You could hardly have been much earlier."

Edwin had gone to the hospital over an hour before Cordelia, to stake out the place.

"It seems your assailant was," said Edwin. "Earlier, I mean. Which means they were in position before I arrived. So I didn't get a chance to see who it was."

"But I don't think he saw you either," said Cordelia.

"Perhaps not. I was quite circumspect in my approach. But let's not get into the habit of referring to this person as if they're male. We want to keep an open mind about whether it's a man or a woman."

"And whether there's just one of them, or more."

"Good point," said Edwin.

It *was* a good one, thought Cordelia, but certainly not a comforting one. An assassin was bad enough, a conspiracy of assassins hardly bore contemplation.

Edwin frowned thoughtfully. "Let's review what we know about this person or persons. They are associated with the yoga centre."

"Or at least they have access to it," said Cordelia.

"Or at least they have access to it," agreed Edwin. "Because they used your pigeonhole to communicate with you."

"And we also know," said Cordelia, "that this must have something to do with the stolen books." She nodded at the books spread in front of them on the table—the rather dull straight-up yoga books and the considerably more interesting Avram Silverlight titles.

"Not necessarily," said Edwin.

"What do you mean?" said Cordelia.

"True, they mentioned the books in their note to you, which was a very effective way of luring you to the hospital for what they hoped would be a lone rendezvous. But perhaps the books were just a ruse. I mean, they were offering the books to you, but they clearly didn't have possession of them."

"So what you're saying is they might have had nothing to do with the robbery, but they just knew about the books and so they used them as bait... Because they wanted to kill me for entirely another reason?"

"It's a possibility we have to consider," said Edwin.

"Not a very encouraging one." Cordelia racked her brains for someone who might want her dead and, despite her best efforts could only come up with one candidate. "What is the threat level with Colin Cutterham at the moment?" Colin Cutterham was the local gangster Cordelia had once made the mistake of pissing off.

And once was more than enough.

She had stolen a superb collection of rare paperbacks that had belonged to him. In fact, had belonged to his beloved deceased mother. In fairness, though, Cordelia couldn't have been expected to know that.

Or indeed, and rather more importantly, to know that Cutterham was a violent career criminal, local kingpin and the vengeful type.

All of which, however, proved to be the case. And explained Cordelia's keen interest in the current threat level.

"Mild to moderate, I would say," said Edwin.

"In other words, green to amber," said Cordelia, who preferred colour coding.

"Yes."

"And we don't think it's him?" said Cordelia.

"We can't rule it out. But it doesn't seem like his style. If he could be said to have a style."

"Which means we're back to where we were," said Cordelia. "Someone who has me in their sights because of the robbery at the ashram."

"It looks like it," said Edwin. "Let's consider possible candidates. I think we can rule out Alfie."

"Why?"

"Whoever was up on the roof of the hospital moved very quickly and nimbly to evade us. From what I've seen, Alfie is too big and too out of shape for that."

"Don't let appearances fool you. According to Lorna, he's incredibly good at yoga."

"Oh, really?"

"Yes," said Cordelia. "The word she used was 'adept'."

"And so we rule Alfie back in?" said Edwin.

"Looks like it," said Cordelia.

"And as for other candidates?"

"Presumably whoever pulled the robbery at the yoga centre. And we have no idea who that is."

"To sum up, then," said Edwin, "we haven't got very far." He sounded a little depressed. Beneath the table, perhaps sensing his master's low spirits, Rainbottle made a sympathetic sound. Then Edwin perked up. He smiled and reached into his pocket. The sensible pocket on his sensible Rohan shirt.

"A little present for you," he said, handing Cordelia an object wrapped in green tissue paper. It was about the size and shape of a fountain pen, though considerably thicker.

She swiftly unwrapped what at first appeared to be an adult toy. But, as she stared at it in embarrassed bewilderment, she realised it was somewhat small for this purpose, not to mention being made of cold, hard metal. Also, it had a ring at one end so you could attach keys, which was pretty audacious for a dildo.

Seeing her puzzlement, Edwin picked it up and showed her how to hold it. He gripped the ribbed cylindrical shaft in his hand with his thumb on the flat base, so the long, blunt conical tip projected from his fingers at the other end. Then he made some stabbing motions with it in the air. "You see?" He smiled at her and held it out.

"It's a weapon?" Cordelia's embarrassment was giving way to interest.

"Non-lethal," said Edwin with a somewhat disparaging, dismissive note in his voice. He shrugged. "But still quite effective."

"You hold it like this…" Cordelia took it from Edwin and imitated his grip on the thing. The cold metal had warmed up a little while he'd held it. The implement was hollow, but nevertheless quite heavy, and very hard. It was evidently made of steel. Cordelia rather liked the feel of it in her hand. It made her feel… what? Safe, strong, competent? "And use it like this?" She repeated Edwin's air-stabs.

"Aim for the head," said Edwin. "I'd suggest the temple, between the ear and the eye. That should discourage someone. Of course, you could aim for the eye itself, but then you'd be looking at permanent injury."

"And they wouldn't be looking at much at all."

"Ha ha, yes," said Edwin.

Cordelia swung the thing through the air. "Not like that," said Edwin. "Overhand, not underhand." He showed her. When he was satisfied she could use it effectively, he said, "Happy birthday."

"It's not my birthday."

"Consider it a late present for your last one," said Edwin. "I hope you don't ever have occasion to use it."

"Thank you." Cordelia felt a transgressive thrill as she attached her keys to what she'd begun to think of as the killer dildo, and put it, jingling merrily, into her bag.

Edwin frowned. "Not in there. Put it somewhere you can get at it in a hurry."

Chastened, Cordelia moved the killer dildo to a pocket of her jeans.

"Better," said Edwin. "Admittedly it won't stop someone dropping a block of concrete on you, but if they get up close and personal…"

"Thank you, Edwin," said Cordelia again. She was genuinely quite touched.

"Sorry I couldn't have been of more help," said Edwin, standing up. "Especially relating to the identity of your assailant. We'll both sleep on things and see if we can come up with any useful ideas. Come on, Rainbottle."

The dog reluctantly stirred and got to his feet. Or paws.

As the two of them headed for the door, Edwin suddenly thought of something else and stopped. "You were supposed to be having a day off from this business. This morning, you said you were taking a day off."

Cordelia shrugged. "I tried. I couldn't have known I'd find a cache of stolen yoga books at a charity shop."

"Well, might I suggest that tomorrow you really do have a day off? And take it easy."

"Okay," said Cordelia. "In fact, I know just how to chill out."

"Good," said Edwin.

"A certain healthy activity that never fails to make me feel better about things."

It didn't take Edwin long to get it. "Oh, no," he said.

"Oh, yes," said Cordelia. "I'm afraid so."

14: FREE LESSON

Cordelia got to the yoga centre early, though not as early as on that recent memorable visit when she'd climbed the tree. Still, she was there waiting when Joni arrived (on her bicycle, being a boring cycling type like Edwin) and was once more the first one through the door of the gift shop as soon as the orange Om blind had been rolled up. Cordelia took considerable satisfaction in telling her that she was here for a lesson. Indeed, for the early morning class, which Mr T would be teaching.

"You can check upstairs if you like," she told Joni. "They'll confirm that my yoga privileges have been restored."

Joni shrugged. "No need," she said.

Cordelia was a little disappointed that she'd given up without a fight. Which was why, as Joni rang up the cost of the lesson on the till (the price had gone up considerably in the period since Cordelia's banishment), she said, "I thought the first lesson was free."

Joni stopped and gave her an angry look. That was more like it, thought Cordelia. "But it isn't your first lesson," said angry Joni.

"It's my first since I was told to go away and never come back. That sounds like a fresh start to me, so ipso facto it's my first lesson." Cordelia wasn't sure that she'd used "ipso facto" correctly, but what the hell. It was worth it to see the expression on Joni's face.

Or was it?

Because the expression on Joni's face, in fact, and very surprisingly, seemed to be that of someone giving Cordelia's argument serious consideration. Then suddenly she shrugged again and said, "All right."

All right? Cordelia was flabbergasted. She watched Joni begin to cancel the sale on the till, unable to quite believe what was happening. "I can just go in?" she said.

"Yes, just go through," said Joni, puzzling over the till. "You remember the way?"

She wasn't sure if this was sarcasm or not (if so, good for Joni) but Cordelia did indeed remember the way. She sauntered through the peace garden—very peaceful indeed, and tranquil at this hour of the morning, though its zen perfection was rather spoiled by the fact that one of the chrome pipes on the wind chimes had come loose from the wooden frame, still attached by its metal cable but dangling on the ground, dragging around in drunken circles instead of hanging beside its friends.

Someone needed to fix that. Someone in orange pyjamas.

Cordelia pushed through the door that led to the changing rooms and the shala. But the pleasure of returning to old haunts was rather spoiled by the intense trepidation she felt as she walked past the bank of pigeonholes on the wall. She found she was deliberately averting her gaze, in case (as in her dream) there was another folded note waiting for her.

This was not a healthy way to behave. If she had to creep in past the pigeonholes as if she was sneaking by the school bully every time she came here, then the whole point of attending lessons was going to be defeated. She'd come here to chill out, to rest and regroup and heal. Not to develop a foolish phobia.

Which was why Cordelia now forced herself to look at the pigeonholes. In particular, she forced herself to look at the one with her name on it.

It was empty.

Cordelia was torn between luxuriating in the feeling of relief that washed over her and despising herself for being so pathetically emotionally fragile in the first place. She went on into the changing room, where there were already a trio of girls getting ready. They'd sidled in past Cordelia while she'd been wrestling with the psychological monstrosity of the pigeonholes. She didn't recognise any of them, but they all seemed to know each other and were chatting happily away.

Cordelia considered introducing herself, perhaps with special reference to her previous disgraced expulsion, but decided that would just be showing off. She got changed, into baggy ecru tracksuit bottoms and a T-shirt that said *668—The Neighbour of the Beast*, and went into the shala. The shala, or less pretentiously yoga studio, or, even less pretentiously classroom, was a big open space with a carpet (still the same thin and threadbare carpet she remembered) with space on it for perhaps 50 students and their yoga mats.

The best places on the floor—either near the open windows for the fresh air fiends, or as far from the open windows as possible for those who were prone to feeling a chill when prone—were already gone. It was like the best spots on the beach being reserved with towels—you had get there quick if you wanted a good one.

Cordelia wasn't that bothered. She was just glad to be back. The place even smelled the same, a compound of incense, soap and a vast variety of deodorants. She found a blank area of carpet in a quiet corner, unrolled her mat and lay down on it. Amazing how quickly it all came back to her. Of course, she had continued her yoga practice at home during her wilderness years, rolling and unrolling her mat on the floor of her little attic room, occasionally with Rainbottle lying beside her and watching her with deep scepticism in his doggie eyes. But when she was practising at home she didn't bother with all the trimmings and refinements, like lying down and relaxing for a few minutes before she started, as was the custom in the class here. Which was a good thing because it meant that, as each punter—sorry, student—came in through the door, they had to stop chatting and lie down silently.

It was all very peaceful.

Cordelia lay with her legs apart, ankles in contact with the mat, positioned at either corner, toes angled outwards. Her arms were spread out at her sides, hands palm upwards, fingers spread. She tensed the muscles in her buttocks and pressed her hips imperceptibly upwards so that the small of her back was hollowed, floating above the mat and not touching it. Similarly, she rocked her head back slightly to create a hollow at the back of her neck, between the base of her skull and her shoulders. Now certain parts on her body were in contact with the floor and other parts were slightly elevated, and she was entirely relaxed. The point of this was to achieve the equivalent of good posture, while lying flat on your back on the floor.

The other thing you were supposed to do was breathe deeply, filling your lungs and taking a small extra breath, then breathing out slowly. Which Cordelia was now doing. And to empty your mind of all your everyday thoughts and concerns. Which Cordelia was not now doing.

But, in fairness, someone was trying to kill her, and that sort of thing did tend to preoccupy you. Indeed, Cordelia would like to meet the yogi who would be able to lie on their mat, mind happily blank, so soon after some fucker had tried to drop a massive block of concrete on them.

Still, even though a beautifully blank mind wasn't going to happen, it didn't do to dwell on such matters, either. Cordelia tried to push away all images of the chunk of concrete, the smashed bench, the red envelope and greeting card… But, as she did so, a nagging little thought tried to make itself known to her. A bit like a name you could almost but not quite recall. And the unsettling thing was, unlike all the stuff she was trying to get out of her head, Cordelia had the powerful feeling this was something she should get *into* her head.

But no luck. The elusive little thought flickered fleetingly then disappeared again.

Maybe if she did manage to make her mind a blank it would come to her…

She genuinely had the feeling it was something important. But it had vanished now, like a glittering fish that had broken the surface only for an instant before diving again, disappearing into the depths.

Cordelia sighed, but passed it off as more deep breathing. She tried one of the yogic tricks for clearing her head, one of Mr T's favourite suggestions for times such as this, which was to concentrate on the ambient sounds of her situation. There wasn't much in the way of these in the room immediately around her, because everybody was doing the same thing she was: breathing deeply and pretending to be emptying their heads while actually obsessing about the minutiae of their lives.

Further afield there was the sound of a lawn mower, a dog barking, the annoying squealing of children running to somewhere or from somewhere, the endless remote droning of traffic on the Upper Richmond Road and even a little bit of birdsong. These were all distant, only just audible, and it really was quite restful to focus her attention on them at the expense of everything else.

Despite herself, Cordelia was beginning to feel quite relaxed. Her breathing was slow and deep, and the floor, solid concrete beneath the thin cheap orange carpet, began to feel like the ocean—massive and solid but slowly swelling, with her body afloat on it like a raft...

This was the other problem with the entire breathe-deeply-and-empty-your-head routine—one did tend to fall asleep.

Cordelia was more exhausted than she had realised. Clearly the events of the last couple of days had worn her out, while leaving her tense and keyed up on a level beyond her conscious awareness or control. But now at last she began to relax properly and profoundly. Before she knew it, she was drifting in that weightless, formless limbo between wakefulness and sleep. Images drifted through her consciousness—rainwater in puddles, dust rising from a recently fallen block of concrete, a bright red envelope...

That was it.

The elusive thought that was trying to break through was now trying again. It resonated with that envelope. No, not the envelope. The card inside it.

Something about the card itself.

Hanging there in her half-waking, half-sleeping limbo, Cordelia almost grasped the thought.

But then the yoga lesson began.

It began with the usual set phrases, the same things that Mr T always said. The words were comfortingly familiar, but not the voice that was saying them. Cordelia found herself rudely awakened by the sound of someone speaking, and it wasn't the relaxing tones of Mr T.

"My name is Devika and I'm here to guide you through your practice this morning."

What? Devika? The Sanskrit name of gobby Joni? What was she doing here? Cordelia's eyes flashed open. She forced herself not to sit bolt upright and stare, but she would in a minute when it was time for everyone to sit up and start their lesson. What the hell was Joni—aka Devika—doing conducting Mr T's yoga class?

Cordelia heard a murmured voice on the other side of the room, near Joni. It must have been someone discreetly asking exactly that same question because Joni said, "Mr Thirunavukkarasu is indisposed. Unfortunately, he won't be able to take your class today."

Cordelia had never known Mr T to miss a lesson. He was rock-solid reliable. What was going on?

Joni was still talking, all too clearly fond of the sound of her own voice. "I am here to instruct you instead. My name is Devika..." She'd already said this and must have realised she'd already said it, because she moved briskly on. "Everyone rise to your feet, please, and stand at the front of your mats to prepare for the sun salutation. Spread your toes, distribute your weight evenly through your whole foot and not just on the heels of your feet or your toes or the balls..."

Balls was the operative word, thought Cordelia. This spiel was pretty much Mr T's routine verbatim, but, coming from dear old Joni in her flat, strained and rather insipid voice, it lacked music and euphony, not to mention conviction. She was like a little kid pretending to be a grown-up. Nevertheless, she cracked on gamely and gave the commands for the sun salute.

As Cordelia went through the moves with the rest of the class, she had a surreptitious but thorough look around. While she'd been lying on her back, trying to clear her head, the place had filled up significantly. The orange-carpeted studio space was almost fully covered with yoga mats, some old and grubby and wearing through in places (like Cordelia's), others brand new and no doubt bought at an extortionate price in the ashram's gift shop. The crowd was mostly women, but there were a fair few men, too. There were at least 40 people; it was a really good turn-out.

Of course, everyone had come expecting Mr T. If they'd known they were going to get fobbed off with Joni, they probably would have all stayed at home eating deep-fried chocolate bars and drinking vodka from the bottle. While watching the shopping channel.

Cordelia caught sight of Alfie in the row opposite her—the room was divided into halves, with the students all facing each other over a narrow band of space in the middle, where the teacher prowled back and forth. Joni was prowling in this now, but with very little conviction. Alfie caught Cordelia's eye and winked at her, and then they all dropped into the downward dog.

The salute to the sun consisted of twelve repetitions of a sequence of postures and stretches done at a moderate-to-fast pace. It was essentially a warm-up routine, which was why you did it at the beginning of the class. For some reason, you always took a breather after the first eight repetitions and stood upright with your arms hanging loose at your sides while your pulse returned to normal before resuming for the final four reps.

It was while they were standing like this, catching their breath, that the door to the shala popped open and the Silver Shrew came in. She did not look pleased. Nor did Joni look pleased to see her. In fact, she looked guilty and scared. The Shrew padded over to where Joni was standing and began to whisper to her in a harsh, hissing undertone.

Cordelia felt that warm, contented feeling you get when you realise someone you don't like is about to be involved in an embarrassing scene.

Joni, with the Shrew hissing in her ear, had ceased to look guilty and scared, and was now looking stubborn and petulant instead. This really did seem promising in terms of embarrassing-scene potential, as did the fact that when Joni replied to the Shrew, she did not choose to do so in a whisper but rather adopted a normal, conversational tone of voice. All the better for all the eager and scandal-hungry among the onlookers (which essentially was everyone, except perhaps for a few holier-than-thou types) to hear what was going on.

"But you promised," said Joni.

The Shrew hissed something, persisting in her disappointingly inaudible whisper.

Joni simply repeated, at the same normal and admirably audible level, "But you promised." And then added, "You said that I could start giving lessons when we had the ashram's anniversary. You promised."

"I did not promise," said the Shrew. She was still hissing but, happily now, either because she'd lost her temper or because she had realised discretion was a lost cause, at a volume everybody could hear.

"Yes, you did," said Joni, sounding like a peevish child. "You promised."

"I promised to *think* about it," said the Silver Shrew, who had transitioned from hissing to snapping, and more loudly than before.

"I explained to you. I explained everything." Joni said this as if it had great significance.

Cordelia wondered what exactly Joni might have explained.

"Nevertheless," said the Shrew, at her most remorseless.

"Well, Mr Thirunavukkarasu isn't here," said Joni. "And someone has to stand in for him and take the lesson, so I stepped into the breach." Joni clearly thought she deserved plaudits for this.

Sadly, the Shrew clearly thought she didn't. "You can't just leave the gift shop unattended."

"I didn't. I locked it up."

"You can't just leave it locked up. What if someone needs access to the centre?"

"Everybody is here for the lesson now," said Joni. "No one else is coming."

"How do you know?" said the Shrew. "And how do you know someone might not come into the shop and want to buy something?"

"It's only for the duration of the lesson."

"Well, we've had to open it again and Harshavardhana is now looking after the shop while I came up here to find out what was going on. And that is hardly an acceptable state of affairs, is it?"

Cordelia could see Joni, rather disappointingly, begin to fold under the impact of the Shrew's implacable logic. "But I've already started the lesson," said Joni, rather pathetically.

"I'll take over," said the Shrew. "You can go back to the shop and allow Harshavardhana to go back to dealing with important matters."

Cordelia wondered what important matters Howdy Doody could possibly be capable of dealing with. But Joni accepted defeat and slunk towards the door, turning just before she went out to say, "We're in the middle of the sun salutation."

The Silver Shrew waited for the door to close behind her and then turned to the class. "Right," she said. "Take a deep breath and stretch your arms upwards…"

The Shrew actually knew her stuff and, as much as Cordelia expected to spend the rest of the class preoccupied with alternately disliking her, gloating over Joni's peremptory dismissal and wondering what could have happened to Mr T, in fact all these thoughts and any other distractions soon vanished from her mind, and she became utterly absorbed in just doing yoga.

She'd thought that returning to class here wouldn't be very different from practising on her own at home. But there was something about doing the postures with a group, and even, grudging credit where it's due, under the guidance of an expert teacher, which added to the whole experience.

Cordelia was pleasurably lost in the swift sequence of stretching and balancing postures. The only time she was really aware of what was going on around her was when she caught sight of what Alfie was doing. They had all just commenced the crow, which effectively involved balancing all your body weight on your hands with the fingers spread on the floor, elbows tucked into the solar plexus, elevated legs folded in behind you and your eyes fixed on a point on the floor in front of you to help maintain balance.

Great for the wrists, but not the easiest of postures to achieve.

But Alfie was having no trouble with it at all.

What was even more remarkable was that he flowed smoothly from the crow into the *headstand*. Cordelia was startled, impressed and more than a little jealous. This was an incredibly cool move and one she had never been able to master herself. It had taken her long enough to master the headstand on its own. And the crow, too, for that matter.

She stared enviously at the old bastard doing his headstand and then she saw his body tip back and, for one tiny instant, half mortified and half gleeful, Cordelia thought he was about to topple over.

But instead he curved his back, spread his legs, arched his feet forwards and brought his forehead towards the floor, but held himself just above it by a dynamic coil of arms and shoulders.

He was doing the *scorpion*. The bastard had segued from the crow into the headstand and from the headstand into the scorpion—a posture that Cordelia had frankly never even aspired to, it was so damned difficult.

And here was Alfie, doing it effortlessly.

He had just achieved one of the most masterful sequences of postures in the whole yoga handbook. And he did it with such ease it was obvious that this was just a common daily occurrence for him.

Lorna had been right. He really was an adept.

* * *

Despite the palace coup by the Shrew (so to speak) it proved to be a good session, and Cordelia emerged from it feeling relaxed, renewed and remarkably free of the worries of recent days. She'd forgotten how good it felt to be in the changing room afterwards, getting into your street clothes again and enjoying the glowing, virtuous sensation of a lesson completed—with the bonus in this case of hearing all the other women in the changing room excitedly discussing the argument between Joni and the Shrew.

When Cordelia came out of the changing room, yoga mat rolled up and hung over her shoulder in her stylish tubular yoga mat bag (pointedly not purchased at the gift shop), she was feeling so relaxed and dreamily distracted that it was an unwelcome shock to come face to face with not only the Shrew herself but also Howdy Doody. They were lurking by the pigeonholes and had apparently been waiting here to ambush her.

"We'd like to speak to you, please," said Howdy, although his "please" didn't sound very sincere.

"Outside in the peace garden, please," said the Silver Shrew. Her "please" sounded even less so.

Cordelia's heart sank but she managed a casual shrug. "Sure," she said. She was clearly about to be fired or get a bollocking for something she'd done or hadn't done or something. As she followed the pair out into the garden, she began to mentally review her recent behaviour to try to identify her transgression and prepare a defence or, at least, a sarcastic riposte.

As she walked past, she made herself take a quick look at her pigeonhole. It was still empty, not surprisingly, but she felt good about having had the guts to check.

Cordelia followed the saffron-clad duo outside, realising with some surprise that, whatever might be in store for her, she felt tranquil and unbothered. If they were going to fire her, so be it. She'd be all right. She'd just sell the books she'd already found on the open market and make enough money to pay off the widow in Richmond for the wonderful John D. MacDonald collection.

And fuck these two.

But it turned out that Howdy and the Shrew didn't want to fire her, or even issue a reprimand.

"We just wanted to tell you that we've checked," said Howdy. "And it's fine if the books you get for us aren't signed."

Cordelia looked into his frank, guileless, freckled face and thought, *Is that all?*

"They have to be in pristine condition, though," said the Shrew, reassuringly true to form.

Cordelia said all that was fine, then left the two of them there in the peace garden and hurried towards the gift shop, eager to see how Joni was taking her recent humiliation.

But as soon as she stepped into the shop, cool with the wash of air from the fan that buzzed quietly and reassuringly high on one corner of the ceiling, all thought of scoping out Joni vanished from her mind.

Because the thought that had been nagging at her ever since she'd arrived here this morning finally broke through into consciousness…

The gift shop didn't merely stock yoga mats. And yoga garb. And yoga knick-knacks and incense and neti pots and yoga books and yoga magazines. Cordelia walked past all this merchandise to the spinner—yes, another one—in the corner by the window. This spinner didn't contain books.

It contained greeting cards.

15: SPINNER

Cordelia spun the spinner with an almost déjà-vu-like sense of certainty of what she was about to find. She didn't hurry, she took her time, savouring the inevitability of it. Unlike books, greeting cards didn't have spines you could read. Because, obviously, they were too thin. But that didn't matter, since each compartment in the spinner contained copies of only one card, the same card that was facing outwards. So you didn't need to rifle through them. You just leisurely spun the (four-sided) spinner and examined the cards facing you.

Nothing on the first side of the spinner. Cordelia rotated it slowly, almost lazily.

Nothing on the second side.

But, on the third side of the spinner, right up the top, at eye level on the left, it stared out at her.

A crazed cartoon rabbit with the word *Surprise!* embossed on it.

Cordelia stood there for a long moment, just looking at it. She studied her reactions carefully for any post-traumatic-type crap, but all she felt was a jubilant sense of achievement and vindication.

She'd guessed right.

Now she reached up and took the card down to reveal a stack of identical ones behind it. The card was sealed in cellophane.

She turned it over. Sure enough, at the back, a bright red envelope nestled snugly behind the card, as well as a small slip of paper that read, *The greeting on this card is "I hope you like your present!"*

She took the card over to the counter where Joni was sitting. Cordelia was so preoccupied with her triumphant find that she was surprised to see Joni looking so mopey and it took her a second to remember why. When she did, Cordelia actually felt a little sorry for her. The girl had been savagely Shrewed, to coin a word. No time for compassion now, though. She held up the card and said, "Would you mind if I just took this out of the shop for a moment? I want to show it to someone. I'll be right back." She didn't need to add this last bit because Joni had already given a mopey shrug.

"Take your time," she said.

Cordelia went back into the peace garden. Handily, Howdy Doody and the Silver Shrew were still there, seated on a bench, deep in what looked like conspiratorial conversation. They were certainly speaking very quietly, which inevitably made Cordelia want to know what they were talking about. But before she could get close enough to have a listen, Alfie came out of the changing rooms.

He immediately ambled over to Cordelia, grinning. "Nice to see you this morning," he said. "Joining in with the rabble?"

"It's good to be back," said Cordelia with unfeigned sincerity.

"Been a while, eh?" said Alfie. "It must be, because I've been coming here for a couple of years myself and I've never seen you around. Before our auspicious meeting the other day, I mean…"

He fell silent and Cordelia wondered if he'd suddenly spotted someone, but she looked up into his eyes and saw they were unfocused, or rather focused on some interior scene. And she realised with a pang of insight that he was thinking about his dead friend, Hank Honeywell.

The first time they'd met, he'd been here too.

Cordelia's heart went out to this bereaved old bastard, and she wondered if she should say something or perhaps put a comforting hand on his arm. Or maybe ask Oral Relief Joni to take him into a private room somewhere for a quick and uplifting session...

But then Alfie rallied and came back from whatever unhappy place he'd been in. He grinned and said, "Is that for me?" indicating the greeting card that Cordelia had been trying to hide—she wasn't entirely sure why. Now she changed her tactics and showed it to him, watching his face carefully.

"No, it's for me," she said. "Or at least it was."

Alfie displayed no obvious reaction beyond perhaps a slight disdain, quickly concealed, for the general crappiness of the card. Nor did he seem puzzled by the cryptic nature of her statement. Just to clarify things a little, she added, "Someone gave me one of these the other day."

Alfie smiled politely. "Nice," he said, with definitely feigned candour.

If he was familiar with this card, for example as the result of having left one on a bench for Cordelia before scooting up to prepare a deadly rooftop trap to spring on her, he certainly showed no sign. She wondered, once more, if anyone could really be that good an actor. Well, of course, some people could, professional actors for instance, but could Alfie?

He was still smiling at her, rather more sincerely now. "Why don't you come back to my place for a cup of tea?" he said. "And maybe a..." He made a gesture of holding a joint to his lips. "Some friends may be dropping by. Some other friends."

Cordelia realised that, by correcting himself, he was including her among his friends. Which was rather nice of him.

"We'll sit out in the garden," he said. "It's a lovely day..."

It was indeed a lovely day, warm and sunny and feeling more like spring than autumn, and this proposal actually sounded like a perfect follow-up to the yoga session, which had left Cordelia chilled but tingling with energy. A bit of weed was just what she needed to capitalise on these sensations. And a cup of tea wouldn't hurt. "I might just do that," she said.

"Tantalisingly provisional," said Alfie.

"I just have a bit of business with…" Cordelia gestured towards Howdy Doody and the Silver Shrew, who were sitting on the bench on the other side of the peace garden, still deep in conversation.

"Have you told them about the books?" said Alfie. "That you've found them?"

"Not yet, but I might be just about to. You haven't told them, have you?"

"I haven't told a soul. My lips are sealed." Alfie pressed two fingers to his lips. It looked more like he was about to blow a kiss than guaranteeing discretion.

"Well, see you soon," said Cordelia. "Perhaps."

"Provisional and tantalising," said Alfie cheerfully "You sure you don't want me to wait for you? I've got the car here."

"No, that's all right. I can always get the bus or a train," said Cordelia, reviewing the public transport options from here to Alfie's place in Putney. She realised that only a few seconds ago she had been soberly considering the possibility that this man might have tried to kill her. Of course, that possibility still existed. But on the other side of the scales, metaphorically speaking, there was the beguiling prospect of trying some of that fabulous weed he was growing in his greenhouse. It was pretty clear to Cordelia which way the metaphorical scales were going to tip.

Alfie shrugged. "Sounds good. Take care." He headed for the gift shop, and Cordelia watched him through the glass panel in the door as he went inside and—as she'd half-expected—strolled up to the counter where Joni was stationed.

Without being too obvious about it, Cordelia moved a little closer to the door and adjusted her angle to get a better view. She could see Alfie and Joni talking. Joni looked thoroughly miserable, on the verge of tears, while Alfie was smiling and turning on his personal charm, clearly trying to cheer her and console her after her skirmish with the Shrew in the shala (a bit of a tongue twister, admittedly).

Well, good luck with that.

Cordelia turned to the bench where Howdy Doody and the Silver Shrew were sitting. They looked a little surprised, and indeed even a bit wary, when she approached them, and they immediately ceased their conversation. Which disappointed Cordelia because she wanted to know what they'd been so deeply preoccupied with. Possibly juggling the teaching schedule and working out who was going to give the lessons in the absence of Mr T. Which reminded her, what the hell had happened to Mr T?

No time to speculate about that now.

Howdy and the Shrew were looking at her.

"Yes?" said Howdy.

"What… can we do for you?" said the Shrew.

Cordelia was pretty sure she'd been about to say, "What do you want?" But that was a little blunt and ill-mannered, even for the Shrew, considering they still needed Cordelia to find their stolen books for them.

Cordelia held up the greeting card with the mad rabbit on it. "You stock this in the gift shop." And, before either of them could say anything sarcastic, she added, "Is it possible to look up and see the last time you sold one?" She didn't add that she also wanted to know the identity of the purchaser, assuming they'd paid by card.

One thing at a time.

"Why?" said Howdy Doody. It was a reasonable question.

"It's part of my investigation," said Cordelia.

"In what way is it part of your 'investigation'?" said the Shrew, putting "investigation" in heavily sardonic quotes for good measure.

"Look," said Cordelia, not feeling like playing any games or inventing any elaborate lies, "help me out with this and I guarantee you'll have your books back by the end of the week." She didn't add that a few of the boring, straight-up yoga titles might be missing, depending on her follow-up with Mac. As that would have spoiled the shock impact of her statement.

Howdy and the Shrew stared at her for a long moment, then turned and looked at each other and then looked at her again and then at each other again.

"I don't see what harm it can do," said Howdy, slowly, clearly turning it over in his mind and trying—and failing—to find a downside.

"You *guarantee* it?" said the Shrew, looking at Cordelia.

"Absolutely. You'll have the books or double your money back." Cordelia wasn't quite sure where this latter bit of hucksterish bravado came from, but it sounded good. Of course, at the moment, their money only amounted to a hundred-quid advance, so Cordelia was merely putting herself on the hook for two hundred pounds, but it didn't matter because she wasn't going to have to pay them anything—they were going to have to pay *her*. Because she already had the books. Save a few pervert-dependent ones.

And those weren't the ones they cared about.

Howdy and the Shrew rose from the bench. Howdy stood and did a long stretch with his legs spread apart and his arms raised above his head, as though surrendering to armed police. Not to be outdone, the Shrew turned back to the bench and, extending one of her short little legs, put her foot on it and bent her head down to her knee, then swapped legs and did the same manoeuvre on the other side.

When the fuckers had finally finished pretentiously indulging in competitive yogic stretching, they sauntered into the gift shop, followed by Cordelia.

Cordelia half-expected Alfie still to be there, engaged in the Sisyphean task of cheering Joni up. But the shop was empty except for Joni herself (who did seem a tad more cheerful, or at least less miserable than before).

The Shrew took the greeting card from Cordelia. "Joni," she said with a ghastly simulacrum of a smile. "Could you please scan this and look it up on our stock-taking database? And check when we last sold one?"

Cordelia could see that Joni was aching to ask why. She hesitated for a moment and the smile on the Shrew's face began to go off as quickly as fish left in the sun. Perhaps Joni recognised this, because she hastily took the card, turned it over and scanned the barcode on the back. Then she began to do an intricate series of actions on the antiquated computer that doubled as a shop till. Judging by the wincing and lip-biting, she wasn't entirely au fait with the system, and it took a fair while to get a result.

During which time both Howdy Doody and the Silver Shrew elected to wait in the gift shop with Cordelia. Cordelia wondered why, then realised they were intrigued about what the hell Cordelia was up to. Fair enough. But it didn't do anything for Joni's rudimentary computer skills to have three people closely watching her as she tried to get the software to cooperate. Cordelia turned away and wandered around the shop, killing time ruminating on the outlandish price of everything, until, finally, Joni said, "I've found it." She sounded positively exultant at her success, then emanated a somewhat hurt silence as no one rushed to congratulate her.

The hurt silence turned into a prolonged and somewhat puzzled silence as Joni struggled with another aspect of the database. Then, after what seemed like hours, she said, "We haven't sold one as far back as our records go."

"And how far back is that?" asked Cordelia.

"Uh… about three years?" said Joni, making it more of a question than a statement.

"Which is when we installed the software," said the Shrew.

Cordelia tried not to feel too disappointed. It was hardly surprising, considering the ugly gruesome cartoon on the card. Or maybe it was only ugly and gruesome to Cordelia because she associated it with recently having been almost murdered.

"That doesn't really tell us anything," said Howdy helpfully. "We've stocked these cards for years. Someone could have bought one long ago."

"Or they could have shoplifted one," said Cordelia.

Both Howdy Doody and the Silver Shrew looked mortally offended. In fact, even Joni looked offended

"What sort of people do you think come here?" demanded the Shrew.

"No one would steal from the ashram," said Howdy.

"Someone stole the books," said Cordelia, not adding that someone had also tried to fucking kill her.

16: FORAGING

Cordelia left the ashram and walked down Abbey Avenue to the Upper Richmond Road (less romantically designated the A205), which she crossed at the pedestrian crossing. She now had the choice of turning left and going to the bus stop to catch a 337, which would involve standing there in the bus shelter, choking on traffic fumes while she waited, probably for an annoying length of time, or turning right and plunging into the beautiful, wild greenery of Barnes Common for a pleasant and unhurried stroll to the train station.

Cordelia turned right.

There was a thin, black tarmac footpath that wound through the common to the station and one could either walk along that or strike off boldly through the woods. Cordelia struck off boldly through the woods. She knew all the routes fairly well and the one she chose now led at first into a shadowy, hushed space, a sort of natural chamber formed by tree canopies that were so overgrown with ivy that light was virtually excluded. The forest floor in here was covered with dead leaves and Cordelia happily shuffled through them, moving between the slender trunks of trees, which rose up like columns in a cathedral.

This was one of her favourite places, its magnificent wild solitude only compromised by the occasional presence of a moody teenager scrutinising their phone and smoking skunk.

Thankfully there was no such manifestation here today and Cordelia savoured the solitude as she moved through the shadows, silent except for the scrunching of dried leaves underfoot. She emerged again into daylight at a point where another footpath ran through the common. Cordelia walked across it and vanished back into the vegetation on the other side. Here was a sunlit clearing with a picturesque fallen tree and, to the right, a water meadow, beyond which she could see the tiny, distant figures of dog walkers. Closer at hand, though, was a familiar figure. A tall woman of at least middle age with long curly hair of an implausible inky blackness. It was Carrie Quinn, the Curry Queen. She was dressed in a quilted blue jacket and baggy blue-and-white striped harem trousers tucked into muddy rubber boots.

She hadn't seen Cordelia and, indeed, was walking away from her, so Cordelia didn't feel any great need to make her presence known. In fact, she would have been reluctant to do so because Carrie was behaving rather oddly, sort of prowling slowly around the fringe of the water meadow where the woods began. Her head was bent low, as if she was looking for something.

Maybe she'd lost a contact lens. Bummer.

Suddenly Carrie fell to her knees and, for an embarrassing moment, Cordelia thought she was about to witness a private moment of religious devotion here in the autumn woods. Perhaps a pagan rite of worship. Which, as far as Cordelia was concerned, would have been much worse than a lost contact lens.

But then she saw that Carrie was carrying a basket. A proper old-fashioned wicker basket. She set it beside her on the ground where she was kneeling and took out a trowel, which she used to dig gently in the earth in front of her, at the base of a tree stump.

Cordelia realised she was *foraging*. And given the time of year, most likely looking for mushrooms, which abounded on the common from late summer to early winter.

Thinking about what the Curry Queen could do with mushrooms started to make Cordelia hungry.

She remembered all the exotic foodstuffs on display in Alfie's kitchen (mushrooms included) and wondered if she might be able to cadge a meal from him...

Cordelia arrived at Alfie's house with her head full of stratagems to get him to cook her lunch. She suspected the old rogue was a serious foodie and that he could probably produce a meal of restaurant standard (this thought reminded her of Carrie's failed restaurant and how Alfie had refused to put any money into it). The question was, which approach would be the least likely to offend and the most likely to succeed, free lunch-wise?

In the event, though, she didn't even get a chance to ask. Her visit to Alfie was brief and rather strange. She'd just arrived and been ushered, promisingly, into the professionally equipped kitchen when the doorbell rang again. Alfie went to answer it gladly. "Looks like the party's started," he chuckled.

But he came back a moment later, looking very subdued. "I'm sorry about this, love," he said.

Cordelia's heart sank. No good ever came of a sentence that began like that.

"Something's come up," he said. "Someone's arrived."

Well, bloody obviously, thought Cordelia. Alfie was looking at her and she could see him come to a decision. "It's Mr T," he said, as if taking her into his confidence on a matter of great importance.

If Cordelia had thought about the matter for a long time, she would have been hard-pressed to come up with a less likely candidate for a sudden appearance here, given his no-show at the yoga centre that morning. Alfie looked distinctly uneasy. "Listen," he said. "Would you mind? This is unforgivably rude of me, having invited you here and everything, but Mr T wants to talk to me alone."

"Oh," said Cordelia, trying to conceal how hurt and offended she felt. "I see."

"I'm sorry. But he'd be very ill at ease if there was anyone from the ashram here."

Cordelia resisted the urge to point out that Alfie was also "from the ashram". "I'll just go, then, shall I?" she said. Anger combined with hurt and offence inside her.

"I know, it's incredibly rude, but Mr T is going through some very heavy shit at the moment."

Suddenly Cordelia felt less angry, hurt and offended and more intrigued. She tried to work out how to get Alfie to tell her what was going on, without baldly asking him. Because that would have been terribly uncool. In the end, what she said was, "Is there anything I can do to help?" She tried to sound concerned and sympathetic.

Alfie shook his head sadly. "I'm not sure there's even anything I can do to help," he said. "But I've got to try. Now, I can see you're pissed off..."

"No, I'm not," lied Cordelia. Or at least it would have been a lie a few seconds ago, but now it was something approaching the truth.

"... and you have every right to be," continued Alfie.

"No, not at all," said Cordelia.

"Especially when I ask you if you don't mind going out the back way," said Alfie. He glanced towards the rear of the house. "It's a terrible thing to ask of someone. But could you go out through the garden? The garage is open and you can get out that way. Sorry for the cloak-and-dagger manoeuvres, but Mr T really doesn't want to see anyone from the ashram right now. He feels bad enough about missing the lesson without being reminded about it. So would you mind terribly, love?"

Cordelia realised that Alfie was already leading her towards the back door of the kitchen, the one that led out into the greenhouse with the giant dope tree whose fruits she wasn't going to be able to enjoy after all. And she began to feel hurt and offended again.

Alfie paused to open a drawer in the kitchen counter and take out a plastic food bag, then he led Cordelia through the greenhouse to the door to the garden and opened it for her, a clear invitation for her to piss off. Cordelia was trying to decide which would be the more cutting way to make a departure—say nothing, or say something terse and icily polite—when Alfie pressed something into her hand. It was the plastic bag he'd taken out of the kitchen drawer. A plastic bag which, it turned out, contained weed.

A huge fucking quantity of weed.

"I didn't want you to go away empty handed," said Alfie. "Sorry, love." He kissed her on the cheek and went back inside.

Cordelia stood there in the garden, holding the bag and reflecting on how quickly even the most grievous offence could be erased by being gifted with a serious quantity of drugs.

She squeezed the fat, green bag happily then unzipped her shoulder rig containing her yoga mat and tried to pack it inside. The weed gift was such a huge mother that she couldn't zip the yoga mat carrier up again, so she took the mat out and unrolled it on the grass, put the weed in the middle of it, like the filling of a giant, hand-rolled cigarette, and rolled it back up again. Once she did this, she found the mat and dope fitted snugly into the shoulder bag, if eased in carefully.

Because she was kneeling on the grass, engrossed in doing this, Cordelia wasn't immediately visible to anyone entering the garden. Which was only significant because someone did now enter the garden, from the garage.

It was the Silver Shrew.

She was an even more unlikely visitor than Mr T. It was hard to say who was more surprised, Cordelia busy with her yoga mat on the ground or the Shrew emerging from the garage when she suddenly spotted her.

They stared at each other for a moment. Clearly neither had expected to encounter the other. The Shrew, to her credit, was the first to recover.

"Is Alfie here?" she said, nodding towards the house.

"Yes, he's inside," said Cordelia. She felt at a bit of a disadvantage kneeling on the ground while the Shrew was standing, so she got up, zipping her shoulder bag shut.

The Shrew turned away from her and headed for the back door of the house, clearly intent on going inside and finding Alfie. Cordelia felt honour-bound to intervene. "He's with someone," she said.

The Shrew turned back and gave Cordelia a look of intense irritation. "I know," she said, and went inside.

Cordelia slung her yoga mat over her shoulder and left, going out through the garage. Any residual anger she'd felt towards Alfie was gone now and replaced with anger towards the Shrew. But what the hell was she doing here? And why was she joining Alfie and Mr T in some kind of private meeting? Alfie had seemed pretty clear that Mr T didn't want to see anyone "from the ashram" and you couldn't be more from the ashram than the Shrew.

Cordelia emerged from the gloom of the garage into the blazing sunlight of the street. She was puzzled about just what was going on in the house—an erotic threesome certainly didn't seem likely, thank heavens—but her prevailing emotion was a small but genuine concern over what was going on with Mr T. He was such a serene, calm little man that it was impossible to imagine him having any personal troubles. But clearly he did.

Cordelia was speculating on what these might be as she made her way homewards. As she left Alfie's road, she spotted a familiar vehicle parked near the corner. It was the ashram's lurid orange van, with a bright red Om symbol painted on either side. So that was how the Shrew had got here. (Cordelia had just assumed she'd flown in on her broom.)

Walking towards Putney station, Cordelia considered stopping at the pervert's charity shop. It was en route anyway and the fact that she was carrying her yoga mat with her would add poignancy to her story of being a novice student who was eager to get her hands on any yoga books they had. But no amount of yoga mats and poignancy would cut any ice with Lipstick Teeth if she was on duty. And Mac the Pervert had specifically said Cordelia should phone the shop.

In addition to these considerations was the fact that she was now carrying a shitload of cannabis and, the last time Cordelia had looked, it was still illegal to be in possession of weed. And whenever she was carrying such contraband she always preferred to go straight home with no detours. Don't tempt fate and so on. She headed for the station and happily hopped on a direct train to Barnes Bridge.

Back at home, contentedly ensconced in her sunny attic room, Cordelia set about turning Alfie's weed (or at least a substantial quantity of it) into edibles. While she was waiting for her Russell Hobbs sous-vide cooker (the 25630, a *Which?* magazine Best Buy) to decarb the weed, Cordelia got on the phone and tried to call the pervert—sorry, Mac—on the number he'd given her. Every time she rang, she got a recorded message that gave the name of the charity shop and its opening times, and invited her to leave a message. Cordelia didn't leave a message because she thought Lipstick Teeth might get it. Indeed, the recorded voice on the phone was a woman's and might even have been Lipstick Teeth, speaking through her encarmined choppers.

No, what she wanted to do was speak directly to Mac. But he didn't answer the phone. Indeed, no one answered the phone and, after a dozen attempts and getting the recorded message every time, Cordelia gave up for the day.

Why had Mac the Pervert given her that number and told her to speak to him directly if no one ever answered the frigging phone?

But it was hard to get too annoyed, what with the mellow autumn sunshine washing in through the window and Alfie's extremely potent weed cooking happily away, destined to be converted to mind-blowing edibles.

All that was needed to make contentment complete was some dog-fondling, preferably accompanied by a cadged cup of hot chocolate. With these twin motives in mind, she went downstairs to Edwin's flat and filled him in on developments, as cryptic, frustrating and inconclusive as they were.

Edwin saw everything in a much more positive light, though. Which, frankly, was his job as far as Cordelia was concerned. That was one reason she'd been so eager to discuss things with him (dog and hot chocolate being two others).

He was particularly impressed with her discovery of the greeting card.

"That was clever of you, to think of looking in the shop at the yoga centre," he said.

"Thank you," said Cordelia, feeling gratifyingly clever

"It's just too much of a coincidence, wouldn't you say? I mean, the copy of the card left for you on the bench, ah… the other night…" Edwin was tapdancing tactfully around any mention of the attempt to squash Cordelia under a slab of concrete, which she appreciated. "It hardly seems likely that they could have obtained the same card somewhere else, although I suppose it's possible."

"No," said Cordelia. "It came from the ashram. I'm sure of that." She didn't have any rational reason to offer for the decisive nature of this assertion. It was a gut instinct.

"But they weren't able to give you any information about who might have bought it there?"

"No, they claimed they've never sold a single one since they've had it on their computer system."

"And you believe them?" said Edwin.

It hadn't occurred to Cordelia that the people at the ashram, or at least Joni, might have been lying. Full marks to Edwin for cynicism and paranoia. Two things which might help to keep a person (in this case Cordelia) alive.

"Well, Joni was reading the information off the computer screen. Or at least pretending to. No one else bothered to check, but they easily could have done." The Shrew, for instance, could have just stepped behind the counter and looked over her shoulder. But she hadn't done that. "And if it was a bluff it was a bold one, which isn't a word I associate with Joni."

"All right, let's assume it's true. No one bought it, yet someone got hold of it…"

"Assuming their stupid system actually works," said Cordelia, "then my guess is that someone pinched it from the shop."

"Would that be easy? Stealing things in there without getting caught?"

"Maybe not something the size of a yoga mat," said Cordelia. "But just about anyone would be able to nick something as small as a greeting card undetected. And they might not even have to. Steal it from the shop while anybody's watching, I mean."

"Sorry, I don't follow."

"If it's somebody who actually works at the ashram, they'd have access to the gift shop when it's not open for business."

"Ah," said Edwin. "So they could steal it at their leisure with no chance of being caught?"

"Right."

"And do you think it's someone who works at the ashram?"

"Not necessarily," said Cordelia. "It could simply be someone who goes there for lessons."

"But we're confident the culprit is someone who's associated with the yoga centre?"

Cordelia liked that Edwin said "we".

"Yes," she said.

"And you've had no luck speaking to your friend at the charity shop?" said Edwin.

"No," said Cordelia, a little thrown by the sudden change of subject. "And let's not call him my friend, shall we?"

"But you'll keep trying?"

"Yes. If they've got the other books I need, I want to get my hands on them. I promised the Shrew and Howdy Doody—"

"Who and who?" said Edwin.

"The head honchos at the yoga centre," said Cordelia. "Sorry, I'd forgotten that I'm the only one who uses those nicknames, though I'm working on spreading them into general use." After all, it had worked with Mr T, hadn't it? "Anyway, I sort of promised them they'd get the stolen books in the next day or two. It was a kind of tit-for-tat in exchange for letting me check on who'd bought the card. Fat lot of good that did me."

"Worth a try," said Edwin, at his most mollifying.

"Having promised them they'd get their books back I'd like to have a complete set to give them, so they don't try to weasel out of giving me my full finder's fee. So that the Shrew doesn't try to weasel out."

"That makes sense," said Edwin. "And, of course, there's another reason it's important to speak to your friend—to your contact—at the charity shop."

"What's that?" said Cordelia.

"He might be able to tell you who donated the books."

Cordelia could have kicked herself for not thinking of this herself. "In other words," she said, "possibly the thief."

"In other words," said Edwin, "possibly the person who's trying to kill you."

17: DOG-FRIENDLY PUB

The next day Cordelia dialled the charity shop again at nine in the morning (they allegedly opened at nine; very unusual for a charity shop, which tended to be casual places staffed by bohemian losers who couldn't hold down a proper job, not least because they couldn't get into work by nine o'clock) and got the recorded message again. She determined to try the number at half-hour intervals. Two-and-a-half hours later, somebody answered. Cordelia was so surprised that she nearly dropped the phone.

It was a woman's voice, and she was sure she recognised it as good old Lipstick Teeth. But Lipstick Teeth didn't recognise her, clearly, because she sounded polite and even friendly. For instance, when Cordelia asked if she could please speak to Mac, Lipstick Teeth said, "Of course you can."

The difference between this courteous, cheerful entity on the other end of the phone and the red-toothed virago she'd encountered face to face was startling, to say the least. It must mean Cordelia hadn't been recognised. But in that case, why was Lipstick Teeth's voice burned into Cordelia's brain and instantly recognisable and not vice versa? She began to feel rather offended. But she didn't have much time to feel this way because Mac came on the line with a guarded "Hello."

"It's me," said Cordelia.

"Thought so. Just a tick." Silence on the line and then Mac's voice was back again. "Just taking the call out of earshot—out of earshot of Beatrice, that is." Beatrice aka Bea aka Lipstick Teeth. "I can talk now. Fire away."

"She didn't recognise me, then?"

"I should say not. She'd never have called me to the phone if she had. Probably would have hung up on you. You really got her angry the other day. She was hopping mad. I've never seen the like. She's still talking about it."

"Well, I'd better not come to the shop, then."

"I should say not. At least not until we can be sure Bea isn't around. We're going to have to wait until she goes on holiday. Which means in November when she goes to Portugal. She does windsurfing in the Algarve."

Making a conscious effort not to picture this, Cordelia, who for obvious reasons had no intention of waiting until November, said, "Listen, Mac..." She was working hard to sound her most pleasant and persuasive.

Clearly the pleasant and persuasive voice worked because Mac immediately offered a very eager and happy "Yes?"

"I guess you're thinking we have to wait until Beatrice is gone so you can show me the back of the shop?"

"Yes, but if you're thinking of trying to sneak in without her seeing you or something like that..."

"I'm not. I have an alternative suggestion. If you wouldn't mind doing me a bit of a favour?" Cordelia really could be pleasant when she tried. And persuasive.

"I suppose not. All right. What is it?"

"I don't need to go into the back of the shop, if you don't mind going in there for me. You have access to the back of the shop, don't you?"

"What do you mean? Of course I have access to the back of the shop. I work here, don't I?"

"Then would you do me an enormous favour and have a look for the books yourself?"

Uncertainty surfaced in Mac's voice. "I don't know. I mean, I don't know which ones you want. How can I know?"

"It's really simple," said Cordelia, at her most honeyed and encouraging. "Just pick out any books about yoga."

"Any?"

"Absolutely anything at all." Cordelia had thought this through carefully. Theoretically she could have briefed Mac to only choose paperbacks, but frankly she didn't trust him to identify what a paperback was. Much better to just tell him to grab anything yoga-related. She might end up with a bit of dross, but that didn't matter so long as she also got all the good stuff.

"Well… all right…"

"And then please let's meet up and I'll pay you for them. You can buy stuff from the shop, can't you?"

"Of course I can. I get a staff discount."

"Well, that's just fine, then," said Cordelia. "But don't feel you have to pass on the discount to me."

"No?" Surprise from Mac.

"No, naturally not. You're doing me a favour. And you should be rewarded for that."

"Oh, all right."

Quickly, so he didn't get the wrong idea—this was, after all, Mac the Pervert—she added, "You should be paid for your trouble."

"Oh, all right." Mac the Pervert sounded a little disappointed. Perhaps he'd been envisioning another, more disgusting, non-financial kind of reward. The notion of which was at least as repellent as the thought of Lipstick Teeth in a wetsuit on a windsurfer in the Portuguese sunshine.

"Buy them with your discount then sell them to me at a healthy profit," said Cordelia.

"Okay." The prospect of a healthy profit sounded like it had cheered him up.

"But the only thing is," said Cordelia, "we need to do this as soon as possible."

"All right."

"How soon do you think you can get the books?" said Cordelia quickly.

"Oh, this lunchtime I should think. When Beatrice goes out for her noodles. She always has noodles from the noodle shop. Like clockwork. She's bound to be gone for at least three quarters of an hour."

Cordelia repressed the weary urge to ask if that was the case then why couldn't she simply come into the shop and look in the back room herself, while Beatrice was safely off the premises noodling. Better just to stick with the plan at hand. "That's wonderful," she said, with somewhat insincere sincerity.

"Then I can have a look and get the books and pay for them and put them through the till, and Beatrice won't need to know anything about it."

"Just wonderful," said Cordelia, and this time she meant it.

"But then how do I get the books to you? Do you want me to bring them over to your gaff?"

Of course not, you pervert. You're not getting within a country mile of my "gaff", thought Cordelia. But she said, chipper and cheerful and polite, "No, let's meet at a pub. Then I can buy you a drink to say thank you."

"Oh, that sounds nice."

Just in case it sounded a little too nice, and again to prevent him getting the wrong idea, the perverted wrong idea, Cordelia added firmly, "This will be a purely platonic drink, you understand, Mac. A purely platonic pint." It was best to put your cards on the table, thought Cordelia, in a situation like this. "I hope that's all right."

"Yeah, that's all right," said Mac with what Cordelia was surprised to find she felt was a somewhat insulting readiness and lack of regret. Wasn't she good enough for a charity shop pervert? "Just so long as it's a proper sort of platonic pint. Cask-conditioned real ale, properly cellared."

Cordelia sighed inwardly to realise that Mac was not only a pervert but a beer snob. "No problem," she said. "We'll see that we go to a decent pub. Where are you based?"

"Based? Where do I live, you mean? My gaff is in Sheen, near the railway tracks on White Hart Lane. You know?"

Cordelia did indeed know. What was more, she knew of the perfect pub there.

They arranged a time to meet, then Cordelia got off the phone and set to work raising some money.

She'd emptied her bank account the other day to pay the widow Fairwell her deposit on the John D. MacDonald jackpot. Since then, the only money that had flowed in had been the 100-quid advance from the ashram bozos, which Cordelia had also paid on to the widow, and the proceeds of the sale of the Sven Hassel books (Nazis, tanks, industrial quantities of slaughter and a cat called Stalin).

But the Sven Hassel money wasn't enough.

She urgently needed some additional funds to pay Mac the Pervert. For the yoga books he was hopefully going to find, of course. But also for something else, something much more important.

She'd need a decent bankroll. And before tonight.

Luckily for Cordelia, she had a plan.

She picked up the beautiful copy of Avram Silverlight's *The Corpse Position* from its place on her table. Ever since she'd obtained the stolen books from Alfie's garage, this relic of the late

Duncan Fairwell's collection had been a duplicate and surplus to requirements, so she'd always intended to sell it.

Well, now the time had come.

Taking the book over to the window where the light was good, Cordelia photographed it and uploaded the photo onto her website and her eBay account, along with some excitable but not entirely inaccurate text about how rare and desirable it was, and how unusual it was for such a fine copy to turn up. The last bits were absolutely true.

Cordelia put the book for sale on Buy it Now instead of an auction because she needed someone to Buy it Now, and she priced it to move.

And move it did. It sold within the hour. Cordelia immediately regretted she hadn't priced it higher, but what the hell. She had topped up her funds and she'd be able to pay Mac the Pervert when she saw him.

Cordelia wasn't entirely surprised at how quickly she'd been able to sell the book. All those emails she'd sent the other day to dealers asking for Avram Silverlight books would have reminded them what collectable items these were, and alerted them to the fact there were buyers out there eager to get hold of them. She couldn't have stirred up more interest in those titles (and increased their market value) if she'd deliberately tried.

In fact, Cordelia wouldn't be surprised if one of the people she'd contacted didn't now get in touch, offering her the very book she'd just sold to *them*.

At a radically inflated price, of course.

Albert's was a tiny gastropub tucked away down an alley near the railway tracks and a patch of allotments between Sheen and Barnes. It was a nice place, characterful, with a good wine list, lots of presumably good beers and ales (whatever the difference was) and excellent food. In fact, it was a gem of a place. The only reason Cordelia didn't go there more often was because she hated the owner. Who was indeed called Albert. She hated him for a couple of distinct but equally legitimate reasons.

Albert had no idea Cordelia hated him and, in fact, it was a bit of a stretch to hate him, but one couldn't help one's feelings and, in the first instance, Albert had made the fatal mistake of going out with someone whom Cordelia adored and felt she should be going out with instead of some shitty chef and pub owner.

How could she not hate him?

She had no idea if Albert was still seeing the person in question, because the whole business was frankly too painful to look into, but the best policy was just to go on hating him.

Not that this stopped Cordelia arranging to meet Mac at Albert's that very night.

And, because she wasn't born yesterday, she took Edwin along with her.

And, since he needed a walk, they took Rainbottle with them.

Cordelia had a wad of cash in her pocket. Provided by Edwin in return for the PayPal funds she'd transferred to him almost as soon as she'd sold *The Corpse Position*. Because cash talks, and electronic transfers are a lot less eloquent, to strain a metaphor.

When she explained why she needed the money and how she'd got it (she was rather proud of the instant book sale), Edwin said, "You could have asked for next month's rent back. You've paid it massively in advance. You could have had it refunded temporarily and paid me again later."

"I did think of that," said Cordelia. "And it's very kind of you. But I'd really rather continue to pay in advance and not presume on our friendship."

Edwin smiled. "You really are the model tenant. I must say, you've turned over a new leaf."

It was true. Cordelia had formerly used every dodge imaginable to avoid paying her rent and only paid it, grudgingly, as late as possible.

But all that had changed when she'd found out how many people Edwin had killed.

Albert's was a dog-friendly pub, so they could take Rainbottle in with them—a prospect that excited him even more than it did his accompanying humans. Fortunately, there were no other dogs currently visiting, so they were spared the indignity of separating combative and/or copulating canines as they made their way to the nicest table—the one with the benches in the little booth in an alcove opposite the pub door.

They settled themselves on the benches on either side of the table and, since this table had an inconvenient wooden base attached to its legs, making it uncomfortable for a dog to lie underneath, Rainbottle jumped up on the bench by Edwin and lay down beside him.

Albert's was a tiny place, only about twice the size of Cordelia's attic room, though with superior wet bar facilities. It had dark wood-panelled walls hung with vintage advertising mirrors or reproductions thereof (the reflective nature of which made the place seem larger than it was). The door through which you entered, and the wall facing out onto the alley, had stained-glass windows which provided a pleasant, subdued otherworldly illumination. The floors were rough-hewn blue Victorian tiles, which meant that if you dropped a glass it was bye-bye and also that, once the place filled up, it became unconscionably noisy.

Luckily it was very quiet at the moment, and Cordelia, Edwin and Rainbottle were the only customers. Albert the owner was not visible but he was audible, remonstrating with the chef in the tiny kitchen at the back of the pub, which was what he spent most of his time doing.

Conversely, very much visible, though not audible, was the beauteous barmaid. Like the late Duncan Fairwell in his bookshop, Albert had a firm policy of only hiring young and good-looking female staff. For some reason, in Albert's case, these were always Australian. The role of these outback sirens seemed to be chiefly ornamental, given their inefficiency as bar staff.

The current incumbent, standing behind the beer taps, was a platinum blonde with startling red eye makeup which at least had the virtue of matching the ribbon in her hair. Far from hassling Cordelia's party, her only customers, to buy a drink, she didn't seem to have even registered their presence, being as she was deeply preoccupied with her phone.

She did glance up, however, when the door opened and Mac the Pervert came in. He was still dressed all in black and he looked like he had washed his hair, which was a bit of a relief but a minor consideration compared to the very promising large plastic shopping bag he was carrying, which bore the legend *Take an old bag shopping* and had a supermarket logo on it.

Mac blinked for a moment to accustom his eyes to the stained-glass gloom of the pub, then spotted Cordelia and company and waved to them. He liked to wave. Smiling, he hurried over to join the trio. Cordelia nippily hopped out of her seat and went to sit with Edwin on the other bench, on the opposite side to Rainbottle.

Ostensibly a piece of politeness to provide the other bench for Mac, this was frankly more a case of pervert-avoidance. She didn't want Mac sitting up close beside her. Also, this way she could look him in the eyes when they were doing business.

"This is my friend Edwin," said Cordelia.

"Good to meet you, Mac," said Edwin, and there was a flurry of handshaking.

"And who's this lovely lad?" said Mac, indicating Rainbottle.

"Rainbottle," said Cordelia.

"Rainbottle? Ha! Top name," said Mac. "Isn't he gorgeous?"

"He's monstrously spoiled," allowed Edwin, patting Rainbottle who stirred his tail politely, well aware he was being talked about.

"Well, that's what they're for, isn't it? Dogs, I mean. Spoiling them, I mean," promulgated Mac.

There then ensued a discussion about dogs, which a frankly bored Cordelia tuned out of. She tuned back in at the end of it so she could ask Mac what he wanted to drink. Unfortunately, this triggered a discussion between the two men about the various beers, or ales or whatever they were, on offer (Edwin was a bit of a beer snob, too) and Cordelia had to tune out again.

Finally, when she found out what the two men wanted— which seemed to be based on the beers with the most ridiculous name (Edwin's rather modest Surrey Hills Shere Drop being easily outclassed in this respect by Mac the Pervert's choice of Tiny Rebel Freakshake Froozie)—Cordelia went to the bar and got drinks for everyone. To her surprise, the red-eyed, platinum blonde Antipodean temptress was not only able to locate all the correct beverages (including a glass of Rioja for Cordelia), do simple arithmetic and work out the change, but she also provided a doggie bowl of water for Rainbottle without being asked.

This rather endeared her to Cordelia, who would have sworn that the girl hadn't even spotted the dog. Maybe Albert didn't hire his harem purely for decorative purposes after all.

While waiting for the barmaid to serve the drinks, Cordelia looked at the rear of the bar where a big retro radio set crouched, looking very imposing and art deco among the gleaming bottles on the mirrored shelf. Cordelia knew that radio all too well.

Luckily the Canberra caryatids employed here were under strict instruction never to play the radio and thereby disrupt the peace and sanctity of this quiet little public house. *Except*—horrifyingly and disgustingly—when Cordelia's *brother's* radio show was on. Yes, Albert the pub owner was a huge fan of Stuart "Stinky" Stanmer. Unbelievably enough, Cordelia's fish-faced sibling was a successful DJ and minor media personality.

This was the second reason Cordelia had for hating him. Albert, that is. Though, of course, she also hated her brother. While that might seem an unusual, or even extreme position, anyone who'd experienced Stinky's rapacious self-serving skulduggery, his spectacularly narcissistic mediocrity, or indeed his cowardly abuse and duplicity, would be likely to endorse it. Indeed, applaud it.

She took the drinks back to the table in two trips, starting with Rainbottle's water bowl. The dog hopped down off the bench and lapped happily as the humans all sipped tentatively at their own beverages.

Then, feeling that she'd waited more than long enough, Cordelia got down to business. "So, Mac, do you have something for me?" She indicated the plastic shopping bag seated tantalisingly on the bench beside him. It had been all Cordelia could do to stop herself snatching it from him and looking inside as soon as he'd sat down.

Mac smiled his unexpectedly charming and not at all perverted smile. "I certainly do," he said. He started to reach into the bag and take stuff out, but Cordelia quickly said, "No, let me, please." Because she didn't want the fool setting immaculate vintage paperbacks on a wet table.

Assuming there were any vintage paperbacks in there.

Mac obediently handed her the bag. Cordelia took a deep breath, then opened it and looked inside.

In a way, she almost didn't need to look inside, because when she took that deep breath, she caught the unmistakable aroma of old paperbacks. With a gentle, languid sensation of triumph, she reached into the bag and carefully began to extract the contents.

Edwin, who understood the dangers of wet tables, moved away from her a little so there was space on the bench between them where she could set the books.

Cordelia could feel her heart beating happily.

The bag contained two stupid hardbacks—*Yoga for Kids*, with a curly-haired moppet doing the tree posture on the cover, and *Yoga for Pets* (by Jean Farrar with an "insight" by Dr Marcus Bach). But, apart from that, it was full of paperbacks. Vintage paperbacks in immaculate, fine or "pristine" (copyright, the Silver Shrew) condition. All of them on the ashram's list of stolen books. And none that *weren't* on the list.

This confirmed Cordelia's suspicion that these were indeed the stolen books themselves. She referred to the ashram list on the phone while the boys talked—more beer chat; deep in concentration, Cordelia hardly registered it—and confirmed with a warm flash of rejoicing that she had now obtained all the books that had been burgled.

Mission accomplished.

Cordelia returned the books carefully to the bag (she'd left her rucksack at home out of a superstition that, if she'd brought it with her, she'd end up with nothing to put in it), using *Kids* and *Pets* as protective packaging around the paperbacks.

Then she interrupted the endless beer talk and negotiated with Mac for a price on the books. His request was so reasonable that she overpaid him. He counted the money and put it away, looking very happy. Almost as happy as Cordelia. Edwin patted a contented Rainbottle and Cordelia carefully stashed the bag of books on the floor between her feet where she could constantly check it was safely present.

Then she got down to the real business of the evening.

* * *

"You've done a fantastic job with the books, Mac," said Cordelia. "Thank you very much."

"You're more than welcome. Thank you for the bonus."

"You're welcome. Now there's something else I'd like your help with."

Mac frowned somewhat dubiously. "You've got all the yoga books in the shop."

"It's not books I'm after now," said Cordelia. "What I'd really like, and what I'd really appreciate your help with…" She was all smiles and charm now, and even did some eyelash fluttering.

"Yes?" said Mac, looking less dubious and more mesmerised.

"I'd really like you to find out who donated those books."

"Donated them?"

"Yes."

Mac assumed a hunted expression. "You mean you want to know who brought them into the shop?"

"Yes, exactly."

"Well, I'm afraid I can't do that. I can't help you. I mean, I'd like to. I really would. But I can't. Data protection. And professional confidentiality. And all that."

Cordelia, who was fairly certain that charity shops didn't have a code of professional conduct and who didn't give a damn about data protection, stopped fluttering her eyelashes and moved to phase two.

She took out all the cash she had in her pocket and put it on the table.

Mac dropped his eyes from her to the cash, with gratifying swiftness. He stared at it and said, "What's that, then?"

"That's the first half of your payment. You get the other half when you find out who brought those books into the shop." Cordelia had no idea where she was going to get the other half of the cash she was promising, but she would worry about that later.

"But I may not be able to give you a name. I mean, we only get names if we do Gift Aid on donations and none of those books had Gift Aid stickers…"

"I don't need a name," said Cordelia. "I just need a description." Mac was still staring at the money. "A really good description."

"You want to know what they look like?" said Mac, looking up from the money and into her eyes now.

"Yes. If you're smart about it, and I know you can be very smart…" Cordelia was in full butter-up mode now and she was aware of Edwin watching her. But she got the feeling he was watching her more with professional admiration than cynical amusement. "Without giving the game away," she said, "you just need to work out when the books came into the shop and who was on duty that day and steer the conversation around to the sort of people who bring things in—in this case books about yoga, and how sometimes it's so funny what people bring in and you wouldn't expect them to have that kind of stuff to donate, and was the person who donated the yoga books the sort of person you'd expect, or were they completely different?" Cordelia examined Mac closely to see if he was getting it. "And then get them to give you a description."

"Yeah…" Mac nodded slowly and looked at them, at both Cordelia and Edwin. He'd clearly concluded (rightly) that Edwin was involved in this too. A pervert maybe, but not a stupid one. "Yeah," said Mac. "I could do that."

"Good," said Cordelia.

"Or I could just get hold of the security camera footage."

18: POPCORN

Cordelia walked home with Edwin and Rainbottle through the cool autumn evening. The bag of books she'd acquired from Mac was a welcome weight, swinging pendulum-steady at her side. Not long after they'd left the pub, they bumped into Lorna, who insisted on walking home with them. Admittedly, she was Edwin's girlfriend, but still it was annoying because it meant Cordelia and Edwin couldn't talk freely.

Luckily, she didn't ask what was in the bag Cordelia was carrying.

As soon as they got back to the house, Cordelia hurried upstairs to her room and took the books out.

She spread them out on her table along with the other recent acquisitions—the ones she'd bought from the charity shop on that memorable day when she'd met Lipstick Teeth, along with, much more significantly, those titles she'd come to think of as "the barbecue books": the complete set of Avram Silverlight's work, which had been lurking in Alfie's garage.

Cordelia stared at them arrayed in front of her. Yes, she was gloating. But she was also double-checking. She could scarcely believe that she'd recovered every single book that had been stolen from the ashram. But she went through the list yet again, carefully crossing off each title in turn. And it was true.

They were all here, all in immaculate or "pristine" (good old Silver Shrew) condition. The ones that were supposed to be signed were all signed.

Yes, these were the originals, stolen and dispersed in various ways, and now here they all were again, reunited and ready to go home. If you could call the Silverlight Yoga Centre "home".

Case closed for the Paperback Sleuth.

The following morning, Cordelia carefully wrapped all the books, put them into her rucksack and set off for the ashram. She'd briefly considered taking her yoga mat, too, and fitting in a lesson. But it was going to be a busy morning, and anyway it would be difficult to wear both the mat in its shoulder bag and the bulging rucksack.

Cordelia walked past the duck pond and Sadie's (her favourite restaurant—she'd have to treat herself to a victory feast here. Maybe invite Edwin, too) to the bus stop by the Red Lion, and caught a 33 that took her all the way to Abbey Avenue, albeit through the irritating stop-start traffic of the morning commute.

She wasn't the first into the gift shop this time and she had to wait while Joni accepted payment for lessons from a queue of eager adherents. When it was finally her turn at the till, Cordelia said, "Could you call Gunadya and Harshavardhana and let them know I'm here." She'd spent her time waiting in the queue productively rehearsing the Sanskrit names of this pair of jokers and willing herself not to say the Silver Shrew and Howdy Doody. Because that would have been unprofessional.

"Do you want a lesson?" said Joni. "You'll have to pay this time." She seemed eager to get that in.

"No thank you," said Cordelia sweetly. And added, all innocence, "Are you teaching today?"

Joni's colour deepened perceptibly. "No," she said, in a somewhat strangled voice.

Checkmate, thought Cordelia with satisfaction. Then something occurred to her. "Is Mr T back?"

"Who?" said Joni.

Cordelia ground her teeth. Joni knew exactly who she was talking about. But she was going to make her say it. So she said it. "Mr Thirunavukkarasu." She stumbled over the name and regretted not having rehearsed that one too. Mr T was so much easier to say, not to mention more fun. It occurred to Cordelia that maybe Joni knew it was she who had coined his nickname and that was why she was refusing to use it. How petty could you get?

"Yes. Mr Thirunavukkarasu is back."

"Is he all right?" said Cordelia. She was genuinely concerned about Mr T, but this didn't seem to count for anything with Joni.

"Yes, he's fine," she said. A rote answer if ever there was one.

"Do you know what the trouble was?" Cordelia knew she shouldn't ask, or at least she shouldn't ask Joni, but she couldn't help herself.

"No, I don't. And it's none of your business, is it?"

"I don't know," said Cordelia. "Since I don't know what the trouble was, I couldn't say whether it's any of my business or not."

"Well, it is none of your business and none of my business and none of anybody's business, anywhere, anytime, anyplace," said Joni.

What an odd thing to say. Cordelia wondered if she was beginning to lose it. But her half-exultant speculation about Joni's brain melting down was interrupted when she suddenly noticed something.

In the wall behind the counter there was a door leading into an alcove and then a corridor that went to the kitchen. Since the door was panelled with glass, Cordelia could see that a bicycle was parked in the alcove. Joni's bicycle.

Cordelia looked at her. "Do you always come here on your bike?"

"I go everywhere on my bicycle. Now, did you want me to phone Gunadya or not?"

"Gunadya or Harshavardhana," said Cordelia absently.

She was thinking of the whispering sound of a bicycle being pedalled swiftly away from the ruins of Putney Hospital on a memorable recent evening.

Joni eventually got through on the phone—it took an unconscionably long time considering she was only calling a room upstairs (you could hear it ringing through the ceiling) and both Howdy Doody and the Silver Shrew were based up there, so they had no excuse for not hearing it and not picking up pronto. Maybe they were too busy playing *Grand Theft Auto* and *Call of Duty* respectively? But someone finally answered, and Joni told them that Cordelia wanted to see them. She then cupped her hand over the phone and smiled a faux-pleasant smile at Cordelia. "Sorry, they're too busy just at the moment."

"No they're not," said Cordelia, and took the phone from her.

Joni gave it up without a struggle and watched with eager interest as Cordelia spoke into the receiver. Probably because she hated the Silver Shrew at least as much as she hated Cordelia.

"Hello, it's me," said Cordelia into the phone.

But it wasn't the Shrew. It was Howdy Doody. "I know," he said. "Joni told me. And, as I told her, I'm afraid Gunadya and I are having a meeting at the moment…"

"I've got the books," said Cordelia.

There was a gratifying silence on the line. And, an agreeable bonus, Joni was staring at her with pleasingly big, surprised eyes. "Come again?" said Howdy.

"I've got the books," said Cordelia. "I've got them here, with me, now." She shifted her shoulder muscles, feeling the reassuring weight of the rucksack. "Do you still want them?" This last bit was obviously a rhetorical question or, if you preferred, a blatant bluff.

But the result was very heart-warming.

"Of course we do," said Howdy, his voice rising about an octave in pitch. "Come up immediately."

By the time Cordelia got upstairs, both Howdy Doody and the Silver Shrew were standing in the hallway waiting for her. They led her into the meeting room. No one said anything. Howdy had clearly briefed the Shrew in the time it had taken Cordelia to get up from the gift shop. As they watched, Cordelia took off her rucksack and set it down on a chair like an obedient child. Then, with a congenial feeling of drama, she opened it up and began to unload blocks of books wrapped in bubble wrap and sealed with transparent tape.

As Howdy Doody and the Silver Shrew watched, Cordelia ceremoniously unveiled the books and put them on the table. She knew what was in each opaque bubble-wrapped block and she'd been debating all morning how she should play this—unwrap the Avram Silverlight titles (the most rare and important finds) first then work her way down to the less significant books? Or the other way around?

Cordelia had decided there was more suspense and excitement and general fun to be had the other way around. She started with the boring, straight-up yoga books, lovingly unwrapping them and setting them carefully on the table in a neat row. When the Silver Shrew saw these her eyes went as wide with surprise as Joni's had downstairs when she'd heard about the recovered loot. Although the Shrew recovered more quickly than Joni and swiftly assumed a poker face.

Cordelia put the books on the table, taking her time. When the first Avram Silverlight title appeared, Howdy Doody gave a little gasp and darted forwards to pick it up. He hastily opened it, no doubt to check that it was signed. As Cordelia put out more Silverlight volumes, Howdy checked a second one and then a third, then he gave up.

"These are the actual books that were stolen?" he said, quietly.

"I believe so," said Cordelia modestly. She felt a mild pang of regret as she put the last book on the table. It was a little bit sad the fun was over.

For a moment the three of them stood looking at the books on the table, then Howdy and the Shrew began to gather them up. For a moment Cordelia thought they were going to hug the books or fondle them. But instead, of course, they began to put them back on the bookshelf. The recently burgled and therefore empty bookshelf.

In little more than a minute and with the commendable minimum of bickering ("This one goes here." "No it doesn't." "No, wait, you're right." "Of course I'm right.") they put all the books back on the shelf.

And then they stood back and looked at it.

It was like the books had never been missing.

Then they turned and looked at Cordelia.

She'd never seen this dour duo looking so happy. Howdy Doody was utterly delighted and the Silver Shrew was, if anything, even more pleased. They stared at her for a moment and then Howdy turned and looked at the bookshelf again, as if the paperbacks might have disappeared the moment he turned his back on them (they hadn't). While he looked at them again, the Shrew kept looking at Cordelia. She was smiling a big, warm smile. She really did look happy.

Finally, Howdy Doody tore his eyes away from the bookcase and looked at Cordelia. "I suppose you'll be wanting to be paid now," he said.

"Yes, please," said Cordelia, feeling deeply peaceful and content. She zipped her rucksack shut and slipped it back over her shoulders. It felt wonderfully light and empty. Cordelia felt wonderfully light and empty too, as though she'd shed her worldly troubles. She resolved to enjoy the sensation while it lasted. Already she could begin to sense, or remember, various worries she had yet to address, like the tiny black specks of carrion birds distantly circling in a clear blue sky.

"Don't forget that we're going to deduct that hundred-pound advance," said the Shrew, bringing everything quickly back down to earth again.

"Oh, let's forget about that," said Howdy Doody, astonishingly.

The Shrew was astonished, too. "What?" she said.

"Let's pay her the hundred pounds," said Howdy.

"We've already paid it to her," said the Shrew, at her pedantic best. Or worst.

"I know," said Howdy. "But let's pay it to her again. As a bonus."

"A bonus?" said the Shrew, as if it was a word she'd seen written down but never actually heard spoken aloud. Then, promptly and utterly unexpectedly, she said, "All right."

"All right?" said Cordelia, unable to quite believe what she was hearing. She felt like the rug had been pulled out from under her. Or rather that the ratty orange carpet had been pulled out from under her.

"We'll pay you the full amount as originally agreed," said the Silver Shrew. "And the hundred pounds, which was originally intended as an advance, will now be considered as a bonus." She was back in pedantry mode and, as if to prove it, she added, "Please send us a new invoice to reflect that."

"All right," said Cordelia.

"Do we have your bank details?" said Howdy Doody. He wasn't quite looking at Cordelia. His head was turned away slightly. She realised he was dying to look at the bookshelf again but wasn't letting himself give in to the urge.

"Yes," said Cordelia. "But I'll include them on the invoice again."

Then they all fell silent. It was as if there was nothing left to say. But there was. Cordelia said, "If you don't mind, perhaps you could expedite payment? I've incurred certain expenses and I need to settle them."

"Of course," said Howdy, giving in to the urge and turning to look quickly at the bookshelf again, then hastily back at Cordelia.

"We'll transfer the funds immediately," said the Silver Shrew. She was still smiling, as if someone had told her the most wonderful, funny story.

Howdy showed Cordelia out of the meeting room and even patted her affectionately on the shoulder as she left. Or maybe he was affectionately patting the rucksack which had so recently disgorged his beloved books.

It was only as she started back down the stairs that Cordelia realised that neither of them had asked her where she'd found the books.

Wasn't that a bit odd?

She didn't have much time to speculate about this, though, because when she reached the bottom of the stairs she saw Carrie Quinn the Curry Queen unlocking the door to the kitchen. Carrie looked at Cordelia and said, "Congratulations."

"What for?" asked Cordelia.

"Finding the books," said Carrie, and she disappeared into the kitchen.

Word certainly travelled fast.

Cordelia wasn't kidding about needing her money soon and having expenses to settle.

When Mac the Pervert had revealed that the charity shop had a security camera, Cordelia had almost fallen off her chair.

Or, in this case, her bench in the pub. But, thinking about it, there was no reason a charity shop shouldn't have a decent security system—Cordelia remembered what Edwin had said to her about burglar alarms when she'd been threatening to break into the place.

According to Mac, it wasn't exactly state of the art, though. A CCTV camera fed a continuous stream of images to an antiquated VHS recorder in the back of the shop. The VHS recorder, of course, used VHS tapes, those enormous cumbersome monstrosities of yesteryear. How big an archive of security footage they could keep was limited by the number of tapes they possessed—which was quite a few, having acquired these things through donations over the years. Most people had no use for VHS anymore, but the technology at the shop worked, so why scrap it for something more modern and more expensive, since it served well enough and everyone—or at least, Mac—knew how to use it and were comfortable with it?

And when they reached the last tape in their archive (the VHS tapes were actually stored, Mac revealed with some pride—perverse pride, appropriately in a pervert—in a plastic dustbin dedicated to solely that purpose at the back of the shop), they simply started recording over them again beginning with the oldest one.

Hearing about this recording over of the past footage alarmed Cordelia but Mac immediately reassured them that the donation of the yoga books would still be safely on tape, by a comfortable margin. "We have about a month's supply of cassettes," he said proudly. Then he suddenly frowned a worried frown at Cordelia. "Do you even know what VHS is?"

It was Cordelia's turn to do some reassuring. "Of course I do," she said, although in fact, she only happened to know about VHS (and indeed Betamax) thanks to her father's obsession with vintage

TV shows, which came with an obligatory adjunct and bonus obsession that involved awareness of obsolete formats.

"You think you'll definitely have the donation—and the donor—recorded?" said Edwin, who liked to make sure that everything was clearly spelled out.

"Definitely," said Mac. "I'll find the tape and borrow it from the shop for you to have a look at."

"But we don't have a VHS player to watch it on," said Cordelia.

"I can probably find one somewhere," said Edwin.

"Don't worry, Edwin," said Mac. "You chaps can come around to my gaff. I have one at home we can use. A VHS unit. We can watch the tape in my sitting room."

"I'll bring some popcorn," suggested Cordelia.

"Just so long as you bring this fellow," said Mac. He leaned over and patted Rainbottle, who acknowledged the courtesy by allowing his tongue to loll out.

"Well, that sounds like a plan," said Edwin crisply. Drinking real ale made him like that. Crisp and a little pedantic. A little more pedantic than usual.

And that was how they'd left it. Mac would need a little time to find the relevant tape, so they'd arranged to meet at his house not the next night but the following one. Which meant Cordelia was at a loose end this evening, indeed for the rest of the day, having taken the recovered books to the ashram first thing in the morning.

The initial euphoria of having proudly presented Howdy and the Shrew with the stolen books had now given way to a feeling of emptiness. By the time she got home, Cordelia felt as empty as her rucksack.

To cheer herself up, she got on the phone and booked a table at Sadic's.

To pay Edwin back for various help and kindnesses (including, although not limited to, saving her life) she booked a table for two. Regrettably, Sadie's was not a dog-friendly restaurant, so they had to leave Rainbottle at home with Radio 3 playing, both to keep him company and to discourage burglars (assuming Rainbottle liked Prokofiev's *Lieutenant Kijé* and the burglars didn't).

Towards the end of their meal, with Cordelia savouring Sadie's excellent house Rioja and Edwin, the beer snob, unexpectedly joining her, Edwin raised his glass and said, "Congratulations on recovering the books."

"Thank you."

"And you said the people at the ashram were pleased?"

"They were grinning like idiots," said Cordelia. "It was really quite heart-warming."

"And you've managed to extract a decent fee from them?"

"It borders on the obscene, which is a good territory for fees to border on, and it should be landing in my bank account any moment." She'd checked before she'd left the house but, despite the Silver Shrew's promise "to transfer the funds immediately", the money still hadn't arrived. Oh well, there was plenty of time between now and tomorrow evening when she needed to pay Mac the Pervert and VHS jockey.

"Well done," said Edwin. "You deserve it." And then he fell silent. It was a somewhat awkward silence. Cordelia decided to puncture it.

"Okay, what else is it that you want to say to me, Edwin?" There was clearly something on his mind.

Edwin took a deep breath. "I'd like to counsel you against dropping your guard," he said.

"Do you think I'm likely to do that?"

"I think it would be an entirely natural thing for anyone to do, having just completed a difficult task. And it may well be that you *can* drop your guard and relax, assuming that whoever tried to kill you was trying to stop you finding the books." Edwin sipped his wine and looked at her.

"And also assuming that, now the books have been found and it's all over, they'll stop trying," said Cordelia. Adding, "To kill me, that is."

"That's the point exactly," said Edwin. "While that may well be the case, and let's hope it is…"

"Yes?" said Cordelia, inviting him to go on.

"While that may well be the case, there are at least three things it's important for us to bear in mind," said Edwin. He set down his wine glass so he could count on his fingers. This was the sort of behaviour—pedantic, finicky—which might once have filled Cordelia with disdain or made her want to laugh out loud.

But not when he was trying to keep her alive.

"Firstly," said Edwin, "whoever was responsible for that attempt on your life may not know yet that you've found the books and returned them. Of course, they'll find out eventually. But we have no way of knowing how quickly that will be. They may try again, not realising there is no point."

Cordelia hadn't considered this horrifying yet absurdly comic possibility. Seeking to kill someone to stop them doing something they'd already done. Whoops. Good old Edwin. You could always trust him to analyse a situation and weigh up the potential for mayhem.

"Always assuming, of course," said Edwin, "that trying to stop you was their motive in the first place. Which brings us to the second thing we must bear in mind: they may be attempting to kill you for another reason altogether."

"One we don't even know," said Cordelia.

"Yes," said Edwin.

"Oh goodie."

"Finally," said Edwin, "there's another immediate possibility I can see, which we must also be prepared for."

"All right, what is it?"

"That the would-be assailant…"

"The would-be assassin," said Cordelia.

"That the would-be assassin was indeed trying to stop you finding the books. And they do indeed now know you have succeeded at your mission…"

"And?"

"And that, consequently, they intend to kill you as revenge for having done just that."

If Cordelia hadn't already said "Oh goodie" in a deeply ironic tone of voice, she would have done so now.

19: ROBOT PASTA

Extremely annoyingly, Cordelia's payment from the ashram still hadn't materialised in her bank account the following day. This normally wouldn't have been a problem but (number one) she needed to pay Mac the Pervert his finder's fee for the charity shop surveillance tape today, and (number two) she had made it absolutely crystal-clear yesterday when she'd handed over the missing books that she needed to be paid promptly. And (number three) Howdy Doody and the Silver Shrew had readily agreed to immediate—nay, instant—payment. But now, getting on for 24 hours since she'd delivered their fucking books, the fucking fuckers still hadn't paid her. Fuck them and their smiling fucking faces and their empty promises.

Admittedly, Cordelia's nerves were a little on edge. She'd drunk too much of that (very good) Rioja at Sadie's last night, which didn't help. And what also didn't help was Edwin's lengthy and scholarly dissertation at their table in the restaurant, interrupted by intervals of diplomatic silence whenever the waitress came and cleared their plates, about reasons why people might be about to kill her. All right—be about to *try* to kill her.

So, surely a certain amount of bad temper and nerves were justified?

And what was she supposed to do when she saw Mac tonight and collected the VHS tape he'd gone to so much trouble to find for her? She'd promised to pay him, and she had no intention of letting him down. And the infuriating thing was, she should have the fucking money to pay him. She should have plenty of money for all sorts of purposes.

But those double-dealing dicks in their orange pyjamas had not paid her as promised.

Cordelia did not put it quite like that in the email she sent, politely and casually reminding them, or at least casually and politely reminding the Silver Shrew, who looked after the financial affairs of the ashram, about payment. And providing, for the third or fourth time, her bank details.

As the day wore on with no joy on the ashram payment front, Cordelia found herself confronted with two choices. Either go to the yoga centre in person and make a fuss, or give them another day or so. Which would involve finding the money she needed tonight from another source.

Going and making a fuss was just a little too uncool and, to be frank, a little too much trouble.

But the alternative wasn't great, either. Finally, Cordelia swallowed her pride and went downstairs to see Edwin and explain the situation to him. He was perfectly fine about it, as she knew he would be. But that wasn't the point...

"The point is," she said, as they walked to Mac's place (or "gaff") later that day, "you shouldn't be put in that position."

"I really don't mind," said Edwin. He was currently gently guiding Rainbottle on their walk, using his bright orange Flexi retractable dog lead. Edwin and Cordelia were taking turns supervising the eager pooch as they made their way from the village green down Willow Avenue. It was a mellow, sunny autumn evening.

"But the point is, you shouldn't have to not mind. The point is that the fuckers should have paid me." Cordelia was still incensed. "And I shouldn't have had to come to you and ask for a loan."

"It wasn't really a loan," said Edwin, at his most mollifying. "You had paid next month's rent massively ahead of time, quite unnecessarily early, really."

"I like paying it early," said Cordelia.

"I know you do and I appreciate it. But I don't mind returning it to you. You can pay it nearer the due date."

"I'm good for it," said Cordelia.

"I know you are."

"Just as soon as those orange pyjama clowns pay me…"

Edwin chuckled. "You really mustn't worry. I certainly don't. It's not like the old days when you used to try and sneak into the house without me hearing you when you owed me money. Which was virtually all the time. Rent week was always particularly exciting. He sounded positively nostalgic.

They made their way from Willow Avenue to the Vine Road recreation ground, past the snack bar (which looked rather sad and abandoned and empty after hours) and the allotments which, here, were raised beds of flowers and vegetables in large wooden boxes. They skirted the children's playground and then, with Rainbottle happily straining ahead, they crossed the pleasant little enclosed bridge over Beverley Brook, which always reminded Cordelia of something out of Monet. It was a perfect evening to be reminded of Monet, with all the colours of the trees and water softly diffused.

Mac the Pervert lived on a road called Railway Side, which was located you'll never guess where. Edwin, a local lad from way back and a bit of a bore, if truth be told, about the history of this area, had been impressed when he'd learned of the address. "Despite appearances, he must have some money to be living there. Or perhaps it's an ex-council property. Lucky chap. It's actually very close to Albert's where we saw him the other night."

"Then he won't have had far to stumble home," said Cordelia.

"He does enjoy his beer," conceded Edwin.

Albert's wasn't the only characterful public house in the vicinity. They were currently walking past The Brown Dog, a singularly appropriate name given Rainbottle's presence. And just up ahead was Mac's "gaff".

It was a tiny house with an even tinier front "garden"—a narrow strip of concrete between the front door and the front gate. Above the front door and just beneath the upstairs windows was a charming square blue plaque with white lettering, which read *Beware of Trains*.

The stretch of road the house was located in was very quiet. Deserted in fact, at the moment.

Which would prove to be very lucky.

While Cordelia restrained an eager Rainbottle, Edwin pushed open the tiny iron front gate in the tiny wall of the tiny garden. It yielded with a screech, and they crowded towards the front door. There was no bell in evidence, so Edwin knocked.

And as soon as his knuckles made contact with the door, it drifted open.

It wasn't just unlocked. It was ajar.

Cordelia and Edwin looked at each other. Rainbottle, looking up at both of them, whined.

Edwin pushed the door the rest of the way open but didn't step inside. "Hello, Mac," he called. "We're here."

Silence seemed to flow out of the house.

Cordelia felt her skin begin to crawl. It didn't help that Rainbottle was now making a continual melancholy whining sound. She looked at Edwin. He had his serious face on.

And then there was the terrible smell that was coming from the house. Cordelia hadn't noticed it until now, or perhaps it had taken a moment to drift from inside. It was a smell of something that had been burned. Repellent and toxic, like melted plastic. It was strange and acrid and penetrating.

Edwin looked at the shadowy interior of the house, a miniscule entrance hall visible through the open door, and then looked at Rainbottle. "Right, old boy," he said. "We'd better tie you up out here." He led Rainbottle back into the street. "No doggie DNA," he said, by way of explanation, as much to Rainbottle as to Cordelia, as he fastened the lead to the gate. It took him a while, but Cordelia wished it had taken him even longer.

She was dreading going into the house. Perhaps sensing this, as soon he had secured Rainbottle, Edwin said, "You can stay out here if you like."

"No."

Cordelia followed him inside. The smell was much stronger and even more horrid. Immediately in front of them was a short hallway and a staircase. The hallway led to a kitchen. The staircase, with worn floral carpet, led up into increasingly shadowed gloom. To their left was a small parlour or sitting room.

"Don't touch anything," said Edwin. He moved into the parlour. Cordelia followed, and almost walked into the back of him when he stopped short.

"Oh dear," said Edwin.

Cordelia leaned forwards so she could look past him. At first, she couldn't see what he was talking about. The room appeared to be empty. There was a fireplace, one armchair, a little sofa, a wooden chair, a small table that looked like it was used for meals (eaten while sitting on the sofa) and a small bookcase. Some remote portion of Cordelia's mind automatically registered the contents of the bookshelves—a few paperbacks, nothing of interest.

All the seats were arranged to face an ungainly dark wooden cabinet with a huge, old-fashioned television sitting on top of it. Underneath that were shelves that contained a satellite decoder, a Blu-ray player and, yes, a venerable VHS machine.

But that was all. Otherwise, as far as Cordelia could see, the room was empty.

Then she saw the legs.

Long thin legs in black trousers, with dirty white sports socks on the feet. They projected from a space between the sofa and the bookcase. Edwin moved over to this area and Cordelia followed him. Although what was coming was all too obvious, she sucked in her breath when she saw Mac.

He was sort of folded up and twisted, half-lying and half-sitting on the carpet in the narrow space between sofa and bookcase. It seemed he'd fallen there. His eyes were closed and his head was on one side.

There was a strange stain around his mouth. A dark yellowish brown.

Edwin eased himself down onto the floor, kneeling by Mac. He leaned forward, moving his face close to the dead man's and, for one horrid, surreal moment, Cordelia thought Edwin was going to kiss him. But he was *sniffing*.

Edwin got to his feet again and impatiently shooed Cordelia out.

They stood silently, crowded together in the tiny hallway. Edwin looked at the staircase and then at the kitchen. He turned towards the kitchen and Cordelia followed him. The burned smell was getting much stronger now.

It was a tiny, grubby, untidy kitchen. The sink was crammed full of dirty dishes and, as if to prove that other behaviours were also available, two perfectly clean plates stood alone in the draining rack. There were stains on the countertops and on the floor.

Looking around, Cordelia found herself thinking, *How can anyone live like this?*

And then she realised no one did. Anymore.

The bad smell was coming from a microwave oven that was crammed between a breadbin and a rack full of beer bottles on the countertop beside the sink. "Here we go," said Edwin.

The door of the microwave was open and inside they saw a deformed black rectangle with a tangled pile of melted brown strands spilling out of it. It looked like a robot had prepared a meal of instant robot noodles and then found them so repugnant it had abandoned them.

It was, of course, a VHS tape that someone had zapped in the microwave.

To say that it was now unplayable was a substantial understatement.

It was quite cold and had obviously been cooked some hours before but the smell coming off it was still intensely toxic and horrid.

"Right, let's get out of here," said Edwin. They moved quickly back down the hallway, through the front door and back outside. It was an indescribable relief to be out in the fresh air again. Rainbottle gave a glad little cry to see them.

While Cordelia was busy taking deep breaths and trying to expel the smell of the burned tape from her nose, Edwin was busy digging in his pockets. He was wearing a Rohan jacket, so these were plentiful and practical. He took out a container of hand sanitiser and a handkerchief and began decontaminating anything they might have touched. Then he untied Rainbottle and they moved away quickly, but not running, leaving the front door ajar as they'd found it.

They didn't see anyone until they were well clear of the house, at which point they tried to slow down to a casual stroll. But Rainbottle was having none of it. He strained on his lead, pulling them along behind him.

"The old chap is in a hurry to get home," said Edwin.

"Clever doggie," said Cordelia. And then, "Why were you smelling Mac's face?"

"Trying to work out what that stain around his mouth might be."

"Any idea what it was?" asked Cordelia.

"Yes," said Edwin. "Curry."

When they reached Beverley Brook and crossed it, Rainbottle, perhaps sensing he was back on home territory, calmed down and slowed his headlong rush, and they were able to resume a more normal pace. No longer feeling like they were fleeing made it easier to talk.

"What do you think happened to him?" said Cordelia.

"Well," said Edwin. "There was no sign of physical violence, so I would say poison."

"You're thinking of the stain around his mouth?"

"That and what we saw in the kitchen."

"You mean the VHS in the microwave?" said Cordelia.

"That's significant, of course," said Edwin. "But it doesn't indicate poisoning."

"But the plates do."

Edwin turned and smiled at Cordelia. "Yes. Precisely. Well spotted."

"They stood out like a sore thumb," she said. "Two carefully washed plates when everything else was still stashed in the sink, filthy."

"Exactly," said Edwin. "It'll be interesting to see if the police spot them."

"Do you think we should call the police?"

"You mean an anonymous tip-off?" said Edwin. "Absolutely not. If we were lucky enough to get in and out of there unseen, and I think we were, then I strongly suggest we don't do anything to spoil that situation." Then, perhaps to change the subject, he said, "Now, what else do those two plates tell us?"

"Two people," said Cordelia.

"Yes. Two people sit down and share a meal. One of them, poor old Mac, has something in his food which kills him so quickly that he doesn't even have a chance to wipe his mouth. Then whoever did it carefully washes the plates in the kitchen sink to remove evidence."

"And cooks the VHS tape in the microwave."

"Yes. I fear there's now no chance of anyone seeing what was on that. They've done a very thorough job of destroying it."

"But why leave it there?" said Cordelia. "Why cook the tape and leave it? Why not just take it with them?"

"I suppose…" said Edwin, thinking it through. "Because a VHS tape is not the sort of thing anybody is likely to have these days, and they wouldn't want to be caught with it, carrying it away from the crime scene."

"Then why not just get rid of it? Throw it away."

"Yes, they could do that. But they'd want to be absolutely sure it was destroyed. Unwatchable. Therefore, they didn't just want to throw it away in a bin or something. They wanted to make sure it was permanently unwatchable. So why not do that right away, there and then?"

"I suppose so," said Cordelia, thinking of the cooked mess of the tape. Unappetising pasta for robots.

"Alternatively…"

"What?" said Cordelia.

"By leaving the tape there, they might be sending us a message."

"A message? What kind of message?"

"I'm not sure exactly," said Edwin. "But it's not a good one."

They walked on in silence for a while and then Cordelia said, "You reckon it was a curry they ate?"

"Yes, or at least that Mac ate." Edwin gave her a sidelong look. "Doesn't your friend at the ashram specialise in curries? The chef."

"She isn't my friend," said Cordelia, rather more emphatically than she needed to. She tried to relax, but it had felt almost like Edwin was accusing her of something. Her nerves were a little on edge. "Yes," she said, "they call her Carrie Quinn the Curry Queen."

"Of course, that doesn't necessarily mean anything," said Edwin. "A lot of people are fond of a curry."

"Just about everyone at the ashram," said Cordelia. "For a start." She looked at Edwin. "Not to mention us."

"I think we can rule the two of us out as suspects," said Edwin dryly. Rainbottle whined for attention. "And you, old boy."

"I should have warned him," said Cordelia.

"What?" said Edwin.

"I should have told Mac that he was getting involved in something dangerous."

"But you didn't know that he was. You had no reason to think so."

"I got him killed," said Cordelia.

Edwin abruptly stopped walking. Rainbottle obediently stopped too, and so did Cordelia. Edwin stared sternly at her and said, "Stop that kind of talk immediately. The only person who got poor Mac killed was the person who killed him. Don't let yourself think otherwise."

Rainbottle murmured firmly in agreement, and they all started walking again.

When they reached the village green, they bumped into Lorna again, almost as if she'd been waiting there for them. Of course, she insisted on walking home with them and that put paid to any further serious conversation.

But whenever she began to blame herself for what had happened to Mac, which was often, Cordelia would make herself remember what Edwin had said. He'd said it with such conviction that he'd made her believe it. And, for the most part, it helped.

But she could still smell the stink of the microwaved tape for days afterwards.

20: YOUR PLACE OR MINE?

Cordelia insisted on paying Edwin back the rent money.

She didn't need it now.

It was no doubt just displaced emotion, after the shock of what they'd discovered in the parlour of the little house on Railway Side, but Cordelia found she had become intensely furious with the Silverlight ashram fuckers, because they still hadn't paid her as promised. So she went to the yoga centre the next morning to confront them. She didn't bother arriving in time for a lesson; she really wasn't in the mood.

But as soon as she stepped into the gift shop she had the dizzying sense that something was wrong. For a start, who should be sitting behind the till but Carrie Quinn, of all people. Carrie was not a member of the ashram staff, as was evidenced by the fact that she was wearing her chef's outfit instead of something fetching in saffron.

"What are you doing here?" said Cordelia.

Carrie shrugged. "Joni's ill, so she asked me to cover for her. Since I was here to serve lunch anyway I said, why not? I can operate a till and it's not exactly a demanding job." She checked her watch—a man's wristwatch, and an expensive-looking one. "And, in a minute, I can go into the kitchen and Harshavardhana can come down off his high horse and take over in here."

Cordelia started to explain why she was here, but Carrie wasn't interested. "Just go ahead," she said.

Cordelia went upstairs. The meeting room was empty and one of the little offices had its door open and was also deserted. The other office had its door closed and Cordelia knocked on it. Howdy Doody's voice called for her to enter.

Howdy was surprised to see her and professed further surprise that Cordelia hadn't been paid yet. "I thought all that was sorted out. Gunadya was supposed to be dealing with it."

"Where is she?" said Cordelia.

"She's away today."

"Then what's going to happen about my payment?"

"It will have to wait until she's back, I'm afraid. I wish I could help you out, but Gunadya's dealing with it."

The circularity of his argument was maddening but flawless, like the smooth, high wall of an impregnable fortress.

Cordelia went back downstairs, even more frustrated and angry than she'd been when she'd arrived. The really annoying thing was that she wasn't even able to vent her frustration on Howdy Doody. He wasn't blowing smoke when he said it wasn't his responsibility, because it was perfectly true that the Silver Shrew was in charge of the ashram's finances in all their myriad money-grubbing facets.

In essence, Cordelia had wasted her time coming here. She couldn't even have a lesson—she quite fancied one now; anything to help calm her down—because she hadn't brought her yoga mat or appropriate clothing. Which was a pisser since she could have snuck in and got a freebie. Carrie on the till didn't give a damn.

At a loose end and in need of a bit of quiet solitude, Cordelia wandered out into the peace garden and sank down on one of the benches. The breeze cooled the sweat on her face. She hadn't even realised she'd been sweating—things were really getting to her. And she mustn't let that happen.

She made herself focus on her peaceful surroundings. The place smelled pleasantly of the herb beds planted around it and a large contingent of the local bird population was busy hopping around in these. Apparently, they'd worked out that the people in orange pyjamas weren't about to discharge shotguns at them.

Cordelia watched the birds and smelled the herbs and tried to empty her mind. But she found herself staring at the wind chimes. No one had fixed the chrome pipe that had come loose and it was still dangling low on the ground, stirring in loose, woozy circles. Cordelia found this disproportionately annoying. It rather spoiled the whole effect.

She was just wondering bad-temperedly whether she should get up and have a go at fixing it herself when the class in the shala ended and people began to trickle out from the changing rooms. As if to rub in Cordelia's disappointment about missing the lesson, they all looked beatifically chilled and cheerful.

After the main bulk of the crowd had dispersed, Alfie emerged. Cordelia realised she had been half waiting for him. He smiled when he saw her and waved. Unlike Mac, he seemed to understand that waving was something you did at a certain distance from people. The thought of Mac—dead with curry on his mouth—brought a sudden savage pain to Cordelia. Like cramps, but worse. She hastened to erase any sign of this from her face as Alfie came over to join her.

She was apparently successful because he was all affable, untroubled smiles as he sat down beside her. "I wanted to see you," he said.

"You could always phone and make an appointment," said Cordelia. "You've got my business card."

"I thought I'd bump into you soon enough," said Alfie. "Congratulations on returning the books."

Word continues to travel fast, thought Cordelia.

"That's one thing I wanted to say," said Alfie. "Very nice work."

"Thank you."

"And the other thing I wanted to say is… I've got another job for you."

Suddenly Cordelia was at full attention. "Really? A paying job?"

"Yes, of course," said Alfie, watching her closely. "I want you to find out who stole the books in the first place."

He let this sink in while Cordelia thought about it, saying nothing.

"Is that the kind of thing the Paperback Sleuth might do?" he added.

"It might well be," said Cordelia.

"Good. I'll pay you double what the ashram paid you for getting the books back."

Cordelia smiled. Suddenly things were looking up. She wasn't even annoyed about the dodgy wind chimes anymore. "Well, in that case, it's *definitely* something the Paperback Sleuth might do," she said.

"Hip hooray," said Alfie. "Thank you. Right, here's the deal. I'll pay you half up front, which you get to keep whatever happens. The other half is paid to you if and when you get a result. How does that sound?"

"You drive a hard bargain," said Cordelia, and they both laughed.

"Okay," said Alfie, suddenly and sombrely, "Now, there's something I have to ask you."

"Okay," said Cordelia. What the hell could this be about?

"Do you already know who stole the books? Before you answer, I want you to know that, if you do, you don't have to pretend you don't. There's no need to look like you're doing more work, launching an investigation, etc, to earn the fee. If you do know already, you can tell me right now and I'll pay you in full. All right?"

"All right," said Cordelia. "But I don't know. I wish I did. Especially with a deal like that on the table. Sorry."

Alfie sighed. "No worries. I didn't really think so, but I thought I'd better check."

"Of course."

"Because you're a very foxy chick."

"You bet I am," said Cordelia.

"Well, let's get started then," said Alfie. He took out his phone. "Give me your bank details."

Cordelia was getting a little fed up with giving people her bank details. But this was very different from the recent maddening tap dance with the ashram clowns. As they sat there, side by side on the peace garden bench with their phones out, Alfie made the payment of the 50 per cent advance. Right there and then in real time. Cordelia watched it go into her bank account.

"Thank you very much," said Cordelia. What a contrast with the slippery, late-paying Silver Shrew. This was the way business should be transacted.

"My pleasure," said Alfie.

Cordelia was positively glowing. If she'd been a pussycat, she would have purred. If she'd been Rainbottle, she would have done some enthusiastic tail thumping. Suddenly it turned out that it wasn't such a wasted visit to the ashram after all.

"Now," said Alfie, gazing pensively across the peace garden, "is Carrie still in the gift shop? I'm going to wait until she's gone before I go in there. Pitiful, I know, but I just don't want to run into her again. It was quite a nasty shock when I saw her in there this morning. I'd rather avoid our Carrie just at the moment…" He edged over towards the gift shop and peered cautiously through the glass-panelled door. "Ah," he said, obviously relieved. "The coast is clear. I'd better dash."

"Okay," said Cordelia. "I'll get started right away on the investigation." She said the last word with a certain vicious emphasis which Alfie couldn't be expected to understand. (It was payback for the Silver Shrew taking the piss out of her.)

"Okay, great," said Alfie.

"Thank you for paying me."

Alfie laughed. "No problem. Oh, by the way, there's a note for you."

"A note?" said Cordelia.

"In your pigeonhole. Bye."

Alfie disappeared into the gift shop, leaving Cordelia alone and feeling suddenly chilled despite the autumn sunlight. And not the right kind of chilled. She stared at the door that led to the changing rooms and the shala. A note in her pigeonhole. Just like in her dream. Her anxiety dream of another assassination attempt by means of bench and falling concrete.

Well, things weren't going to turn out like they had in her dream. For a start, if they wanted to meet her at the hospital, she'd make damned sure she took Edwin with her. The fierce warm triumph of this decision vanished immediately—no, wait a minute, what was she talking about? She wouldn't go to the bloody hospital at all. Why would she? She wouldn't be that stupid...

These and other similar thoughts occupied Cordelia on what felt like the extremely long walk through the door, past the changing rooms and to the pigeonholes.

Yes, there was a note for her.

Cordelia stared at it.

It was on pale blue paper this time, so at least her would-be assassin was ringing the changes. It took Cordelia a remarkable and embarrassing length of time to force herself to put her hand into the pigeonhole and pick up the note. (What was she expecting? A poisonous snake to spring up and sink its fangs into the big vein on her wrist? A miniature guillotine to come down and chop off her hand? There was actually a rather groovy Robert Bonfils cover painting which depicted exactly that last scenario. Was it for *Operator Five*? Some pulp hero, anyway...)

She finally reached in and picked up the note. It was folded in half with her name handwritten on the outside. That was new too. And it was written in dark blue fibre-tip pen, in rather girlie handwriting, loose and flowing with an unnecessary amount of curves and loops. Cordelia opened the note to reveal more girlie handwriting.

Hi Cordelia, We need to talk. It's very important. Please ring me right away.

Then there was the number of a mobile phone.

It was signed *Joni*.

Cordelia put the number into the address book on her phone. Since she didn't know Joni's last name she entered it under last name Blowjob, first name Joni. And she tried dialling the number as she walked home along Vine Road, as soon as she was clear of the traffic noise on the main road.

To her surprise—normally nothing was this easy, was it?—Joni picked up right away. As she heard her voice, Cordelia felt an irrational flash of relief that the people you phoned couldn't see the name you'd chosen for them in your address book.

"Hello? Cordelia?"

How did Joni know it was her? If Cordelia's name came up when she rang, that meant Joni must have her number. In which case, why leave the note in the pigeonhole in the first place? What the hell was she up to? Standing in the sunshine on Vine Road in the beautiful autumn sunshine with the charming wild water meadow spread out on one side of her and a row of magnificent moguls' mansions on the other, Cordelia felt herself being swallowed in a rising tide of paranoia.

"Hello? Is anyone there?" said Joni's anxious little voice.

"Yes, it's me. Cordelia. How did you know it was me?"

"I didn't," said Joni. "But I hoped it was. I've been sitting with my phone all morning, waiting for you to call."

"Why?" said Cordelia.

"I need to talk to you."

"All right, talk." Cordelia started to walk again.

"We have to meet up," said Joni.

"Why?" said Cordelia.

"There are some things, lots of things I can't tell you over the phone."

"Why not?" said Cordelia. She was quite enjoying this terse, staccato way of addressing Joni. It felt very grown-up and businesslike.

"Please, please let's meet up. It's very important. It's about the robbery at the ashram and everything that's happening. It's about Hank Honeywell and Mr Silbert and everything. The whole situation."

"Who's Mr Silbert?" said Cordelia, genuinely baffled.

There was a pause on the line and then Joni said, with great sarcasm and considerable anger, "Alfie. Alfie *Silbert*."

Her reaction was so ferocious that Cordelia found herself automatically apologising. "I'm sorry, I don't think I've ever heard his last name."

"It doesn't matter," said Joni, although clearly it did. "Anyway, we have to meet up. As soon as possible. Can you come to my place?"

Still wrongfooted about Alfie's last name, Cordelia almost found herself agreeing to do this. But she caught herself just in time and put her foot down. (It might still have been the wrong foot, but to hell with it.) "No," she said, very firmly. "You can come to my place."

"Your place? Come to your place? I don't know…" said Joni, sounding simultaneously indecisive and angry, which was a fairly impressive feat.

"My place or forget it," said Cordelia, also getting angry but, in her case, being *very* decisive. The whole nerve-shredding aftermath of last night's body discovery had come back full force as soon as Alfie had mentioned the note in her pigeonhole. And since Joni had left the note, it was all Joni's fault. In fact, everything was Joni's fault. This wasn't a rational assessment, true, but, at that moment, Cordelia was well beyond rational assessment and was a whisker away from telling Joni—and indeed, any random passer-by, including the innocent-looking young mother who was approaching with twins in a pushchair— to just fuck off.

Perhaps sensing this, a rather contrite-sounding Joni said, "All right. Could you give me your address, please?"

Cordelia did so and set a time for Joni to arrive (more firmness), then went home and told Edwin they were expecting company.

Edwin was delighted. He didn't exactly rub his hands together, but he did start humming a happy little tune.

Cordelia had made it very clear that Joni was potentially the psycho behind everything, including the murder (blunt instrument) of Hank Honeywell and (poison) of poor Mac the Pervert. Joni's strange insistence on meeting in person rather than talking over the phone, her refusal to give any hint as to what it was really all about (beyond tantalising generalities), her attempt to get Cordelia to come to her place rather than vice versa... all these only strengthened the notion that Joni might be up to no good, and indeed have murderous mayhem in mind.

Which, of course, was why Edwin was delighted.

Edwin, although at first glance a Rohan-wearing, *Guardian*-reading dullard, had considerable hidden depths, as Cordelia had discovered only last year.

In fact, her lovable landlord was, if you wanted to be pedantic about it, a serial killer.

Not a creepy-collector-of-grisly-trophies-type serial killer, but rather a vigilante and social engineer. In other words, if Edwin thought the world was better off without you, watch out.

Cordelia had learned all this when he'd helped her dispose of a body. (This sounded terribly sordid, but it was the body of a hitman who'd been sent to kill Cordelia. So fair enough.)

Soon after that Edwin had purchased an elaborate security system for the house—closed-circuit television, silent alarms—a protective measure against the same vengeful gangster, Colin Cutterham, who'd unleashed the hitman on Cordelia.

Now Edwin was happily restoring all this technology, which had been operating in a scaled-back mode, to its full working glory. And, although he didn't discuss this with Cordelia, she knew he'd soon be making a selection of useful weapons.

All in all, if it turned out that Joni *wasn't* coming around this evening to try to kill Cordelia, Edwin was going to be seriously disappointed.

Cordelia had suggested a seven o'clock arrival time. Joni had tried to insist on making it earlier, but Cordelia had stuck to her guns. She knew Edwin would want to be fully prepared and she didn't want to rush him.

As seven o'clock approached, Cordelia, sitting with Edwin and Rainbottle in their little downstairs flat, found herself getting unbearably tense. On the one hand, there was the worry about what Joni might try to do if she really was the assassin. On the other hand, there was the issue of how let down Edwin would be if she wasn't.

And whatever happened, it would be Cordelia's responsibility.

It was a pity that Cordelia reached maximum tension so soon. She should have left some margin for feeling tenser when seven o'clock came and went and Joni didn't show. Cordelia gave her half an hour—actually, 27 minutes—and then rang her. Joni's phone went straight to voicemail.

Cordelia kept trying, at 15-minute intervals, then ten-minute intervals, and then, at eleven o'clock, when it had become obvious that Joni was neither going to answer her phone or arrive on their doorstep, Edwin prevailed on her to go to bed.

"There's no point both of us staying up."

"Both of us?" said Cordelia. "You're not going to stay up, are you?"

"Of course I am," said Edwin, gesturing at the three laptops on his kitchen table, each one showing a different variety of angles from the numerous security camera feeds (including the spectral night-vision ones). "It's actually not a bad tactic," he said.

"Not a bad tactic?" said Cordelia. "You mean not turning up?"

"Turning up very late, when everyone has abandoned any hope of seeing you." Edwin smiled. "In other words, when they've dropped their guard. Quite a clever tactic in fact."

Cordelia left him happily watching the laptops with Rainbottle contentedly at his feet and went to bed in her attic room. Perhaps worn out by the non-stop emotional stress of the day, she fell asleep instantly and was lost deep in dreamless oblivion until about four in the morning when she was awakened by the zombie-baby scream of a fox canoodling in somebody's garden.

It was still solid darkness outside, save for streetlights and the occasional passing car. Cordelia pressed her nose to the window, watching the road below as if Joni was going to come pedalling up on her bicycle. Eventually the window fogged up with her breath so she couldn't see anything, and Cordelia turned away, put on a robe and went downstairs.

She tapped tentatively on the door of Edwin's flat and then opened it, calling, "It's just me."

"I know. I can see you from about seven different camera angles," said Edwin.

Cordelia didn't say that she'd anticipated as much but had decided it was just as well to err on the side of caution and knock, and thereby not spring any surprises on her ready-for-action, heavily armed and by now sleep-deprived landlord.

Things in Edwin's kitchen were pretty much as she'd left them, except Rainbottle's cushion had been transferred to a chair beside his master and he was now lying on it and snoring heavily.

In contrast, Edwin was wide awake and looking a little haggard and disconsolate.

"You know, I'm beginning to think she might not show up," he said.

21: FROZEN

Carrie wasn't behind the till in the gift shop today. Which should have been a relief. Not because there was anything unwelcome about Carrie herself, but just because seeing her there had been such an unsettling departure from routine. Unfortunately, Carrie had been replaced by someone who seemed even stranger in the role.

Mr T.

"Hello, bad penny," said Mr T, smiling at Cordelia.

"Is Joni here?"

"Joni…" said Mr T.

But before he could say anything else the door behind him opened and the Silver Shrew looked at them. "Cordelia," she said. "Could you come up to the meeting room, please?"

Mr T gave Cordelia an odd look as she followed the Shrew up the stairs. It was as if he was trying to tell her something, to convey something with the soulful gaze of his eyes. Cordelia didn't have time to think about this, though, as the Shrew led her into the meeting room and closed the door behind them. So much for the circulation of fresh air. "Have a seat, please," said the Shrew.

Cordelia perched on the edge of a chair, ready for a quick getaway. She didn't like the feel of any of this. Howdy Doody was nowhere in sight, and somehow that made things worse.

The Shrew sat down across the table from her. "First of all, I have to apologise for the late payment of your fee."

Ridiculously Cordelia, who, up to this instant, had been brimming with rage about exactly this matter and was quite ready to debonairly break a chair over the Shrew's head, now suddenly felt the urge to put the woman at her ease. "Oh no, it's all right," she heard herself saying, to her own chagrin and amazement. "That's fine."

Fine? Fucking hell.

"The thing is," said the Shrew, "we find ourselves in a difficult and embarrassing situation." She looked Cordelia right in the eye. The Shrew had hard, dark little eyes. Direct and candid.

"You don't have the money," said Cordelia with an odd mixture of relief, surprise and contempt.

"Oh no, on the contrary, we have a great deal of money in the ashram's account. But we can't access it. Our bank account has been frozen."

"Frozen?" said Cordelia. She repressed the foolish compulsion to make a joke about this not being the weather for it—it was another unseasonably hot autumn day.

"Yes, we're under investigation for money laundering."

"What?"

"It's all total nonsense, of course, but the bank is required by law to look into it and, until we're in the clear, our account has been frozen and we don't have access to any of our funds. That's where I was yesterday, at the bank trying to sort out this nonsense. It's very annoying and very awkward, as you can imagine. But the bank has certain set procedures they are required to follow and we just have to wait patiently until they complete them." The Shrew smiled. A rare sighting of a Silver Shrew smile. "Or rather, wait *im*patiently. Meanwhile, you have our deepest apologies about the late payment."

"Well, it's not really late," Cordelia found herself saying. "In fact, you were paying me early…"

"And you deserved to be paid early. You did a splendid job for us." The Shrew glanced at the shelf of paperback books, all present and correct again. Then she turned back to Cordelia. "So you very much deserve to be paid."

Cordelia was on the verge of saying that there was really no hurry, but she managed to stifle this treacherous utterance before it got past her lips.

"And you certainly will be paid, just as soon as this absurd block on our account is lifted." This seemed to conclude the Shrew's peroration, and she began to rise from her chair.

But before she could do so, Cordelia said, "Where's Joni?"

The Shrew froze, half in and half out of her chair, and gave Cordelia a strange look. It seemed to be the day for it. "I thought you knew," she said, sitting back down.

"Knew what?"

"She came off her bike last night. She's in hospital with a serious head injury."

Cordelia surprised herself by going through with her original plan of having a yoga lesson—luckily Mr T abandoned his post at the till to conduct it (presumably Howdy Doody or maybe even the Shrew replaced him in the gift shop). An additional surprise was that Alfie wasn't present in the class. Like Mr T, he was a stalwart and never missed one. Where was he?

It was only at the very end of the session, while emerging from the relaxation and stretching bit, that it occurred to Cordelia to start worrying about exactly why Alfie might not have turned up.

She could think of at least two possible explanations, neither attractive.

First of all, that he'd been responsible for what had happened to Joni and had now done a runner.

Secondly, that none of that was true and, instead, something had also happened to *him*.

Cordelia swiftly rolled up her mat, stuffed it in her bag, hurried to the changing room, pulled her street clothes on, and had her phone in her hand as she emerged into the peace garden. Fortunately for her peace of mind, Alfie answered right away and told her to come straight over.

Cordelia found him, as he'd told her to expect, sitting in the garden behind the house. He hadn't told her to expect him to be smoking a large doobie, but that could more or less be taken as read. As she joined him, he offered her a puff. Cordelia shook her head—the head she wanted to keep clear.

"Let's go inside," said Alfie. "It's too hot out here and I've got this feeling, I've had it all morning, that someone's watching me. Have you ever had that feeling? Of being watched?"

"No," said Cordelia. "I've read about it, but it's not something I've ever personally experienced. What's it like?"

"It feels like ants crawling on the back of your neck. Mind you, in my garden, ants *could* be crawling on the back of your neck."

Alfie led the way indoors, through the greenhouse. As they passed the massive cannabis plantation Cordelia repressed the fleeting urge to curtsy or genuflect in respect. She followed Alfie into the kitchen, where he parked his big smouldering joint in a Tintin ashtray. (A Tintin *ashtray*? That must date from a simpler, more innocent age. Innocent of pulmonary disease anyway.) Then he began to open cupboards, drawers and the refrigerator. Seemingly at random.

"Would you like something?" he said as he peered into the refrigerator, the bright light from its interior causing his eyes to glow. He closed the fridge and looked at her. "I could make us something to eat."

Cordelia felt a gratifying sense of a plan coming together, although that particular plan had been formulated on quite another day. "Sounds good."

"Okay, I've got some curry that Carrie made. A Carrie curry…" He took a hanging saucepan down from its hook under a cabinet.

Cordelia felt her throat tighten. "Actually," she said, "on second thoughts I don't think I will have anything."

Alfie looked at her. "Don't have an appetite?" He shrugged. "You know, I don't think I do, either. It was just the dope. Phantom appetite, or the munchies as they're also known." He hung the saucepan back on its hook and retrieved the spliff from Tintin. He took a deep lungful of the burning weed and slowly exhaled it. With the smoke bleeding out of his mouth and nostrils, wreathing his bearded and rather noble old face, he looked like some kind of hippy temple adornment, a doped-up deity decoratively carved and emanating real smoke to awe the gullible parishioners.

"You heard about Joni?" he said.

"Yes," said Cordelia.

"What did you hear?"

"She came off her bike."

"Someone *knocked* her off her bike," said Alfie, examining the spliff as if surprised to find it in his hand.

"How do you know?" said Cordelia.

"All right," said Alfie combatively. "Maybe they didn't knock her off her bike. Maybe they asked her politely to stop and, when she got off her bike, they hit her on the head with a piece of concrete."

"A piece of concrete?" said Cordelia. Of course, there was a lot of concrete scattered around London and the fact that someone had tried to kill Cordelia with a piece of it and now, apparently, the same or a similar thing had happened to Joni, was pure coincidence.

Of course it was. Absolutely. Sure…

Alfie nodded. "Joni was found lying in a field beside the road with her bike on the ground beside her and her head conveniently on a big chunk of concrete. And when I say conveniently, I only mean…"

"Convenient for the person who did it," said Cordelia. "For the assailant."

"Yes," said Alfie. "It's not like this was a piece of waste ground, full of rubble."

Like the ruins of Putney Hospital, thought Cordelia.

"It was a field on the common," continued Alfie. "And it was all grass and trees as far as the eye could see, except for this one lump of concrete that just happened to be there." He looked at Cordelia then looked at his spliff. "And Joni's head just happened to come into contact with it." He took another toke, blew out the smoke and said, "A bit of a coincidence, eh?"

"How do you know all the details of the accident?" said Cordelia, feeling suspicion worm through her.

"Carrie went and looked at the scene," said Alfie. "The scene of the crime."

"And how did she know where to look?" Cordelia's suspicion was a mercurial thing, shifting and twisting, but not diminishing.

"The police contacted her."

"Why her?" said Cordelia.

"Carrie is Joni's landlord. Landlady? Land-person? Anyway, Joni lives in Carrie's house. And pays rent."

Cordelia had the sudden weird feeling that she and Joni were doppelgangers. And Carrie the landlord was Joni's equivalent of Edwin. "She doesn't live in the attic, does she, Joni?"

"No, in the basement," said Alfie.

Cordelia felt an odd sensation of relief. She realised that sitting here, breathing Alfie's secondhand smoke meant she was getting fairly well-baked. So much for trying to keep a clear head.

"More's the pity," added Alfie. "Bad feng shui, living in a basement. Very bad for the energy flow. I ought to know. I've lived in enough of them."

"You say Carrie went and had a look at the crime scene? And told you all about it?"

"Right," said Alfie. "She thought the whole thing was as dodgy as I do."

Cordelia reflected that this was one way of describing the situation. Another would be that Carrie had put these thoughts in Alfie's head, and he'd accepted them unquestioningly and uncritically.

"You don't believe me, do you?" said Alfie suddenly.

Cordelia had the unsettling feeling that her own head was made of glass and he could see inside. She was definitely feeling the effect of that secondhand smoke.

"It's Carrie who I'm not sure I believe."

"Well, I went and had a look, too. And it's just the way she described. Grass everywhere and this one chunk of concrete that looks like someone put it there. I mean, of course someone put it there. How else did it get there? But I mean someone put it there…"

"Deliberately," said Cordelia.

"That's it," said Alfie. "Deliberately to use it on Joni."

"Then, what's your theory, that someone driving a car…"

"A car or some other vehicle," said Alfie pedantically.

"That they knocked Joni off her bike…"

"Yes."

"And they did it with such surgical accuracy," said Cordelia, "that she landed exactly headfirst on this piece of concrete?"

"No," said Alfie patiently. "They knocked her off her bike and she was stunned or shaken. And, while she was stunned or shaken, they hit her on the head with the piece of concrete."

Blunt force trauma, thought Cordelia, feeling a cold flow inside her as if she'd just swallowed ice water. "How big is this piece of concrete?"

"About the size of a loaf of bread."

"So someone could pick it up and use it as a weapon..."

"Oh, yes," said Alfie.

"How badly hurt is Joni?"

"They thought she was going to die at first," said Alfie. Then he suddenly shook his head violently. "No, wait a minute, maybe that's just what *I* thought. I'm trying to think what they said exactly. This is all filtered through Carrie, you understand... Let me think. Serious head injury... unconscious when they brought her in and still unconscious now... but she's young and strong and healthy..." Alfie looked at Cordelia. "Of course, when I heard them talking like that, I started to get *really* worried."

"Poor Joni," said Cordelia.

"She's young and strong and healthy," said Alfie, apparently without irony. "Listen, I'm going to make some coffee. Would you like some?"

"Yes please."

Alfie set about making coffee. This was an elaborate procedure at the best of times, but now, with a very stoned Alfie doing it and a not-much-less stoned Cordelia watching him, it seemed slightly more complicated than enriching uranium. Time seemed to slow down to a majestic monolithic crawl as various implements, accoutrements and accessories were brought to bear on the slippery problem of converting little brown beans into a warm fluid.

At some point during the procedure, Cordelia got up from where she'd been sitting and wandered around the kitchen, looking at things. Most of the wall space was dedicated either to cupboards or to hanging utensils. But the occasional blank spot was occupied by a poster.

As Cordelia had observed before, the two kinds of wall decorations Alfie favoured were pictures of nudes or of rock groups. Most of the latter were of the Who, clearly a favourite band, but here in the kitchen was a big one of the Rolling Stones, and it was really quite striking. As Cordelia studied it, strange thoughts began to stir in the back of her mind.

And she suddenly remembered her conversation with Joni about Alfie's last name.

Silbert.

Alfie Silbert.

Initials AS.

Strange thoughts now began to stir in the *front* of Cordelia's mind.

Alfie came over and joined her. "Nice, eh?" he said, looking at the poster.

"Sorry?" said Cordelia, coming back from a long way off. And then, having arrived, "Yes, it is nice."

"It came with my copy of *Let it Bleed*. That was their album." He paused. "Do you even know what an album is?"

"Yes, of course I do." Cordelia reflected that you didn't need to be a vinyl detective to know that much.

"It's still kicking around here somewhere. The album, that is. A little the worse for wear, though. I should have framed it, like that poster. To preserve it. But it wouldn't have been so easy to roll spliffs on it then. Or to play it, for that matter. Great album."

"You're a big fan of the Rolling Stones?" said Cordelia carefully.

"Oh yeah," said Alfie. "Brian Jones era, mostly. Not that that would mean anything to a youngster like you. But he was the founding member of the band. A great multi-instrumentalist. Died in a swimming pool, full of drugs. It was quite the done thing in the sixties."

"The swimming pool was full of drugs?" Cordelia was only half-listening. She was putting things together in her head.

Alfie laughed. "No, *he* was full of drugs."

"Did you grow up in Putney, Alfie?"

"Yes. Born here."

Cordelia was thinking… initials AS, grew up in Putney, food lover, yoga expert, Rolling Stones fan… And then there was his odd insistence that the ashram should recover the stolen books. "Do you have any tattoos?" she said.

He gave her a strange look. "Why do you ask that?"

Cordelia turned to look him in the eye. "Because I don't think you died in 1999."

22: DROP THE BODY

"Died in 1999...?"

Alfie slowly began to smile as realisation dawned. "Oh, you mean my Wikipedia entry?"

"Yes, I do."

"Yeah, they've got that wrong, haven't they?" he chuckled. "But I certainly wasn't going to correct them, even if I knew how. I've found it very handy on more than one occasion for people to think that Avram Silverlight has dropped the body and departed this mortal coil."

"And you've got a tattoo of a lotus on your chest?"

"Yes, do you want to see it?"

"No thanks, that's all right."

"Joni wanted to see it," said Alfie. He sounded sad, nostalgic and like he was about to say something else. So Cordelia didn't say anything. "That was at the Christmas party," he eventually added. He was silent for a moment. Then he said, "I was the man who established the ashram. But I stopped going to it in the last century."

"Before your death," said Cordelia.

He chuckled. "Long before that. Some time in the eighties. I kept up my yoga practice, did it scrupulously every day, wherever

I was. Mostly here, in the front room. But I didn't go anywhere near the ashram. That chapter of my life was over. That's what I thought. That's what I'd decided. But then, in recent years, I began to miss the place. You can do yoga on your own, you know, but it's not the same."

"I know," said Cordelia. "I found that out when I came back."

"One day I just thought, why not? Sneak back to the old ashram and have a look around. Attend incognito, so to speak. Under a pseudonym. Though, of course, Alfie Silbert is my real name: Alfred Reginald Silbert. Avram Silverlight was only ever a nom de plume. But no one need know that. No one was going to recognise me. Unless I told them who I was, no one would have any idea. It was as simple as that. I just started going back there and taking lessons. Paying for them, which was kind of amusing considering I'd founded the ashram. I helped to build it. I financed its creation. But it was quite a kick, just lining up with everyone else and paying for my lessons." He looked at Cordelia, grinning. "Then I bought the annual yoga pass because it was cheaper than paying every day."

"And no one suspected?"

He shook his head. "Why would they? But it was funny passing unrecognised… Funny strange, I mean. And also funny fun." He smiled his most roguish smile. "I like a bit of fun. And I never would have been unmasked. But then at the Christmas party I suddenly got nostalgic. I wanted to have a little moment. When no one was looking, I snuck off upstairs and went into the meeting room. It hadn't changed that much. I was looking at the pictures on the wall."

"And your books," said Cordelia.

"Yes, those too. I never kept copies, you see. I had lots at various times, but over the years I just gave them away to people. And then, as the decades passed, they became scarce and valuable and hard to find. Each year I said to myself I should track down a set of them, hire someone like you to find them for me." He winked at Cordelia. "Hire a Paperback Sleuth. But I never got around to it and every year they became more difficult to get. But it didn't matter…"

"Because you knew they had them at the ashram."

"That's right. I knew they had a full set of the books safe and sound there. It didn't matter if I didn't have them here. But when someone stole them… it was a nasty shock. One hell of a nasty shock. I thought they should have taken better care of them. Kept them in a locked case or something."

"Which is why you threatened to cut the ashram out of your will."

"That's right. That happened at the Christmas party, too. My announcement about my will, I mean. It wasn't an announcement really. I just took Harshavardhana aside and had a quiet word with him. I'd been thinking about doing it for quite a while." He looked around at the big, disorderly house. "This place is worth quite a bit. And I've got the cottage in France and one in Wales…"

"Really?" said Cordelia. Holy shit, her generation had really missed the boat when it came to buying property.

"Yes, all paid for by the books. Anyway, along with everything else, it amounts to quite a lot of money. My estate. And I was thinking about what should happen to it when I don't need it anymore." He looked at her. "Not that I have any intention of dropping the body any time soon."

"Of course not," said Cordelia.

"But I wanted the money to go to a good cause. And what better cause than the ashram? I'd created it with my money in the first place, so it only seemed natural to give the rest of it to them, when the time came, to continue the good cause. So I told—"

"Howdy Doody," said Cordelia.

"Who?"

"That's what I call Harshavardhana."

"Great name!" said Alfie.

Cordelia felt a warm glow of gratification. But then, Alfie was very stoned. And so was she.

"So I told Howdy Doody," said Alfie. "I mean, I didn't tell him who I was or where the money came from. Just that they'd be getting it."

"Was he pleased?" said Cordelia.

"Chuffed to the bollocks," said Alfie, smiling reminiscently. His smile faded. "Mind you, there was someone who wasn't so pleased. When she found out."

"You mean the Silver Shrew?" said Cordelia.

"The Silver Shrew. Is that Gunadya?"

"Yup."

"Another great name. And yes, I suppose her, too. I mean she wasn't too pleased when she discovered that she couldn't boot me out for bad behaviour, that they were stuck with me no matter what I did." He snorted. "Because money talks, even in the holy sanctity of the ashram. But it wasn't her I was thinking of. I was thinking of Carrie. Curry Queen Carrie Quinn. She was supremely pissed off."

"Why?" said Cordelia. Then she answered her own question. "Because you hadn't put any money into her restaurant."

"That's right. I'd refused to bail her out. Or rather, I refused to join her in a sinking boat by lending her the money that wouldn't save her restaurant." He shook his head. "Carrie can cook. And she's a terrific lay…"

Two dinosaurs writhing in a swamp… Cordelia winced inwardly. And perhaps outwardly too, because Alfie quickly said, "Sorry, too much information. What I'm saying is that Carrie has some great qualities, but she has some very bad qualities too. Like being unreasonable. Supremely unreasonable. Not to mention *resentful*. Oh my, very resentful."

Cordelia hoped he wasn't going to rehash this old grievance again. He'd already explained it in detail to her, and Lorna, on the day they'd found Hank Honeywell's body.

But whatever else he was, Alfie wasn't a bore. He had a sensitivity about other people, as he now demonstrated very neatly by saying, "But you know all that. The thing is, she felt I *owed* her the money. Which is totally batshit, right? Then when she heard I'd promised all this money to the ashram instead of giving it to her, she went nuts. Absolutely nuts. And like I say, totally unreasonable. It's hard to enumerate all the ways she was unreasonable. For a start, it's my money, right?"

"Right."

"And then there's the fact that I'm not actually *giving* it to the ashram. Not while I'm alive. They only get it when poor old Alfie is dead." He chuckled. "Not a minute before. Now, that's a very different situation, isn't it?"

"Yes," said Cordelia.

"Maybe if Carrie had asked me to put some money for her in my will, for her restaurant, rather than demanded it upfront, I might have done it. Though, of course, it wouldn't have done any good, because she needed—or at least *wanted*—the money right away. And I must say it would have been a very unwise thing to do, leaving a large sum of money for Carrie in my will."

"Why?" said Cordelia.

Alfie grinned a savage grin. "Because Carrie is a rather ruthless lady. If she knew there was a nice little payoff coming to her when Alfie dropped the body, she might well find a way of hastening that dropping of the body."

"You mean she'd…" Cordelia hesitated then wondered what she was being so delicate about. "She'd kill you?"

"Sure," said Alfie, cheerfully and without hesitation.

"I can't believe that," said Cordelia.

"Of course not," said Alfie. "But that's because you don't know her as well as I do. Like I say, she's a ruthless lady. And, of course, there's no love lost between us. Not anymore."

A thought suddenly occurred to Cordelia. "Does Carrie know you're Avram Silverlight?"

"Nope," said Alfie. "Only Joni knows." He smiled at Cordelia. "And now you, of course." Then he paused and the smile faded. "Unless Joni told Carrie."

"Why would Joni tell her landlord?" said Cordelia.

"Well, Joni and Carrie aren't just tenant and landlord. They're quite tight. Carrie was teaching Joni to cook. And Joni's apparently showing promise. Personally, I think she should pack in any notion of teaching yoga. Forget all about becoming part of the ashram."

Cordelia realised that Alfie was talking about Joni as if she wasn't lying unconscious in hospital with a serious head injury. But it seemed unnecessarily pedantic, not to mention cruel, to point this out to him.

"She isn't really out out for yoga teaching," said Alfie. "But she would make a really good apprentice for Carrie, and Carrie needs one. Joni could still come to the ashram and practise there, but she should go into business with Carrie. Like I say, Carrie needs the help, though she'd never admit it, and then Joni wouldn't have to worry about dealing with Gunadya—the Silver Shrew, ha!—or any of the other shit at the ashram. It would be a perfect solution." He sighed. "But, of course, neither Joni or Carrie will listen to me… Isn't it funny how people can't seem to see their own best interests?"

"It is funny," said Cordelia, who'd often thought much the same thing herself.

"But to go back to what you were saying…" said Alfie.

What was I saying? thought Cordelia, lightheaded with revelations and passive dope smoking.

Luckily Alfie offered a précis. "You're right, why would Joni tell Carrie who I really am? I asked her to keep my identity secret and she was very scrupulous about that. Poor Joni... I know you don't like her."

This came out of nowhere and Cordelia started to protest, but Alfie waved her to silence. "I can understand that," he said. "But I saw a very different side of her than most people do. It all started that night at the Christmas party."

"I know," said Cordelia. "It's the stuff of legend at the ashram."

Alfie chuckled. "I suppose it is. I guess everybody knows. Did Lorna tell you?"

"Yes."

"Well, it was naughty of me, of both of us. But it was sort of a magic moment. I'd just told Howdy Doody that the ashram was in line to get all this nice, juicy cash and he practically danced a jig. Consequently he was happy, and I was happy that he was happy. And everyone else was having a good time at the party— one of Carrie's finest curries was on offer. That woman may have her flaws, but my goodness, she can cook. And I'd had a little smoke beforehand, so I was getting the full benefit from the food and the Christmassy vibe and everybody's great positive mood, and I was feeling very mellow and a little nostalgic. Which is why, while everybody was happily chatting and noshing on the curry and nobody was looking, I just slipped away upstairs to the meeting room. Like I said, I was up there, looking at my books and the photos and all the other souvenirs, and having a little private moment. Of reflection."

"It didn't stay private, though, did it?"

"No, I think Joni saw me leave the party. Or maybe she was checking something upstairs like she said, though what there was to check I can't imagine. Anyway, she barged in on me. I was having this lovely, private moment, all alone there in this room full of memories in the dark. Almost nothing had changed and, if I squinted my eyes, I could imagine that half a century had dropped away and I was back there in the days when we first built the place. For a moment it seemed like all those years were just an illusion and I could step back into the past..." Alfie looked at Cordelia.

"But then Joni came in and blew it," said Cordelia. Then, realising what she'd just said, felt herself suddenly start to redden.

Alfie was grinning from ear to ear. "Well put. But you were right. My mood was spoiled when she barged in and ordered me out of the meeting room, told me to go back down to the party, that I shouldn't be in there. That I didn't belong."

"That must have annoyed you," said Cordelia.

"I shouldn't have let it bother me, but it did. And I told her that nobody belonged there more than I did. Of course, she didn't believe me. So I showed her my photo on the wall."

Cordelia remembered the black-and-white photo of the bare-chested young titan.

"And I said, 'That's me.' But she didn't believe that either. So I showed her my tattoo." He smiled. "That gave her pause, all right. But then she said that the tattoo didn't prove anything. Two people could have the same tattoo."

"True," said Cordelia.

"I suppose I should have just let it go, gone back down to the party and shut up. But I'd already gone too far. My ego had become involved. I'd let the cat out of the bag and told her who I was and she didn't believe me. Which meant I had to prove it."

"And how did you do that?" said Cordelia.

Alfie smiled. "By opening the safe. I told you the place hadn't changed much. They hadn't even bothered to change the combination."

"You remembered it after all those years?"

"Of course. I'd chosen it, using numbers that were significant to me. You know, dates of significant events in my life. And I just pulled back the curtains and spun the dial on the safe and it popped open. And Joni stood there staring at me. She believed me all right and…"

"She popped open too," said Cordelia.

Alfie laughed. "In a manner of speaking. And there we were, having a little romantic interlude when the Silver Shrew burst in on us."

"That must have been a bit of a mood killer," said Cordelia.

"It was a bit."

"I take it you'd safely closed up the safe again."

"Yes," said Alfie, "and closed the curtains. And I'd already sworn Joni to silence about my secret identity."

Speaking of silence, there was now a long pause. And then the smell of coffee suddenly made itself known to the two stoned fools. "Hey, I must have finished making the coffee," said Alfie. He went and poured two cups and came back. They sat and sipped in further silence. It was good coffee but not really worth the wait. Nothing could have been.

Sitting there, thoughts adrift, Cordelia put two and two together and realised that Alfie was the mysterious missing link in the ashram hierarchy—he was the one Howdy and the Shrew would have had to check with when Cordelia had asked if replacement copies of the books needed to be signed.

She was quite pleased with herself for working this out.

Eventually Alfie said, "And now can I ask you some questions?"

"Of course."

"Okay, so where did you find the stolen books?"

"Well, various places," said Cordelia. "But I guess you're most interested in the Avram Silverlight ones. Your ones."

"Yes," said Alfie. "Where did you find my books?"

"In your garage," said Cordelia.

"*What?*"

"Do you remember when you sent me out there to put the hibachi in the car?"

"On the day of the picnic," said Alfie.

"Right. I thought I glimpsed something then, just out of the corner of my eye. I didn't really process it at the time because we were rushing around. But it was in the back of my mind. And then, when Lorna and I came back from the common, after we found Hank… I had a proper look and there they were. All the books, in that red barbecue. Just sitting inside it."

"Just sitting inside it," echoed Alfie in a voice hollowed out by surprise. "So you took them then?"

"No, I came back that night and broke into your garage. Or I would have done, but it wasn't locked."

Alfie began to laugh. He laughed until tears ran down his cheeks and then he wiped his eyes and sighed. "What a hoot," he said. "They were in my garage all along? We were tearing our hair out trying to work out where they'd gone, and they were here all the time?"

"Yep," said Cordelia feeling proud of herself. The Paperback Sleuth strikes again.

"But you have no idea who put them there?"

"My first thought was you."

"Me?" said Alfie.

"Yes."

"It wasn't me," he said.

"So I gathered," said Cordelia. "I kept watching you for giveaway signs. But you didn't give any away."

Alfie put down his coffee cup and looked at her. Then he smiled and snapped his fingers. "Wait a minute. That's why you wanted to borrow the red barbecue?"

"I didn't really want to *borrow* it…"

"But you wanted to confront me with it," said Alfie.

"That's right," said Cordelia. "It must have seemed pretty weird and suspicious, I suppose."

"On the contrary," said Alfie, "you had me completely hoodwinked. I just thought you and Edward…"

"Edwin."

"… you and Edwin wanted to borrow it and have a barbecue. You completely fooled me."

"I'm glad," said Cordelia.

"And that convinced you I was innocent?"

Cordelia smiled. "Nothing could convince me of that."

Alfie smiled back at her. She could see how pleased the remark made him.

"But," said Cordelia, "that and other things did seem to indicate you hadn't pinched the books."

"What other things?"

"The way you were so pleased when I told you I'd found them. In the peace garden that day."

"Oh yeah. Oh well, so we've eliminated me as a suspect. And I'm very pleased about that. But where does that leave us?"

"I don't know," said Cordelia candidly. "But I'll notify you as soon as I have any useful leads. Now can I ask you a question?"

"Sure," said Alfie.

"Why do you want me to find out who stole the books?"

"Well, to tell the truth," said Alfie, "I think I know who did it."

"*What?*" This time it was Cordelia's turn to say it. She felt entirely blindsided by this disclosure, and the rush of emotions it engendered. Including shock, anger and a sense of betrayal. If Alfie knew, then why the fuck was he playing weird games with her? But then she remembered the large sum of money that was now in her bank account. If Alfie was playing weird games with her, he'd paid handsomely for the privilege. She took a deep breath and said, "Not that I don't love the money, but if you know who did it, then why did you hire me…?"

"I *think* I know who did it. But I'm not sure. And I want you to confirm or deny, so to speak."

"Okay," said Cordelia. "Are you going to tell me who you think it was?"

Alfie looked at her for a moment and then said, simply, "Hank."

Cordelia thought of Hank, in his daisy-decorated jeans jacket, dead on the common. "And why do you think he might have stolen the books?"

"It's just the sort of prank he would have pulled. A Hank prank." Alfie smiled a nostalgic smile. "Good old Hank."

"Now you want me to clear his name?"

"Not really, I'm perfectly happy if Hank did steal the books."

"Then why not let sleeping dogs lie?" said Cordelia, thinking for a moment of a snoozing Rainbottle.

Alfie grinned at her. "Are you trying to talk yourself out of a job?"

"No," said Cordelia, but she found she was tightly gripping her phone in her pocket, as though Alfie might somehow take back the money he'd paid into her account.

Alfie sighed and looked away from her evasively for a moment, then back at her again, meeting her eyes. "I think that if Hank took the books, it might have something to do with why he was killed."

"So if I find the book thief…"

"We might learn who the killer is."

"Okay," said Cordelia. "By the way," she added, "you didn't kill him, did you?" She kept the tone light and conversational.

Alfie didn't seem at all offended by the question. "No. Hank was my best friend. And incidentally, the cops have already looked into me as a possible suspect and ruled me out."

"Why were you a suspect?"

"Because he was staying at my place."

"And how did they rule you out?" said Cordelia.

"I was up in town at a Black Midi gig and there's plenty of footage of me on socials, at the exact time he died, cavorting in the mosh pit in front of the band, in a manner unbecoming a man of my advanced years. Would you like to see some of that footage?"

Cordelia smiled. "No thanks."

"Your loss."

"I'll be okay," said Cordelia. "How do the police know the exact time Hank died?"

"He was wearing one of those things on his wrist which records your physical activity. And it recorded exactly when he ceased to be physically active. Poor Hank. Poor old sod."

Well, that sounded incontrovertible. Alfie fell silent, and Cordelia wasn't sure if he was mourning his friend or absorbed in other thoughts. Apparently the latter, because he then said, "Both Hank and Joni ended up lying on the common with their heads bashed in." He looked at Cordelia. "There's an odd similarity there, don't you think?"

"There are differences, too," said Cordelia. "Joni's still alive."

"Not for the lack of someone trying. Maybe they were interrupted. The spot where they found Joni was right by the road. Much more exposed and public than where Hank was. Maybe someone drove past and spooked the killer, and they didn't have time to make sure they'd finished the job."

Cordelia nodded. "That sounds plausible."

"It does, doesn't it?" said Alfie.

"But what about a motive?"

"As far as Joni's concerned, I have no idea," said Alfie. "But in Hank's case, we're working on the assumption that it was to do with him stealing the books."

"But if Hank was killed for stealing the books and it wasn't you who did it," said Cordelia, "then the only other people with a motive would be someone at the ashram. After all, they're the ones who were robbed. Someone at the ashram acting out of a spirit of revenge or retribution."

"Right. Revenge or retribution."

"Still, I must say I don't think that's very likely," said Cordelia.

"Because they're too spiritually advanced and chilled out to want revenge or retribution?" said Alfie.

"Because I can't see either Howdy Doody or the Silver Shrew beating Hank to death with a whisky bottle for stealing some books."

Alfie shook his head. "When you put it like that, neither can I."

"Anyway," said Cordelia, "just to clarify…"

"Okay, clarify away," said Alfie.

"You're hiring me to find a book thief, not to identify a killer."

"That's right," said Alfie.

He didn't sound particularly convincing.

23: DEAD LETTER

Cordelia's phone rang.

It was an unknown caller, so she answered with a certain amount of trepidation, even though she was now safely ensconced in her attic room, coming down from the dope smoke at her meeting earlier in the day with Alfie. Maybe that was why she was feeling trepidation. Because of the dope smoke.

"Hello, Cordelia? This is Carrie Quinn."

"Oh… hello, Carrie."

"I got your number from Alfie."

For all of Alfie's protestations about the bad blood between them, and wanting to avoid her and all the rest of it, Alfie and Carrie seemed to be in constant touch, virtually living in each other's pockets.

"Ah… good," said Cordelia.

"I'm calling you because of Joni."

"How is she?" said Cordelia.

"Well, I was at the hospital today and they're guardedly optimistic, whatever the hell that means. But that's not what I meant when I said I was calling because of her. Naturally I'm happy to give you an update. But that's not why I called. I called because she left a letter for you."

"What? A letter for me?"

"Sorry, that makes it sound like a suicide note or something, doesn't it?" said Carrie.

Yes, it bloody does, thought Cordelia, her heart pounding. She didn't say anything, though. She didn't quite trust herself to.

"No," said Carrie, "what I mean is a letter. A proper letter. Sealed in an envelope, addressed to you. With a stamp on it."

For a moment Cordelia was about to deny that Joni had her address. But, of course, Cordelia had given it to her last night when she'd arranged for Joni to come over. Was it really only last night? Christ… "Okay," said Cordelia warily.

"I found it when I looked in her room," said Carrie. "After the accident. It was sitting there in full view. Almost as if…"

"Almost as if she wanted it to be posted if anything happened to her," suggested Cordelia.

"Yes, that's more or less what I thought," said Carrie. "Either that or she'd planned to post it herself and just didn't have the chance to do so. In fact, when I found it, my first thought was to post it for her."

"Okay," said Cordelia, again.

"But then I thought, why not just hand it over to you? In person."

"Okay," said Cordelia. It was becoming a habit.

"It seems somehow safer that way. I'd be absolutely certain you'd received it if I gave it to you in person."

Because she couldn't say "Okay" again, Cordelia said, "Good idea."

"Then can you come around and collect it?" said Carrie.

Experiencing just a suggestion of déjà vu, Cordelia said, "It would be better if you came over here."

"Sorry," said Carrie. "That's not going to happen."

Cordelia said, or began to say, firmly, "I really would prefer—"

"You have to come here," said Carrie. "If you want the letter."

With a sinking feeling, Cordelia realised that Carrie was going to outdo her in the firmness sweepstakes.

"Unless you want me to open it and read it to you?" said Carrie.
"No," said Cordelia quickly. She most definitely did not want that.
So she took Carrie's address and they arranged a time.

Carrie's house was on the opposite side of Putney to Alfie's, as if to denote the much-advertised bad feeling between them.

There was a bright pink Post-it note on Carrie's front door saying, tersely but comprehensibly, *In back garden*. Cordelia went around the side of the house and into the garden, which was almost a textbook example of contrast with Alfie's chaotic jungle. This place was attractive, orderly and highly productive. There was almost no lawn, just thin strips of grass that ran between planting beds. And these did not contain flowers, but rather vegetables. Vegetables of every imaginable variety.

Which, if you were Cordelia, wasn't that wide a variety. There were many specimens she couldn't identify.

But she could certainly identify the ones Carrie was currently working on, bent over with a trowel in her hand and doing whatever things a gardener does with squashes. Carrie looked up as Cordelia approached, her sweaty face bright red.

"My god, those squashes are amazing," said Cordelia. And she wasn't being polite. The squashes had a kind of grotesque beauty. They were all different shapes and colours and combinations of colours—stripes were the least of it.

"Thank you," said Carrie.

"There's a greengrocer's in Barnes that has a display of those in its window. Very similar."

"Where do you think they get them?" said Carrie with a kind of acid modesty.

"Oh," said Cordelia. "You give them to the shop?"

"I sell them to the shop. Well, let's get you that letter."

Carrie led her back around to the other side of the house, up the steps to the front door, pausing to peel the pink Post-it note off it, opening the door (unlocked, Cordelia noted) and leading her into cool, fragrant semi-darkness.

Once through the door, Cordelia could just about make out a chest of drawers with bicycle accessories spread out on it (pump, a repair kit, a spare seat). Edwin would have been in his element, thought Cordelia, then she realised with a pang that these things must belong to the hospitalised Joni—it was impossible to imagine Carrie on a bike. There were some Carrie-related items on the sideboard, though. Gardening stuff: gloves, rolls of wire, packets of seeds.

There was also a large, hand-painted ceramic salad bowl. Cordelia knew it was a salad bowl because the hand painting featured salad ingredients—tomatoes, mushrooms, lemons, garlic and some notably badly executed lettuce. It didn't contain salad, though. It contained various sets of keys, junk mail and the sort of stuff that comes through a London letterbox.

Carrie was staring into the salad bowl. Then she reached into it and began searching through the junk mail and leaflets. Her hands were dirty from grubbing in the earth. After a brief, rather violent search, she stopped.

She looked at Cordelia with bafflement. But it was a sort of angry bafflement, as if Cordelia might be to blame for it. "It's not here."

"My letter?" said Cordelia. She'd already begun to feel intensely possessive about this missive, which she had never seen and only heard about.

"Yes. Your letter. It should be there. Right there." She inspected the salad bowl with disfavour. "I put it there so it was ready for you to pick up."

They both stared at the disappointing salad bowl as if expecting a magic trick or minor miracle. But the letter didn't materialise.

"Perhaps you put it somewhere else," suggested Cordelia.

"I did *not* put it somewhere else," snarled Carrie, embarrassingly all too easily decoding the subtext of Cordelia's suggestion—dotty old woman forgets where she puts things. "I put it *there*. I did not put it anywhere else."

Nevertheless, there then ensued a detailed search of most of the ground floor of the house. With no results. Or at least no positive results. Carrie's temper, never good at the best of times, became particularly ugly.

"Could it be downstairs?" suggested Cordelia.

"Downstairs?"

"In Joni's room."

"It *was* downstairs in Joni's room. I brought it *upstairs* and put it *there*." They were standing by the famous salad bowl again.

"Well, could it be upstairs?" said Cordelia.

"Upstairs?" said Carrie.

Cordelia was ready to believe that Carrie was going to deny that the house had an upper floor.

"Should we look?" said Cordelia.

"No," said Carrie. With what in other contexts would have been admirably steadfast finality.

There followed a long, tense silence. Cordelia was prepared, if Carrie suggested that they should forget about the letter and instead sit down and have a nice little curry together, to turn quickly and without ceremony flee through the front door.

To this end she kept a constant eye on her line of retreat.

At last Carrie said, with a great attempt at politeness and serenity, "The letter was here. It was here just an hour ago. Before I went out to the garden."

"Could someone have taken it?" said Cordelia, deciding not to be embarrassed to propose the obvious.

"No," said Carrie, again with monumental finality. But then she wavered. "No one has been here. Except…"

Cordelia pounced. She felt, after all this nonsense, she was entitled to a pounce. "Except?"

"Mr T popped around earlier. To collect some veggies. But he wouldn't have touched it."

"Wouldn't he?" said Cordelia. No one was a bigger fan of Mr T than herself. But frankly, at this point, she would have been prepared to accept aliens or poltergeists as a solution if there were pointers to indicate them. Like the aliens or poltergeists having popped around earlier to collect some veggies.

Carrie gave Cordelia a look. But, for once, it was more a thoughtful look than an angry one. Almost like they were conspirators in some dubious enterprise together. Or about to be. She took out her phone and turned her back on Cordelia, then wandered up the hallway. There was a pause while she impatiently tapped her foot. And then her foot suddenly stopped tapping and Cordelia was immediately all attention.

"Hello? T? Yes. Hi. Yes, I'm glad. No, my pleasure. Cook the courgettes first or they'll be past their best. Right, listen, T, did you happen to see a letter? Addressed to Cordelia? It was   What? Oh, did you? Well, why did you do that? I see. And did you? I see. Well you might have thought to tell me. No. Well, yes, I am a little angry. Think nothing of it. Goodbye."

She rang off, rather abruptly, and looked at Cordelia. It was a weary look.

"He took the letter and posted it. He thought he was being helpful."

"So, there's nothing to do except wait for the letter to arrive?" said Edwin. He was at home, with Rainbottle making noises in the background, and Cordelia was still in Putney, speaking to him on the phone as she made her way to Alfie's. She felt the need to talk over what had just happened. With Alfie, but first with Edwin.

"Correct," said Cordelia into the phone. "Assuming it doesn't get lost in the post."

"Well, it shouldn't," said good old reassuring Edwin.

"And assuming that Mr T really posted it."

"Well, that is quite another matter. Do you know if it was first- or second-class?"

"Second-class."

"Oh, Christ," said Edwin. Summarising Cordelia's own feelings on the situation quite nicely. "Who knows how long that will take to arrive…"

"Exactly," said Cordelia. "Oh, by the way, I meant to say, we don't have to go ahead with the barbecue."

"Why not?" Edwin sounded disappointed.

"I've explained to Alfie it was all a ruse."

"But we've got the sausages," said Edwin. Then, meditatively, "I suppose we could just grill them on the stove…"

"Listen, I've got to go."

"All right," said Edwin. "Be safe."

When Cordelia arrived at Alfie's, she found him smoking what looked like exactly the same spliff as before but was, no doubt, just the latest in a long sequence. With that in mind, it was impressive he was still so lucid. And upright. They went into the sitting room (patchouli-smelling gloom and a multitude of ethnic cushions, plus those giant speakers), where Cordelia told him the saga of the letter, concluding with the question that had impelled her here.

"Do you think it could be Mr T?"

"What could be Mr T?" said Alfie.

"That he could be responsible for everything," said Cordelia.

"Stealing the books?" said Alfie.

"Everything."

"You mean killing Hank?" said Alfie.

"Yes."

"Holy fuck," said Alfie, rising from his armchair, then abruptly losing his balance and sitting back down again. Maybe he wasn't so lucid and upright after all. He stared at Cordelia. "I think you're nuts," he said.

"Why?"

"Well, why do you think Mr T might be the culprit?"

"Besides stealing my letter?" asked Cordelia.

"He didn't *steal* it," said Alfie. "He posted it."

"Allegedly," said Cordelia, "There's also the fact he's been behaving strangely lately. Like missing a lesson. He never misses a lesson."

"Oh, that," said Alfie. He sighed and looked at her speculatively, as though he was making up his mind whether to tell her something. "That's all about his daughter."

"His daughter?" Cordelia had been vaguely aware that Mr T had children. He sometimes mentioned them in class.

"Yes," said Alfie. "She's seriously ill."

"Oh, I'm sorry," said Cordelia conventionally but truthfully.

"That's why he missed his lesson the other day. And that's why he came around here. You remember, you were here and I very rudely asked you to go?"

It was rather rude, thought Cordelia. She said, "Yes."

"Well, that was because Mr T had come around here to score some dope. It helps his daughter with her condition. Genuine medical need. But he wouldn't have wanted anyone to know. Either about his daughter being ill or about him scoring dope for her. Do you see?"

"Yes," said Cordelia. She did.

"He's a very private man. I hope that explains all the skulduggery and intrigue, and my bad manners."

"It does," said Cordelia. "But it doesn't explain him taking my letter from Carrie's and posting it."

Alfie shrugged. "Mr T is a bit of a busybody. He probably thought he was being helpful."

"All right," said Cordelia.

"You don't sound convinced."

"I'm not, entirely. But I'll keep an open mind."

"You can't say fairer than that," said Alfie. "Would you like to stay for a curry tonight? I've got a bunch of people coming over."

"I'd love to," said Cordelia. "But I have other commitments." The "love to" bit was a lie, but not the other commitments.

"Anything exciting?" Alfie's eyes gleamed salaciously under his bushy grey brows.

"A wake on a houseboat."

"Oh, another one of those."

Cordelia laughed. "It's at one of those big houses on the river in Richmond. The widow is going to empty her husband's wine cellar. She says it needs drinking up now that he's gone, and she isn't interested in wine."

"But he was, was he? The dead husband?"

"Oh, yes. Apparently, there's going to be some amazing stuff. It's a pity I'm not a wine expert."

"I'm not either," said Alfie. "But I'd give it a go. Maybe I should crash this party."

"I'm sure it would be easy," said Cordelia. "And there are going to be fireworks."

"See you there, then."

"I thought you were having people over for a curry tonight?"

"Oh, damn, you're right. Life's so complicated."

24: FIREWORKS

Cordelia didn't exclusively read crime fiction, and in fact, not long ago, she'd gone on a rather highbrow Somerset Maugham binge, motivated by the discovery—at a very reasonable price in a charity shop in Chiswick—of a beautiful set of vintage Penguin editions with the Derek Birdsall/Harri Peccinotti covers. These were particularly beautiful because you could set them side by side to form a vast panorama (a bit like the Pauline Baynes covers for the Ballantine *Lord of the Rings*, although that panorama wasn't quite so vast), and they were damned hard to find.

Anyway, in the course of this reading binge, Cordelia had happened to devour *The Painted Veil* (1925), a much-underrated early novel by Maugham, which told the story of Kitty Fane (great name), a young English housewife taken out to Hong Kong in the 1900s, and of her destructive extramarital passion for a handsome cad she meets there. They have a searing affair before Kitty is torn away and forced to go on an odyssey, involving much non-cad-related suffering, with her husband in mainland China. Consequently, Kitty becomes sadder but wiser, a much more mature party girl, and looks back with disdainful detachment on her devastating infatuation. At last, she knows she is cured forever.

But as soon as she returns to Hong Kong and bumps into the cad, despite all her newfound wisdom, she helplessly plunges right back into her torrid affair with him.

Well, this was a bit like that, minus the cholera epidemic and colonial attitudes...

Because as soon as Cordelia arrived at the widow Fairwell's big house in Richmond and walked across the wide green lawn down to the river, gleaming with reflected lights as the evening darkened, and joined the heaving party throng on the houseboat, she spotted someone.

A beautiful person called Agatha.

Now, Cordelia had *not* had a searing affair with Agatha; in fact, she'd only ever exchanged a few innocent words with her. But last year Agatha had been the focal point of a major, indeed incapacitating, crush. Obsession might not have been too strong a word, though perhaps a trifle unkind. And Cordelia, having undergone something of an odyssey of her own, had by now thought she was quite over it.

But as soon as she glimpsed Agatha, looking especially fantastic tonight in a woolly pink cardigan, black rollneck and skinny grey jeans, Cordelia felt a lurch in her chest and knew she was not entirely cured yet.

Agatha was here with her friend, a white girl with black hair and blue eyes. Set beside Agatha, she just kind of faded away, at least as far as Cordelia was concerned, but under normal circumstances the black-haired, blue-eyed bombshell would have been the most beautiful woman in the room—or, in this case, on the houseboat.

The boat had a name painted on its side, *The Flushed Bust*, and a cartoon rather in the style of Saul Bass, which depicted a blushing busty maiden in a bikini, with diagonal shading lines indicating the eponymous flush across her face and ample cleavage.

The name was a punning, or perhaps spoonerised, reference to the name of Travis McGee's houseboat in John D. MacDonald's series of novels: *The Busted Flush* (because McGee had won it in a poker game). Unlike McGee's floating party pad, however, the widow's houseboat really was like a house. A little house floating on the river.

A long, narrow Frank Lloyd Wright house: a bungalow mounted on a thin, buoyant foundation, the house or bungalow bit consisting of big picture windows, panels of red wood and strips of stainless steel. The long, flat rectangular roof of the bungalow, accessed by outside staircases at either end and an indoor one in the middle, was an open deck with yellow tubular guard rails that ran around its perimeter and matching yellow tubular uprights which held a corrugated steel roof above it, creating a large sheltered-yet-alfresco area like a roof deck or giant balcony.

This was ideal for a party on a mild autumn evening such as this, and doubled the floor space on the boat for people to stand around getting drunk.

Getting very drunk.

On either side of the central stairwell in this roof deck were long, rectangular tables covered with pink cloths, on which were bottles of wine. Dotted around the space were smaller, circular tables with, rather less interestingly, bottles of beer on them (lager, of course) and, even less interestingly, bowls of food. The dense crowd of party guests filled the deck but was, predictably enough, at its thickest close to the wine tables.

The wine tables were on the side of the deck that faced inland and it was impossible, at least at the moment, to get anywhere near them. A crowd of greedy wine connoisseurs formed a human shield, like the crush at an incredibly busy bar. Agatha and the bombshell must have arrived early because they were near the front of the crush, at the far end of the deck in relation to Cordelia, and sipping happily away.

Immediately in front of Cordelia were two beefy men wearing dark blue waterproof jackets with a stag's head and crossed oars, and the words *Richmond Bridge Boat Club* printed in white on the back.

"Is there any more of that Château Angélus, Barney?" said one of them.

"No, that other bugger nabbed the last of it," replied his companion.

Barney sounded bereft.

Over their shoulders Cordelia gazed helplessly at the wines on display, ranked bottles like obedient soldiers lined up to go to their doom. She stood there for a few minutes, staring at the impossible-to-reach but no doubt fantastic wines, and listening to the boat clubbers' conversation—they had no idea what the festivities were in aid of, had never met their hostess and certainly hadn't been invited; they'd got word of the wine, though, and smartly turned up to plunder it, which confirmed Cordelia's suspicion that this would be a very easy party to crash. It was a pity Alfie hadn't come along.

Finally, she gave up and retreated to one of the small, round tables where the bottles of beer were on offer, as well as a selection of segmented fruits—wedges of oranges, lemons and limes. Cordelia didn't need detailed instructions. She selected a bottle, Mexican lager, and stuck a segment of blood orange in the neck of it. Then she proceeded to wander among the noisy crowd, occasionally unplugging the orange from the bottle, squeezing a little of it into the beer (as she understood the correct procedure to be), having a sip and then plugging it back in again.

All the while casually trying to keep her eye on Agatha.

Cordelia was beginning to get a bit bored and fed up—a classic hazard for her at parties. It was almost dark now, and the big white house looked ghostly and regal, sitting on its broad lawns against a deepening blue sky. Then suddenly all its windows flashed a pale pink, reflecting a starburst above the trees, and a sharp little explosion racketed between the house and the river.

Of course, *fireworks*.

There was a unanimous excited sound from the crowd and the throng of people moved in a body to the other side of the deck, abandoning the wine tables. This would have been the moment to go after some of the high-end red or white, but Cordelia was drinking lager now and, besides, she was intrigued to see what was going on up above.

She set her bottle down on one of the small tables and went to join the crowd, peering out over the river, just in time to see a vast red flower blossom in the sky, symmetrically reflected in the darkness of the Thames below. A loud explosion racketed back and forth in echoes from the stone face of the house behind them, rattling bottles and glasses on the houseboat.

Now an intense globe of pale blue glowed high above as if someone had used a giant cigarette to burn a hole in the black backcloth of the night sky, revealing the daylight behind it. Cordelia went and retrieved her lager—she was going to get pissed and really enjoy the pyrotechnics. The piece of blood orange had fallen out of her bottle. She took a long pull then stuck it back in, returning to the crowded rail in time to see the blue sphere develop streaks of yellow that radiated from its centre. These in turn exploded and emitted whistling banshee shrieks.

Cordelia didn't think she'd ever seen such a fantastic firework display.

It helped that the beer on an empty stomach suddenly had her feeling light-headed and a little spaced-out; almost high.

There were green and yellow starbursts and a series of glittering white explosions, which consisted of intricate filaments that then exploded in turn, miniature versions of the mother firework that drifted in the sky like silver thistledown.

There was a patriotic sequence of developing pyrotechnics, first red then white then blue. These were followed by fetching confections in violet and green, then an enormous yellow fireball, then a small but intensely white teardrop shape that burned upwards on a zigzag course, like a squiggling spermatozoa seeking to impregnate the night.

Each new detonation was accompanied by appreciative oohs and aahs from the crowd. Cordelia looked at the people watching the fireworks and saw Betty, the widow Fairwell, in a crush of gawkers, her charming face reflecting the coloured lights as she stared skywards.

Cordelia had come here with the intention of combining the party with collecting her John D. MacDonald novels. Thanks to Alfie, she now had the funds to pay the widow in full.

But it was clear that Cordelia wouldn't be able to do this tonight. Betty obviously had her hands full looking after her guests and supervising the party and, if she did have a quiet moment, she should spend it enjoying herself and not transacting business with Cordelia.

It had been a silly idea. Well, perhaps not silly, but overambitious. No problem. Cordelia would collect the books another time. Now she'd just relax and enjoy the show. She sipped her beer and watched the fireworks. Or tried to watch them.

She was finding the flaming colours in the sky just a little too bright, a little too piercing. It was giving her a headache to look at them, so she dropped her gaze and watched the pretty explosions reflected in the water. The reflections down in the river seemed somehow gentler, cooler and easier on the eye than the real things up above.

Cordelia set her half-empty beer bottle down on the floor at her feet. Not good manners but she didn't have the energy to take it to a table and dispose of it properly. And she certainly didn't want another. One had been more than enough. She really should have eaten something before she started pouring lager down her throat. Oh well.

The strategy of watching the fireworks in the water worked very well for a while. In fact, it was downright soothing. Even the loud bangs as they went off began to seem comforting and distant, like thunder when you're safe in your bed.

Cordelia decided she actually would like to *be* safe in her bed and made a firm decision to leave as soon as the fireworks were concluded. A bit dull of her, but there you go.

If only the bright colours didn't hurt her eyes. Or rather, hurt her head. Their piercing gleam seemed to cut painfully right into her brain. Why was that? Oh, of course, how silly of her, she'd inadvertently started looking up into the sky again. No wonder it was painfully dazzling. She was supposed to be watching not the fireworks themselves but their dream-doubles in the river below.

All Cordelia had to do was lower her gaze from sky to water. *Look down, Cordelia.* She tried to do so then realised she was *already* looking down.

Or was she?

Wait a minute, which one was sky and which one was river? The two had become fatally confused. In fact, the whole concept of up and down (or was that two concepts?) was now hopelessly muddled.

For a vertiginous moment, Cordelia couldn't work out which was which, air or water. Air, water...

What about earth and fire? Those were the four essential elements, weren't they?

Well, the fire was in the sky, and the earth, lovely firm earth, wasn't far away. She just needed to step off the houseboat and back onto terra firma, the widow's lawn. Actually, it might be a good idea to do that now. Get off the houseboat and head home, home to her lovely attic room and her lovely quilt of New Zealand wool, so soft it was like lying in a heap of snow, but *warm* snow.

Yes, time to go home. Just take a deep breath and clutch the handy handrail in front of her to steady herself, take a last look at the pretty polychrome pyrotechnics in the river and then say goodbye.

But suddenly the river had become turbulent, its surface bellying and swollen as if something huge was swimming just below the surface. And the surging swell was rocking the boat and lifting it. Alarm compounded the queasiness in Cordelia's stomach. Why was no one else reacting to this? Everyone was carrying on as though nothing was happening, while the houseboat lurched, shifted, tilted underfoot...

Cordelia staggered to the edge of the roof deck, increasingly unsteady and increasingly queasy, and she got to the far end and went down the stairs. It was quieter down there—all the party people were upstairs. It was a relief to be quiet and alone in the dark. The hot sweat on her forehead cooled in the river breeze. The end of the boat—the aft? the stern? the butt?—was nearby, which was handy as there was suddenly a molten convulsion in her guts.

Cordelia moved briskly to the edge of the boat and leaned out over the dark water just in time to vomit.

She moaned and doubled over, too weak to stand.

Strange things were happening. There was a band of darkness at the edge of her vision and it seemed to be growing. Her head swam.

She was blacking out. Why was she blacking out?

Best not to do that while leaning out over the river.

Safety first...

Cordelia was trying to sit down when someone grabbed her from behind and threw her into the water.

* * *

Cordelia would later give herself a hard time for not twisting around to get a look at whoever had thrown her off the boat.

But as she plunged into the murky Thames she was concentrating, although concentrating was probably too strong a word, on trying to hold her breath as she stared at what was directly in front of her.

Lying face down in the water as she was, what was directly in front of her was the river bottom. Mud, weeds and a dispiriting number of beer cans. The bottom was not far below her and Cordelia might even have been able to stand up with her head above the water.

If she hadn't, at that moment, blacked out.

25: RIVER SMELL

Cordelia woke up with no clear understanding of where she was...
Except that she wasn't at the bottom of a river.

Which, for the first few minutes, was good enough for her.

She just lay there with her eyes closed, listening to the party
sounds outside, coming from the distant but not too distant
houseboat, and tried to piece things together in her mind... The
sounds were outside, so she was *inside*. And since they were
distant but not too distant, she assumed she was inside Betty
Fairwell's house.

Something smelled not especially pleasantly of the river and
Cordelia gradually realised it was her, or rather her hair, which was
still damp.

Damp, but not soaking wet. And the rest of her was dry and
wrapped in a soft pink towelling robe that smelled strongly (and
arguably only slightly less disagreeably) of synthetically scented
laundry liquid.

Cordelia could sense both intense nausea and a spectacular
headache crouching somewhere nearby, just outside her immediate
range of consciousness, and waiting to pounce if she made one
false move. Opening her eyes seemed all too likely to be just such
a move, but eventually she decided she must do it.

She opened her eyes and discovered that she was in one of the downstairs rooms in the widow's house, with windows facing out towards the lawn and the river. It was a kind of intimate little sitting room or study, with dark green carpeting. Hanging on the mint-green walls were framed prints of vintage art deco American Penguin covers by Robert Jonas: *Murder in Fiji* (John Vandercook), *Market for Murder* (Frank Gruber) and *Great Murder Stories* (by America's Foremost Mystery Writers). Cordelia appreciated Jonas's fabulous paperback art but, just now, she could have done without the murder theme.

There was also a glossy black desk, a small white linen-covered sofa and a pair of matching armchairs. All the colours were restrained, muted, soothing. Which was just as well because Cordelia felt bright colours would cause her brain to explode.

No more fireworks, please.

Cordelia was lying on the sofa, and sitting nearby in one of the armchairs, quietly watching her, was a young woman.

The black haired, blue eyed friend of Agatha's.

There was no one in the other armchair, or at the desk or elsewhere in the room.

In other words, there was no sign of Agatha.

"How are you feeling?" said the young woman.

"Not great," said Cordelia. She was embarrassed to discover her voice was a rusty croak; the creaking of a coffin lid in an old horror movie. "But better than…"

"The alternative?" suggested the woman.

Cordelia nodded, but very carefully so the top of her head wouldn't come off. "What happened?" she croaked. "I mean, after I went into the water?"

"Well, you made quite a splash. To coin a phrase…" The woman grinned at her. "But not many people paid much attention. They were all too busy having a good time."

"But not you?"

"I thought it sounded like someone had gone overboard, and so did my friend. So we went to have a look."

"And you went into the water and pulled me out?" Cordelia felt tears of gratitude begin to sting in her eyes.

"My friend went into the water." The woman smiled. "I just helped pull you out, from the warm, dry comfort of the boat deck. That was the smart way to do it because my friend is the one who's really good at swimming."

"I know," said Cordelia.

These two husky syllables were greeted with an agreeable amount of blue-eyed surprise.

"Tinkler told me," she added. "Didn't Agatha save *him* from drowning once?"

"Something like that," said the woman, her eyes now narrowed. "Tinkler and I were an item for a while."

The woman nodded as if this confirmed a theory. "Are you Stinky Stanmer's sister?"

Cordelia felt like crying again, this time at the unfairness of it: to be known to the world only by such a dubious distinction. "Yes," she said. "Sorry."

"Oh, don't apologise. It's not your fault. And besides, Tinkler said you hate him as much as we do."

"At least," said Cordelia. "My name's Cordelia, by the way."

"I'm Nevada."

"Where's Agatha?" said Cordelia, trying to put a casual note in her croak.

"She went home to change. She lives in Richmond. Not far from here."

Cordelia didn't volunteer that she already knew this. Instead she said, "What happened to my clothes?"

"They're hanging up in the bathroom to dry. We washed them

out as best we could, but you're going to have to do it properly when you get home."

"Thank you."

"Your phone's a goner, I'm afraid." Nevada said this last bit with a sort of comradely certainty, as one who'd been there herself. "But your cards and cash are okay. And this…" She took out Cordelia's keys, attached to the self-defence weapon that Edwin had given her. The one Cordelia had dubbed the killer dildo. Nevada evidently knew exactly what it was because she gave it a sardonic, appraising look. "Expecting trouble?" she said.

"Much good it did me," said Cordelia. "But thank you anyway. For everything."

Nevada shrugged. "All part of the service. You should really thank our hostess. She provided the bathrobe you're wearing and said we could put you in here to lie down until…"

"I woke up," said Cordelia.

"Until you *sobered* up."

"I'm not drunk," said Cordelia. Through the clotted fog that enshrouded her, she felt a combination of indignation and truculence. "I only had half a bottle of beer."

"And you think your drink was spiked?"

"Yes," said Cordelia, bracing herself for some heavy-duty humour-the-nutcase scepticism.

But Nevada just nodded thoughtfully. "I reckoned it must have been something like that."

There was silence in the small room. For Cordelia's part it was a surprised silence. "Why?" she said.

"People, even very drunk people, tend to wake up when they fall into cold water," said Nevada. "Not pass out."

"I didn't fall in," said Cordelia. "Someone pushed me."

There was more silence, though, oddly enough, not a surprised one. Then Nevada said, "You said you were drinking a bottle of beer? Do you remember what kind of beer it was?"

"Something Mexican. It had a slice of blood orange in the neck."

Nevada nodded and got up.

"Where are you going?" said Cordelia.

"If I can find your beer, we have a friend who can analyse it. Well, a friend of a friend." She went out.

Despite strenuously trying to stay awake, Cordelia fell asleep almost immediately. But she woke again as soon as the door opened and Nevada stepped in, empty-handed and not looking entirely pleased.

"No luck?" croaked Cordelia.

"No luck. Your bottle's been tidied away, emptied and put in the recycling. No need to read anything sinister into that…" She sighed and sank back into an armchair. "Our hostess has hired some very efficient staff for her party."

"How long were you gone?" said Cordelia.

"About five minutes."

As far as Cordelia was concerned it could have been five hours.

"Did you fall asleep?" said Nevada.

"Yes."

"I'm not surprised."

Cordelia forced herself to sit up with some semblance of alertness. "I'd really like to say thank you to Agatha," she said, striving once more for a casual tone. "Is she coming back?"

"I doubt it. I think she's going to call it a night. And I think you should, too. I've phoned Tinkler and he's going to come and pick you up. I asked our hostess and you can go home in that bathrobe if you like." Nevada grinned. "Tinkler's seen a lot worse."

Cordelia nodded, with great care so as not to cause her head to burst like a soap bubble. She was impressed with Nevada's efficiency. What a good idea to enlist Tinkler. He was a mutual friend with whom she'd had what she was reluctant to dignify with the term "affair", but it amounted to that, so what the hell… They'd had an affair for a few months, last year. "Thank you," she said. "That means I don't have to dress in my wet clothes."

"That's the idea." Nevada looked at her phone. "We'll get your things and put them in a bag. Tinkler should be here in about five minutes."

"I really do appreciate everything you've done—I can't thank you enough."

"I'm just glad he wasn't too stoned to drive," said Nevada.

Tinkler did indeed arrive within five minutes and drove Cordelia home with the minimum of stupid questions. He didn't even stare at her bare legs. Much. When they got to her house in Barnes, he pulled over and stopped the car and looked at her.

"Nevada said someone tried to drown you."

"Yes."

"And you don't know who did it."

"That's right," said Cordelia.

"Well, she says if you feel the need for a bodyguard, she can do you a deal."

"Tell her thanks, but I'll be okay."

"She really knows her stuff," said Tinkler.

"I'll be okay."

"Okay," said Tinkler doubtfully.

Cordelia felt a bit bad turning down the offer, and without explanation. But Edwin would have her back and she wasn't at liberty to enlighten Tinkler, or anyone, about her landlord's extra-curricular activities and special skill set.

She said goodnight to Tinkler and scurried for the front door of Edwin's house, barefoot in a bathrobe, clutching her bag of clothes in one hand and her keys in the other, attached to the killer dildo.

Please don't let anyone see me, thought Cordelia. Not least because it looked like Tinkler was dropping her off after attending an orgy.

Perhaps he thought so, too. Because he beeped his horn cheerfully as he drove off into the night.

Cordelia immediately put her clothes in the washing machine then set about having a hot bath and a very thorough shampooing to remove the smell of the river from her hair and elsewhere. The bathroom was near the door of Edwin's little flat and, before she went in, she heard the sound of classical music coming from that direction. Given Edwin's routine, he was probably watching a concert on BBC Four, with his loyal mutt at his side.

She decided not to bother Edwin just then with the details of what had happened to her. But, the following morning, she gave him a full briefing. After his initial (and rather gratifying) alarm, Edwin became all business.

"Now, if someone tried to kill you at this party, then the first question is…"

"How did they know I'd be at the party," said Cordelia.

Edwin nodded approvingly and Rainbottle gave a guttural little utterance of approbation. "Could they have followed you there?" said Edwin.

"I suppose it's not impossible, but it seems very unlikely," said Cordelia. "Unless they've got me under surveillance at all times. Possibly using drones." This was a rather unsettling thought.

But Cordelia agreed with Edwin when he said, "Very unlikely. Did anyone know you were going to be there?"

"Yes," said Cordelia. "Alfie."

"Well, we'd better go and pay Alfie a visit then," said Edwin.

26: SAFFRON RICE

Cordelia's SIM card had survived its impromptu immersion and the first thing they did on leaving the house in Edwin's car was to buy her a low-end replacement phone (the dead phone had also been a cheapo one, hence this wasn't a big step down). Barnes being Barnes, there wasn't a cheap phone shop locally, so they went to Putney High Street.

It was on their way anyway.

After they bought the phone and set it up, they headed for Alfie's. This involved driving past the charity shop where the murdered Mac had worked, so, by the time they reached their destination, Cordelia was in a turbulent and angry mood, to say the least.

Edwin, by contrast, was as chilled as the proverbial cylindrical green salad vegetable.

He parked near Alfie's house and, as they walked to the front door, he said, "Let's not ring the bell."

"All right."

"Let's surprise Mr Alfie."

Mr Silbert, thought Cordelia. But she said, "Okay."

They were prepared to sneak around to the back garden by way of the garage, which was open, but, in the end, they went in through the front door which was, in classic Alfie style, unlocked. Edwin held the door open for Cordelia then closed it quietly behind them.

The house was silent and still. Cordelia's flesh began to creep and somewhere deep in her nose she could still smell the angry ghost of the burned videotape. The thought of Mac's little house beside the railway tracks was almost unbearable.

When they heard the sound of Alfie clearing his throat, it was an enormous relief. After he finished clearing his throat, he started to hum a merry little tune. Cordelia and Edwin looked at each other then headed in the direction of the humming.

Alfie was in his kitchen. The kitchen was warm and steamy, and a saucepan happily bubbled on the stove. A rich, aromatic, rather woody smell hung, pleasantly intense, in the air. Alfie was perched at the counter. In front of him was a large pestle and mortar made of what looked like green marble with some traces of reddish brown mush in it, and a white-and-yellow plastic food container with cartoon bumblebees on it. Less eccentrically, there was also an assortment of cooking ingredients: a bottle of extra-virgin olive oil, the remains of some red onions, a bag of basmati rice and a small, transparent plastic box secured with lavender ribbons, which contained tiny dark red strands.

Alfie looked up as Cordelia and Edwin came in and his face lit up. "Hey!" he said, rising happily from his chair. "Cordelia and Edwin. Definitely not Edward but Edwin."

"Definitely not Edward," said Edwin coolly.

Cordelia wondered, yet again, whether Alfie could really be that good an actor.

He turned his beaming countenance on Cordelia. "How was the wake on the houseboat?"

He really couldn't be that good an actor.

"We were very nearly having a wake for Cordelia," said Edwin quietly.

Alfie stopped beaming. He stared at Edwin, then at Cordelia. "What happened?" he said.

"Someone tried to kill me," said Cordelia. She was rather appalled to find her voice had a tearful wobble when she said this. How infuriatingly girlie. What made it worse was that Alfie immediately came over and gave her a bear hug. What made it even worse still was that Cordelia then burst into full-blown weeping in his arms. She felt foolishly secure and safe wrapped in his stoned old hippie bulk. Alfie smelled pleasantly of sundry cooking aromas and also his expensive aftershave, whatever it was. Cordelia wept uninhibitedly and happily.

Eventually she stopped crying and Alfie released her.

Edwin didn't seem at all embarrassed to have witnessed this display of emotion. He was now sitting, quite relaxed, in the chair where Alfie had been.

"What's that?" he asked, pointing at the box of little red fibres.

"Saffron. Saffron stamens. The real stuff, from Iran. Not the fake stuff from America and god knows where."

"You're making saffron rice?" said Edwin. He sounded genuinely interested.

"Right," said Alfie. "To go with my curry." He tapped the food container with the cartoon bees on it.

"Sounds good," said Edwin. He then added, conversationally, "Did you happen to mention to anyone what Cordelia was doing last night?"

Alfie shrugged. "Hell, yes. A wake on a houseboat? With fireworks? I think I've told everyone I've spoken to."

"And how many people is that?" said Edwin.

"Quite a lot," said Alfie. "Do you want a list?"

"When did you tell them about it?" said Cordelia, anxious to recover some cred after her girlie display of emotion.

"Today… This morning… I've been on the phone and on my socials…"

"Did you tell anyone yesterday?" said Cordelia.

"Yes," said Alfie. "Carrie."

"When?" said Cordelia.

"Just after you left here," said Alfie.

Edwin and Cordelia looked at each other. Plenty of time to prepare plans, get to Richmond and make an attempt on Cordelia's life.

Like Alfie's, Carrie's front door was unlocked. Cordelia wasn't surprised because it had also been unlocked the other day when she came to get the letter. Once again, she and Edwin went in without ringing the bell and entered a silent house. Once again, they ended up in the kitchen.

There was no merry humming this time. Just more silence. Plenty of cooking smells, however. It looked as though Carrie had been preparing an industrial quantity of curry. There were professional catering-sized cooking implements in evidence, all washed and gleaming now.

The curry had evidently been transferred to the containers, which were stacked six deep on the counter. White-and-yellow containers with cartoon bees on them. No mystery where Alfie got his, then.

No sign of Carrie, though.

"Maybe she's in the garden," said Cordelia. "I guess we should have checked there first." Then, in a horrid echo of Mac's sitting room, she saw the legs on the floor. Fat, bare, pale female legs with sandals on the grubby feet. Edwin saw Cordelia's face and looked where she was looking.

He moved swiftly to where Carrie was lying on the floor between the counters, which is why she'd been out of sight when they'd first come into the kitchen. "She's still breathing," said Edwin abruptly, and he took out his phone.

Cordelia moved around behind him to get a better look. She tried not to look too directly at Carrie—it seemed unfair to stare at someone when they couldn't stare back at you.

Carrie was in a navy-blue skirt and a blue-and-white striped T-shirt. There was a yellow stain—curry, no doubt—on the shirt. And a dirty fork lay on the floor beside her, where evidently she'd dropped it, with a smear of curry on the tiles beside it. The tiny mess seemed strangely transgressive in the otherwise immaculate kitchen. Cordelia noticed there was a plate of curry on the counter. Carrie had evidently been sampling the stuff she'd just cooked.

Edwin was busy talking on the phone, getting an ambulance, but Cordelia didn't really take in what he was saying. She was looking at the food containers with the cartoon bees on them.

"Alfie," she said. She took out her own phone and called his number.

It went straight to voicemail, of course. She tried again and again. Then, because it was obviously pointless, she gave up and hung up

Edwin was watching her. He'd put his own phone away.

"No reply?".

"No reply."

Edwin was looking at the bumblebee containers. "You have to get over there and warn him," he said. "Stop him eating—"

Yes, bloody obviously yes. But "Yes," was all Cordelia said.

"I'll have to stay here and wait for the ambulance." Edwin took out his car keys. "Can you drive?"

Cordelia's heart slammed. Alfie's life was at stake and here she was, scared of having to drive a car across Putney.

It was horrible but true.

Edwin must have read something in her face, or her hesitation, because he said, "I've got a better idea. Come on." They hurried out to the car, Edwin still holding the keys. He unlocked the back and took out something that looked like a unicycle that had been mangled in a major industrial accident.

It wasn't that, though. Cordelia recognised it as a folding bicycle. Edwin had a folding bicycle in his car. Of course he did.

It was a green and black and silver contraption with the name Brompton on the side.

"You can ride a bike, can't you?" said Edwin as he unfolded it.

"Ah…" *Pull yourself together, Cordelia.* "Yes, yes of course."

Edwin finished unfolding the bike. "This will be quicker than a car in the traffic anyway."

There's an old saying. "It's like riding a bicycle. You never forget how."

Well, this was true enough. Cordelia hadn't been on a bike since she was a kid, but she was able to saddle up, start pedalling and set off as if minutes rather than years had elapsed since the last time she'd ridden one.

It wasn't the riding of the bicycle per se that was the problem.

The problem, which Cordelia had clearly foreseen and which was the reason for her hesitation when Edwin had asked her about it, was that Cordelia had never tried to ride a bike in London traffic. In the sort of hellish traffic Putney could offer on a sunny autumn day like this.

The back streets weren't so bad, though quite hair-raising enough. The really bad bit was crossing Putney High Street.

Cordelia was subjected to the obnoxious blaring of car horns on no less than three occasions as people decided they disapproved of her lack of experience, smarts and agility in the traffic stream. On the fourth occasion, someone actually buzzed open the window of his BMW and shouted savage and only semi-coherent obscenities at her in an old Etonian accent.

By the time she reached Alfie's street—a cul-de-sac, thank all the gods—she was completely drenched with sweat and her heart rate was through the roof. But, as she gratefully abandoned the bike in front of the house and ran for the front steps, her heart rate increased dramatically.

What was she going to find inside?

The first thing she found, as she pushed open the front door, was blaring music. It was coming from the big speakers in the sitting room and it was so loud that Cordelia would have covered her ears, but she could only cover one because her other hand was occupied by clutching the killer dildo.

(She felt very exposed and alone without Edwin at her back and she wanted to be ready for anything.)

Cordelia looked in the sitting room, the source of the pounding music. But, of course, Alfie wasn't there. She headed for the kitchen. There was no point calling out to him because he wouldn't hear her over the thunderous music.

Alfie was in the kitchen.

He was in the same place where he'd been sitting earlier. Except now there was a plate in front of him. A large, gleaming white plate that provided what, in other circumstances, would have been a pleasing aesthetic contrast with the golden pile of saffron rice and the darker yellowish-brown of the curry. The curry that had just come out of the plastic container with the cartoon bees on it.

Cordelia knew it had only just come out of the container because not only was Alfie still alive and well and fully conscious, but he was also just now lifting a clean fork off the counter beside his plate and starting to dig into the curry.

Cordelia was coming in through the door of the kitchen and Alfie was on the other side of the room. Although he hadn't seen her, he was certainly within earshot and, in normal circumstances, it would have made sense for Cordelia to yell for him to put the fucking fork down.

Except for one thing...

Alfie was wearing headphones and listening to music.

He was playing music at top volume on his big fucking speakers, blasting through the house, and simultaneously listening to music on his fucking headphones. *More* music. Who did that?

But, much more to the point, he had now loaded a hefty forkful of curry and was lifting it towards his mouth.

Cordelia shouted. Of course, he couldn't hear her.

She could never reach him in time. She was about to watch helplessly while...

No.

Cordelia threw the killer dildo.

She aimed it at Alfie, at his maddening, obstinate, eccentric, music-listening head. But Cordelia wasn't very good at throwing things (she used to hide in the library during PE at school).

And she missed.

However, the killer dildo landed right in the middle of Alfie's plate of curry, spattering the stuff.

He looked up in astonishment. Astonishment that rapidly turned to scandalised anger.

But he didn't put the fork in his mouth, which was the main thing.

"Why were you listening to music on your headphones and playing it out loud on your giant speakers?" Cordelia felt entitled to ask this question.

"The music I'm playing on the speakers is the original LP," explained Alfie patiently. "And I wanted to compare it to the new, remastered version. But I only have the new remastered version on download, so I had to listen on my headphones, and then I got into it and forgot I was also playing it on the record player." He looked at her. "Does that make sense?"

"Not really," said Cordelia. "But it doesn't matter." She'd collapsed into a chair opposite Alfie and she felt so exhausted that she didn't think she would ever get up again. Alfie was sitting where he had been before. The only things that had changed were that he'd taken off his headphones, turned off the thunderous music in the sitting room, and removed his plate and set it beside the sink where neither of them would have to look at it. He'd wanted to throw the food away, but Cordelia had stopped him. The police, or someone, would want to analyse it.

"You're sure it's poisoned?" said Alfie.

"Carrie's was."

Alfie's brow creased with worry. For all his avowed friction with the Curry Queen, he seemed very concerned about her. "You said she was…"

"Edwin's with her. Waiting for the ambulance."

"Do you think she'll be all right?"

"I have no idea," said Cordelia wearily. *Mac wasn't*, she thought. "I'll phone in a minute and find out what's happening."

"Okay," said Alfie.

He seemed cowed, polite, obedient. Very unlike Alfie. That made Cordelia feel bad. She sighed. She wanted to just sit here in this kitchen doing nothing and, above all, thinking nothing, but she forced her mind into motion.

"Okay," she said. She must have said it with a certain abrupt authority because Alfie looked at her alertly, all attention, like Rainbottle when he sensed a walk was in the offing. "There's one thing that's for certain," said Cordelia.

"Good," said Alfie. "What?"

"Although the curry was poisoned, it wasn't Carrie who poisoned it."

Alfie winced at the mention of Carrie's name, but nevertheless he said, "Isn't that two things?" which was a lot more like the old Alfie.

"However many things it is, we need to work out who did this to her, and... tried to do it to you." She'd almost mentioned the unfortunate dead Mac, who she wasn't supposed to know anything about. "Now, when Carrie brought the curry around for you," Cordelia nodded at the box with the cartoon bees on it, "did she mention she might be seeing someone else?"

"She didn't bring the curry around," said Alfie. "It was... what's your name for her? The Golden Mongoose?"

"The Silver Shrew," said Cordelia, feeling a thrill of appalled inevitability.

27: KILLER BEES

"The Silver Shrew brought this curry?"

"She said she was helping Carrie by delivering them for her, because Carrie had her hands full."

"Okay," said Cordelia. "Wait, *them*? She was delivering more than one of these?" Cordelia's gaze dropped to the food container with its merry cartoon bees, formerly so cute and innocent, now quite deadly looking. Killer booo, in fact.

"Yes," said Alfie. "She'd already dropped one off with ah... Howdy Doody." He seemed pleased to have remembered Cordelia's nickname for Harshavardhana, thereby regaining lost ground after the Golden Mongoose débâcle.

Cordelia got on her phone to the ashram straight away. She was no fan of Howdy, but she had no desire for someone to find him lying on the floor with his legs sticking out. His long, orange-pyjama-clad legs.

The ashram answered immediately, or at least a recorded voice did. With maddening inevitability, Cordelia was going to be compelled to leave a life-and-death message on voicemail (before haring over there in person) to tell them that the ashram's most respected and beloved—well, respected anyway—senior member and financial controller was actually a murderous psycho.

Oh yes, and she was probably also the one who'd stolen the books and redecorated their meeting room with the contents of her lower bowel.

As Cordelia tried to work out how on earth to put all this into words, the recorded message miraculously vanished and instead she heard Howdy Doody's welcome voice on the line. "Silverlight Yoga Centre."

"Harshavardhana, this is Cordelia."

"Oh hello, Cordelia. If this is about you being paid—"

"It's not. It's about you not being poisoned."

Having thus got his attention, Cordelia proceeded to fill Howdy Doody in. When, again with maddening inevitability, he refused to believe her, she put Alfie on the line.

And Alfie, to his credit, did an impressive job of putting the fear of god—and poisoned curry—into Howdy. He finished with the words, "And for Christ's sake don't touch any of that muck in the box with the bees on it." Then he hung up.

"Did you convince him?" said Cordelia.

"Not entirely," said Alfie. "But he's not going to be in any hurry to tuck into his lunch, which is the main thing. Now, could you please check on Carrie?"

Cordelia phoned Edwin. "Did you get to Alfie in time?" he said.

"Yes, in fact he wants a word with you."

Once more, Cordelia surrendered the phone to Alfie, who asked for an update on Carrie and then fell silent except for the occasional "Uh huh" and "Okay", then handed the phone back to Cordelia. He still looked worried, but less worried than before.

Cordelia took the phone and asked Edwin, "What happened?"

"While I was waiting for the ambulance, one of Carrie's neighbours came over for some veggies from her garden. Turned out she was a nurse. Very officious, take-charge type. So I let her take charge. It was perfect. I was able to sort of slip into the background when the ambulance came. They've just gone."

"How is she?"

"Still alive and now in good hands. It looks like we found her just after she ate the stuff, which is good. Anyway, I was about to come and get you at Alfie's."

"Don't bother," said Cordelia. "The traffic's diabolical. Meet me at the ashram." She told him about the packed lunch for Howdy Doody, delivered by the venomous Shrew. "I want to make sure he believes us."

"And once he does," said Edwin, "he should be the one to report this mess to the police."

"Good idea," said Cordelia. "For a start, he's probably the only one who can tell them the Silver Shrew's real name. As opposed to her Sanskrit one."

"Good point."

"I'll see you there in about half an hour—if you don't mind, I'm going to leave your bike at Alfie's. You can pick it up later, if that's all right?"

Edwin laughed. "That's fine," he said. "Had enough cycling for one day?"

"Yes, thanks." Cordelia hung up and turned to see that Alfie was holding something wrapped in several layers of paper towel.

"Do you want this back?" he asked.

It was the killer dildo. "Yes," said Cordelia. After all, it still had her keys attached to it. She put it back in her pocket, but only after washing it very carefully to remove any traces of the curry it had landed in, using a pair of rubber kitchen gloves that Alfie gave her and which they threw in the rubbish afterwards.

Better safe than sorry.

"Well, I'd better be going now," said Cordelia.

"Don't eat any curries," said Alfie, rising to escort her out. "At least not any delivered by the Silver Shrew."

"I didn't realise you two were so friendly," said Cordelia.

"We're not, I'm happy to say." They went out of the kitchen into the hallway. "In fact, I should have smelled a rat when she delivered it."

"Why?"

Alfie paused by the door of the sitting room, erstwhile home of blasting music. "Because she hates my guts. I mean, she never liked me. She thought that I embodied values that were the opposite of all the values of the ashram." Amusement gleamed in his eyes. "The opposite of all the values of Avram Silverlight. What a hoot, eh?"

"Yes," said Cordelia. Although "ironic" might have been the word she would have chosen.

"But ever since that Christmas when I was caught in flagrante with Joni, and the Silver Shrew discovered she couldn't boot me out of the ashram, she's *really* hated me. So, like I say, I should have smelled a rat."

"Or smelled a shrew."

"Or, indeed, smelled a shrew, but I didn't. Because I'd genuinely ordered a curry from Carrie and I was waiting for it to be delivered. So when the Shrew turned up with it and said Carrie had asked her to help out with the delivery, I believed her, because Carrie has recently been getting very chummy with her."

They continued towards the front door. "But if the Shrew hates your guts…" said Cordelia.

"And vice versa, to be honest."

"And vice versa," said Cordelia, "what was she doing here the other day?"

"What other day?"

"When you sent me away because you were having a private chat with Mr T."

"Yeah, sorry about that. But the Silver Shrew wasn't here that day."

"Yes she was."

They were at the front door now and Alfie had been reaching to open it for her. Now he lowered his arm.

"What do you mean?"

"I saw her out in the garden. She'd just come in through the garage. She said she was on her way inside to see you."

"Well, she wasn't," said Alfie. "And she never came inside."

"She was lying," said Cordelia, putting it together. "Or rather, bluffing." But why?

"Oh well, she's committed worse crimes than that. And, by the way, it looks like you've earned the rest of your fee."

"The rest of my fee?"

Alfie smiled. "If the Silver Shrew is the culprit, you've solved the case. Assuming she stole the books..." His smile faded. "And did everything else."

"The books," said Cordelia. Of course. "That's what she was doing in the garage. The Shrew was looking for the books."

"The books in the barbecue?"

"That's right. I'd just told her and Howdy Doody I could guarantee the return of the books by the end of the week."

"So..." said Alfie thoughtfully. He reached into his pocket, took out a battered-looking spliff and ignited it. "So... she was the one who put the books in the barbecue."

"Right," said Cordelia. "And she thought they were safely hidden there."

"Then when you said you'd got them, she raced over here to check if it was true." Alfie breathed out dope smoke. It seemed to be helping him with problem-solving, despite all the propaganda to the contrary.

"That's it," said Cordelia, feeling another tiny piece of the puzzle fit into place. "I'd better be going. I said I'd meet Edwin."

"Can I give you a lift to the ashram?" said Alfie.

"No thanks, the traffic is…"

"Diabolical, I heard you telling him. Well, if you don't mind then, I'll stay here." Alfie looked back towards the kitchen. "And make myself something else to have with my saffron rice."

28: WET SHOES

Cordelia walked happily up Putney Hill. It was a wonderful sensation to be on foot again after her nightmare bicycle odyssey.

She was thinking that, if the traffic situation was better at the top of the hill, she might catch a 337. But the traffic situation wasn't better at the top of the hill and even contemplating catching a bus was madness, so she abided by her original plan and went into the railway station.

When her train pulled in, after a longish wait on a crowded platform, Cordelia hopped on it and managed to bag her favourite seat. She settled down for the brief, three-minute journey to Barnes station. As she relaxed and watched the scenery whip past, she realised that she needed to go to the loo quite badly and, indeed, had needed to for some time.

No problem. As soon as she got off the train at Barnes, she hotfooted it into the thickly forested section of the common that lay between the station and the main road. Ideal wee-in-the-woods territory. Cordelia was quite alone so, as soon as she saw a suitably comfortable and concealed spot, she left the footpath and disappeared between trees and bushes.

Birds sang on the branches above her; she heard the slithering scramble and territorial squawking of a squirrel high up on a trunk;

in the far-off distance there was the faint roar of cars on the road. Cordelia slipped out of her shoes—her cherished, natty Ecco two-strap black slip-on trainers—and took a step or two back from them, so there was no danger of them getting splashed; not that such a thing had ever happened to her, of course.

Absolutely not.

Categorically not.

Never.

And then, shoes safely distant, she unzipped her jeans, pulled down her knickers and bent down to squat on her heels and... blessed relief.

One reason that humans tend to associate bodily functions with shame, and demand privacy, is because it is at such moments that we are particularly vulnerable.

Cordelia had occasion to reflect on this as she heard, from nowhere, the abrupt, brisk crunching of someone approaching through the undergrowth. Whoever it was didn't seem to merely be passing by, or just be in the general vicinity or something. Instead, it appeared they were coming directly and deliberately at her.

Cordelia, spooked, told herself not to be silly, but nonetheless finished quickly, stood up, pulled her knickers back on and reached down to tug up her jeans—

Just as a figure came hurtling out of the trees towards her.

Cordelia's first, panicked thought—that she was being attacked by a pervert (not the late Mac)—was almost instantly replaced by the realisation she was being attacked by the Silver Shrew.

The Shrew was dressed in baggy orange trousers, a quilted jacket of a slightly paler shade of orange and bulbous hiking boots. She wore sunglasses, her silver hair was scraped back in a bun and, on her back, she had a rucksack—orange, of course, with an Om symbol on it.

Which seemed inappropriate because the Shrew was pulling out of it a savage-looking device that consisted of a long, thin cable with a gleaming cylindrical chromed weight on the end of it. As the Shrew held this over her head and set it whirling in a worrying-looking blur of savagely whistling metal, Cordelia's brain helpfully identified it as that loose part of the wind chimes from the peace garden, which had recently been dangling so annoyingly.

Now adapted as a lethal weapon.

Just how lethal was vividly demonstrated as the Shrew brought the spinning metal weight down on the spot where Cordelia had been an instant earlier and it bit deep into a fallen log with a wet chopping sound, slicing away the dark bark and revealing the pale wood underneath, deeply gouged.

Meanwhile Cordelia was scrambling to pull on her jeans, which were still currently around her ankles. Not something that's easy to accomplish while also trying to run for your life. As the Shrew pulled the metal weight out of the log and set it spinning again, closing in on Cordelia, Cordelia thought *fuck it* and abandoned any attempt to pull on her jeans and simply slithered the rest of the way out of them and ran, leaving them lying there, abandoned on the ground with her shoes.

She ran through the woods, barefoot and wearing only her knickers (and admittedly her top), fleeing half-naked through the underbrush, pursued by a remorseless killer with an unusual weapon, just like a stupid girl in a horror movie. Cordelia liked to flatter herself by thinking she wasn't stupid, though.

That was when she realised that, by abandoning her jeans, she'd also abandoned her keys and, more importantly in the current situation, her only weapon. The killer dildo.

Oh, fuck.

So, as she ran, she began to frantically look for a suitable replacement weapon. A fallen branch, handily club-sized, suggested itself for this purpose. Cordelia scooped it up, only to have the rotten wood fall apart in her hands. She dropped it and resumed running. The pause for the treacherous branch had lost her precious fractions of a second and the Shrew was disconcertingly close on her heels now; close enough for Cordelia to hear the distinctive whistling of the chrome pipe as it scythed in a circle over the Shrew's head, as if signalling its eagerness to be deployed in Cordelia's direction.

Equally eager for this not to happen, Cordelia changed direction, leaving the primitive trace of a footpath she'd been following and crashing through some dense foliage into a clearing where, lying in a patch of sunlight as though put on display especially for her approval, was another usefully club-sized branch.

A sucker for punishment, Cordelia snatched this up, fully expecting it to be as (literally) rotten and useless as the last one. But, to her satisfaction, it was a solid, hard and weighty length of wood. Cordelia stopped running and, holding it clutched in her sweaty hands, turned and waited.

She didn't have to wait for long.

The Shrew came blundering through the bushes into the clearing, spinning the chrome wind chime above her head. She came to a sudden, screeching stop, startled to find that Cordelia was no longer fleeing her but facing her.

And holding a fair-sized wooden club, which she now threw in the Shrew's face with satisfying accuracy, so the Shrew had to fling her hands in front of her face to protect it. And, in doing so, released the spinning metal weight that, thanks to its rotational momentum or radial velocity or whatever you call it, went shooting away to disappear into the woods.

When the Shrew realised she'd lost her weapon, she gave a forlorn little yelp that in different circumstances—very different circumstances—might have been touching. Cordelia didn't stick around to be touched, in any sense of the word, and instead turned and fled back the way she'd come.

She felt positively undressed without her jeans and shoes, and she headed smartly back to collect these. Behind her, she could hear the Shrew blundering through the boscage in search of her flown-away weapon.

But her chances of finding it were agreeably miniscule. Or, from the Shrew's point of view, disagreeably miniscule.

The Shrew must also have realised this because, a moment later, Cordelia heard her abandon the search and head her way again. Of course, the Shrew might not have *abandoned* her search.

She might have *succeeded* in it...

That didn't bear thinking about. Anyway, by now, Cordelia was back at the spot where she'd deserted her garments and was hastily tugging on her jeans.

She'd accomplished this assignment but annoyingly hadn't yet had time to slip her shoes back on when the Shrew reappeared.

The good news was that the Shrew had not found and retrieved her lethal wind chime bolero. (No, wait a minute, it wasn't a bolero. What was such a weapon called? A bola. Not Ebola. *A* bola.).

The bad news was that, as soon as she spotted Cordelia, the Shrew reached into her Om rucksack and took out something new.

It looked like a fat wooden truncheon or billy club, until Cordelia recognised it as one of the stakes from the peace garden used to separate tiers of pebbles into neat zen islands.

It was interesting how a garden dedicated to peace was proving such a rich source of deadly weapons.

Potentially deadly weapons.

Instead of fleeing again, Cordelia was now standing her ground, with her back to a big, friendly tree. Which was almost a very bad mistake, because the Shrew lunged at her with no warning and with remarkable swiftness (yoga was very good for the reflexes), swinging the wooden stake.

It came down, a whisker away from Cordelia's head, with a crushing smash against the trunk of the big, friendly tree.

But Cordelia also did yoga, and her reflexes were pretty good too. By the time the Shrew had swung at her and missed, Cordelia had pulled the killer dildo out of her pocket and hit the Shrew in the head with it.

Exactly as Edwin had shown her.

29: BACK AT THE ASHRAM

The Shrew made a sound compounded of horror, pain and what Cordelia could only describe as intense disappointment, as if hitting her with the killer dildo had been a flagrant violation of the rules of engagement.

Then the Shrew reeled away from her, crashing off through the undergrowth, clutching her head. Cordelia stood there for a moment, catching her breath. After that, finally, she put her shoes back on.

When she was quite sure the Shrew was nowhere nearby and wasn't about to spring out at her, she set off.

When Cordelia got to the ashram, Edwin and Howdy Doody were waiting for her in the peace garden. They got up from the bench where they'd been sitting, then sat back down with her between them. After her recent adventures, Cordelia rather appreciated the comforting presence of a tall man on either side of her.

The first words out of Howdy Doody's mouth were, "I didn't believe you."

"Then why did you change your mind?" said Cordelia, for clearly he had.

Howdy gave a deep and rather heart-rending sigh. "I went

and looked in Gunadya's office. I looked on her computer. Do you know what I found?"

"Lots of research about poisons," said Cordelia.

Howdy nodded sadly. "Yes. And not just that. She's been embezzling the ashram's funds. She's done her best to empty our account."

"It's lucky it was frozen, then," said Cordelia. But, as soon as she said the words, she realised the truth. "Your bank account wasn't frozen, was it?"

"No—was that what she told you?"

"Yes. That was supposedly why she couldn't pay me."

"I'm afraid I don't know when we will be able to pay you," said Howdy. He sounded as though he was going to cry.

To change the subject, and thereby avoid this embarrassing prospect—and also because she'd just spotted the wind chimes with their missing component, recently adopted for the Shrew's bola of death—she told Howdy and Edwin about her skirmish on Barnes Common.

"You may want to tell the police that was the last place she was seen."

"I will," said Howdy Doody, standing up. "I've already given them her description and a description of the ashram's van."

"Has she taken that, then?" said Cordelia. Gaudy and highly distinctive, it wasn't the ideal choice for an escape vehicle.

Howdy nodded and turned to go, then turned back. "I just don't understand how she could do it," he said. He seemed like a little lost boy. He looked all around him. "The ashram was her whole life. She was completely dedicated to it."

"I didn't want to say so in front of him," said Cordelia. "But I think that's exactly why she did it."

"How's that?" said Edwin. He was driving the two of them back home, heading along Vine Road.

Cordelia said, "The Shrew did it precisely *because* she'd dedicated her whole life to the ashram." She glanced at Edwin, who was concentrating on slowing down for a cyclist. "But I couldn't explain that, since I couldn't tell Howdy that Alfie is actually Avram Silverlight. It's not my place to blow his cover."

"But you think the Shrew knew," said Edwin. "You think his cover was blown to her?"

"Yes, and I reckon it was Joni who blew it," said Cordelia, beginning to wish she hadn't used the word "blown" in connection with Joni and Alfie. "Joni knew who Alfie was. She was sworn to secrecy and she kept the secret for a long time. But, in the end, I think she spilled the beans to the Shrew."

"Why?" said Edwin.

"Because Joni was desperate to start teaching at the ashram and be awarded her Sanskrit name and all that. Pathetic, but there you go."

"Not pathetic to her," said Edwin.

"Yes, well that's it exactly. It was her little dream. Poor Joni. And the Shrew had got her hopes up by saying that Joni might get her wish on the ashram's anniversary." Cordelia remembered the argument Joni and the Shrew had had in the yoga lesson. "I should have paid more attention when I heard that."

"Why?" said Edwin again. They were approaching the first railway crossing and, ever the cautious driver, he slowed down once more.

"The paperbacks were stolen the day after the anniversary. Or rather, the robbery was *discovered* the day after. Thinking about it, they were probably stolen on the night of the anniversary itself."

"What are you thinking?" said Edwin.

Cordelia was actually thinking about how Joni had said to the Shrew, *"I explained to you. I explained everything."* It had seemed significant at the time, but she'd had no idea why. Now she did. "I think when the anniversary arrived and the Shrew didn't give Joni what she wanted, Joni cracked."

"And she told the Shrew who Alfie really is?"

"Yes," said Cordelia. "She told the Shrew the truth about her beloved ashram, to which—as Howdy Doody said—she had dedicated her life. Joni revealed that the saintly man who had founded the place not only wasn't dead and safely canonised, he was actually this impertinent, fornicating reprobate whom the Shrew despised. And the Shrew flipped out. That would explain not only stealing the paperbacks but also her so-called 'dirty protest', literally spreading shit around the place."

"Desecrating what had once been holy," said Edwin.

"Exactly," said Cordelia. They'd got past the first railway crossing but had been caught at the second one, with barriers descending. Now, while they sat waiting for the train to pass, she took out her phone and called Alfie.

"What's happening?" he said.

"Well, I was just almost killed by the Shrew," said Cordelia.

"Holy fuck…"

Cordelia gave a brief account of recent events and then said, "But that's not what I'm calling about. I wanted to ask where you were the night the paperbacks were stolen."

"Why, am I still under suspicion?" said Alfie.

"No," said Cordelia.

"Well, I was at a gig."

"Black Midi?" said Cordelia.

"No, it was Wet Leg this time. Do you need proof?"

"Not at all," said Cordelia.

"Pity, because I've got some great selfies."

"Just one other question," said Cordelia. "Was Hank staying in your house at the time?"

"Yup."

"Could he have been there while you were away at the gig?"

"Yes, definitely," said Alfie. "Never a great concertgoer, old Hank."

"Okay, thanks."

"Do you want to tell me what this is all about?"

"I'll fill you in when I know for sure," said Cordelia. They said their goodbyes and she hung up.

The train rumbled past, the barriers rose and Edwin drove on. "So what have you learned?" he said.

"I was thinking about where I found the books," said Cordelia.

"In the barbecue?"

"Yes, the significance hadn't clicked before. But there they were, stacked in a barbecue, with a can of lighter fluid and one of those things you use to make a spark and start a fire."

"Start a fire…" said Edwin. He was beginning to see it, too.

"That's right."

"You think someone was planning a book-burning?"

"Yes," said Cordelia. "I'm working out the timeline. The Shrew does the robbery, she goes to Alfie's house, planning to burn his beloved books in front of him."

"In revenge," said Edwin.

"That's right, in revenge for what she saw as a betrayal of her values and ideals and, in fact, her whole life. So she puts them on the barbecue with the burning materials, all ready to go and torch them before his very eyes. Just one problem…"

"Alfie wasn't at home," said Edwin.

"Correct," said Cordelia. "But Hank was."

"And you think Hank saw the Shrew?"

"Yes," said Cordelia. "When she realised Alfie wasn't at home, she took off. But not before Hank registered her visit. And either then or later, he discovered the books in the garage."

"Which meant he knew that she'd committed the robbery," said Edwin.

"That's right," said Cordelia. "And he arranged a little meeting with her on the common. Just the two of them and a bottle of expensive whisky."

"And he was going to blackmail her?"

"One thing I haven't mentioned," said Cordelia, "partly because it's so implausible, is that Hank quite fancied the Shrew."

"And therefore he would agree to stay silent about the robbery in exchange for sexual favours?"

"Don't look now, because you're driving," said Cordelia. "But I'm shuddering."

Edwin chuckled. "In that case, she would have had a right to defend herself," he said.

"I agree, and although I wouldn't want Hank to have his head smashed in with a whisky bottle, my sympathies would have been or her side…"

"If it had been a one-off act of self-defence," said Edwin.

"Yes," said Cordelia. "Instead of the start of a killing spree."

30: GRASS WIDOW

You wouldn't have thought it would be too difficult for the police to apprehend a small person in bright orange clothing driving a bright orange van with a bright red Om symbol on it. But nonetheless the Shrew seemed to have eluded capture.

"She's slipped through the net," said Cordelia.

"I'm not sure the police can even afford a net," said Edwin, "after a succession of Conservative governments."

In any case, it was hard for Cordelia to feel entirely secure with the Shrew at large, given that this personage had tried to kill her on three (count them) separate occasions.

So when it came time to go to Richmond to collect the books she'd bought from Betty Fairwell, Cordelia took Edwin with her. And Rainbottle. They drove over and dropped Cordelia at the widow's house and then, having seen her safely inside, Edwin took his keen canine for a leisurely walk.

Betty Fairwell greeted Cordelia at the door and graciously accepted the return of her borrowed bathrobe (freshly laundered) with a merciful lack of comment. Then they retired, as was becoming traditional, to the sitting room, where Cordelia's heart began to beat a little faster at the sight of the bags containing her beloved John D. MacDonald paperbacks. She paid Betty what she owed—in cash, of course—and, as the widow carefully counted it, quite without embarrassment, Cordelia reciprocally opened the bags and checked their contents.

Then they both relaxed.

Cordelia watched as Betty Fairwell began not drinking lager for once but, rather surprisingly, smoking weed. Or grass, as she called it. "Would you like a hit?" she said, offering Cordelia a very neatly rolled joint.

Cordelia declined for reasons of wanting to keep a clear head in case someone tried to assassinate her.

"It's really good grass," said Betty. "Are you sure?"

"Yes, thanks." Cordelia watched the widow fondly as she smoked, and came to a sudden decision. Before she could change her mind, Cordelia reached into the bag containing both copies of *Weep for Me* and took them out. "There's something I have to tell you," she said.

Betty Fairwell gave her an odd look, as well she might.

"You see these books?" said Cordelia, rather redundantly because, even if the widow was smoking cannabis for glaucoma, she would have had no trouble seeing them at this distance. "They're very rare."

"Really? Well, good for you."

"No," said Cordelia. "I mean really rare."

"And why's that?" said Betty.

"Because John D. MacDonald suppressed the book. He forbade his publisher from reprinting it after these two editions."

"That seems rather a silly thing to do."

"It was," said Cordelia. "You see, he thought it wasn't up to his usual high standard and that it was derivative."

"And was it?" said Betty Fairwell.

"Well, it's a classic noir story in the manner of James M. Cain. But I think it's absolutely brilliant."

"And he was wrong to suppress it?"

"Yes, he was," said Cordelia. "But the point is, these copies are worth a lot of money."

The widow's eyebrows made an attractive shape of enquiry. "Really? How much?"

Cordelia took a deep breath. "A lot more than I've paid you for them," she said.

"How much more?"

Cordelia looked at the books in her lap. "Well, they're both in fine condition..." She picked up the second printing, Gold Medal 884, with its Barye Phillips cover art. "This one is worth at least 100 quid. Maybe 200..." She set it aside and picked up, gingerly and delicately, the first printing, Gold Medal 200, which featured a virtually identical cover painting, but this one by Owen Kampen. "And this one, which is a true first printing... It's worth..." She repressed the impulse—microscopically but reprehensibly present—to lie and said, "If it goes to auction, maybe as much as a thousand.

"A thousand? Good heavens." Betty Fairwell took the book from Cordelia and examined it. Then her gaze flicked upwards and met Cordelia's, her rather lovely eyes with their vastly dilated, stoned pupils. "And do you intend to auction it?"

"Hell no," said Cordelia fervently. "They're both going into my library and staying there."

Betty smiled and gave her back the book. Cordelia wiped her hands before she took it—a shameful sweat had sprung out on them at the thought of losing these beauties.

"In that case you must have them."

"How much more would you like me to pay you for them?"

The widow gave her an ironic assessing look as she puffed daintily at her joint. Finally she said, "Not a penny."

"Really?"

"Consider it a reward for your honesty."

"Well, that's a first," said Cordelia. And they both laughed.

"I find it interesting, by the way, that you refer to it as your library," said Betty.

"What else would I call it?" said Cordelia, putting the books away with great care.

"Your book collection. That's what Duncan always called his."

"Well, a collection is something you put away and never look at," said Cordelia, after a moment's thought. "A library is something that's constantly in use."

"Well put," said Betty Fairwell.

What Cordelia had first intended to say was that a library is alive while a collection is dead. But she felt a little hesitant to use a word like "dead" in front of the recently bereaved. "By the way," she said, "how are you doing?"

"Oh, you know," said Betty, moving her hand in the air as if writing with the smoke of the joint.

"I never asked you…" said Cordelia, taking the plunge. "How did Duncan die?"

Of the various reactions she might have anticipated from the widow, a joyful burst of mirth would not have been high on the list.

But that's what she got.

When she stopped laughing, Betty Fairwell said, "Oh, Duncan's not *dead*. When I said I'd lost him, I merely meant he'd run off with one of the floozies he hired to work in his shop."

"My god, really?"

"Yes, they've fled to Ibiza, where no doubt they're both dancing to pounding techno music and having sex on the beach while he pursues the will-o'-the-wisp of his midlife crisis. Wait, do I mean will-o'-the-wisp?"

"As good a term as any," said Cordelia. "Do you think he'll come crawling back to you?"

"If he does," said Betty, "he'll find both his book collection and wine cellar sadly depleted."

She laughed merrily, fragrant, illegal smoke spilling from her pretty little nostrils.

EPILOGUE: POIROT AND WALKIES

The Royal Mail had a statutory obligation to deliver 93 per cent of first-class letters by the following day. Now, being a privatised shit show, they constantly failed to meet this obligation.

So, for *second*-class letters the understanding was that they would be delivered some time before the heat death of the universe.

That wasn't the exact wording, but it might as well have been...

Anyway, the second-class letter from Joni, so helpfully posted by Mr T, did eventually turn up. But, by then, not only was Joni herself out of hospital, but so was Carrie, and the Silver Shrew had been arrested—in North Africa, of all places—and was awaiting deportation or extradition or whatever you called it.

From these various sources, Cordelia had assembled a fairly comprehensive picture of what had actually happened. So, one gleaming morning when rain showers were alternating with brilliant October sunshine, she set out with Edwin and Rainbottle on a walk.

And also to complete a small but long overdue task...

"All right," said Cordelia. "Now, this is like the bit at the end of a Poirot novel in which he explains exactly what happened. With the difference that there won't be a dramatic last-minute unmasking and nabbing of a culprit."

Rainbottle made a small sound as if to indicate his relief at this. He walked at their side as they crossed the village green, steering well clear of the duck pond to avoid undesirable bird-chasing. "Fire away," said Edwin.

"Okay, so let's establish a timeline."

"Establish away."

"I suppose," said Cordelia, "that everything starts way back in the 1960s when a young Alfie Silbert steals a Rolling Stones record and is banged up as a consequence."

"That's a rather harsh punishment for stealing a record."

"He committed a break-in to get hold of it," said Cordelia.

"That's pretty extreme," said Edwin.

"That's our Alfie. And then, because it's the only book in the prison library—or, rather, the borstal library—he reads about yoga and discovers his true calling in life. Then, under the pseudonym of Avram Silverlight, he writes a series of bestsellers drenched in drugs and murky mysticism. Using some of the proceeds from these, he establishes the Silverlight Yoga Centre, which we all know and love. Then, a decade or two later, he drops out of the picture, ceasing to attend the ashram, and people eventually assume he's dead."

"All right," said Edwin.

"Meanwhile, out there somewhere, a young and impressionable (and not yet Silver) Shrew discovers the works of Avram Silverlight, avidly devours them and experiences a road to Damascus moment. She's discovered her true calling. She will devote her life to yoga and she makes a pilgrimage to the Silverlight Yoga Centre. Over the years, starting at a lowly level, she works her way to the top at the ashram. All the while thinking that Avram Silverlight's books are the gospel truth, so to speak, and the reverend Avram himself is nobly dead."

"Got it," said Edwin.

Rainbottle murmured as if he, too, got it.

"Now, things really start to happen a couple of years ago when Alfie, aka Avram, who is very much not dead, decides to start attending yoga lessons at the ashram again."

"Incognito," said Edwin.

"Absolutely incognito."

"And, of course, no one remembers or recognises him."

"Most of them not having been born when he was last there," said Cordelia. "But he makes quite an impression on his first visit. People take note of his ratty old yoga mat and also the fact he roars with laughter when he's told by Joni-behind-the-counter that his first lesson there is free."

"Because, of course, it wasn't his first lesson there," said Edwin. "Not by a considerable margin."

They were now approaching the little bridge across Beverley Brook and Rainbottle began to surge ahead, restrained only by his orange retractable lead.

"He impresses everybody with his yoga skills," said Cordelia. "And he begins attending the centre regularly, having rediscovered his taste for it. He becomes a familiar figure there, quite a popular figure, though certain people on the staff are appalled by his Rabelaisian, not to mention proletarian, character. Namely the Silver Shrew, who really doesn't like him. But apart from the fact that she finds him distasteful for being insolent, bawdy and charming, she doesn't have any real grounds to get rid of him. She can't boot him out, because his behaviour is actually exemplary."

"Until the Christmas party," said Edwin.

"Right. Which is when it all really begins to kick off."

Cordelia and Rainbottle and Edwin had now reached the bridge, and Rainbottle made his traditional attempt to break away, head down the bank and jump in the water. At least it was traditional whenever there was another dog splashing in the brook, which there was now. Two of them, in fact.

"At some time during the party, Alfie slips away and goes upstairs to the ashram office to reminisce," said Cordelia as Edwin firmly steered Rainbottle away from the amphibious mutts and made him walk across the bridge like a good dog. "And Joni goes upstairs, finds Alfie and gives him a bollocking. 'What are you doing in here, you don't belong in here' sort of thing."

"But, of course, he does belong in there," said Edwin. They were safely across the bridge now, away from watery temptation, and Rainbottle overcame his disappointment and began happily snuffling at the alley as they walked along it.

"Exactly," said Cordelia. "He probably belongs there more than anyone else. And he decides to reveal who he really is. First by showing her his tattoo, as also seen in a photo on the wall, and then, when she's still sceptical, by opening the safe. This is the wall safe, behind some drapes. Only the Silver Shrew ever uses it and the only other person who has the combination is Howdy Doody. So, when Alfie just casually opens it, Joni opens her..."

"*Heart* to him," said Edwin. He really was an old romantic. He reeled Rainbottle in a little closer as they approached the end of the alley and the busy road ahead.

"And they're in the middle of this, ah, heart-to-heart encounter," said Cordelia, "when the Silver Shrew comes in, presumably wondering what's taking Joni so long and eager to take advantage of the chance to give her hell, which she enjoys doing to her underlings at every possible opportunity."

"And she walks in on them," said Edwin.

They paused and waited for a gap in the traffic, then sauntered across the road and into the trees. Which was very nearly the title of a Hemingway novel.

"Catches them in flagrante, yes. And she's outraged, as only a Shrew can be. She immediately demotes poor Joni, who was about to become a full-blown, no pun intended, yoga instructor at the ashram with a Sanskrit name and everything. She also tries to take action against Alfie and boot him out. But Howdy Doody overrules her because Alfie has promised to give them a big, fat cash gift in his will. And money talks."

"Unfortunately, it does," said Edwin. They'd emerged from the trees and crossed a second, far less busy road, and were back in the trees again. Not just trees but all sorts of bushes and undergrowth. Wait, was that *Cannabis sativa* growing there? Cordelia would have paused to check it out if Rainbottle hadn't been happily hurtling ahead, Edwin allowing him a lot of play on the lead now as they left the traffic safely behind.

"Now most of this we knew before," said Cordelia. "What we didn't know was Carrie's role in the whole thing. For a start, believe it or not, Carrie had set about making friends with the Shrew. They'd always been on civil terms but, when Carrie heard about Alfie's will, she began a major charm offensive on the Shrew. Because Carrie thought he was giving money to the ashram when she felt he should be giving it to *her*. So she sets about trying to enlist the Shrew in a conspiracy."

"A conspiracy?" said Edwin. Rainbottle had now dragged them out of the trees and onto the big, open field where people sometimes played cricket or sat on the benches smoking dope. Only one of these activities appealed to Cordelia, but neither was taking place at the moment.

"That's right," said Cordelia. "Carrie wants Alfie's money for herself, but she's willing to split it with the Silver Shrew, especially since the Shrew—as the ashram's financial officer—is the perfect person to syphon off the funds."

"You mean embezzlement?" said Edwin.

"It's an ugly word," said Cordelia. And they both chuckled. "And at first," continued Cordelia, "the Shrew refuses to even consider such a plan. Like Howdy Doody told us, the ashram was her whole life. She certainly wasn't going to steal from it."

"But that changed," said Edwin.

They'd now crossed the field and were approaching the footpath to Barnes railway station.

"That did indeed change," said Cordelia. "Ironically enough, on the ashram's anniversary. The Shrew had promised Joni that her time of disgrace would come to an end on that day. That's what Joni says, and I believe her. I also believe her when she says the Shrew reneged on her promise. That would be a totally Shrew-like thing to do. And when she does so, Joni is desperate. She thinks she'll never get her Sanskrit name or get to teach students. Naturally she begs the Shrew to reconsider. And, in desperation, she tells the Shrew who Alfie really is, thinking that will make all the difference."

"Very unwise," said Edwin.

"Well, Joni wasn't wrong about the news having a big impact on the Shrew. Unfortunately, it was the wrong kind of impact. At first, of course, she doesn't believe Joni. But Joni tells her how Alfie opened the safe and, crucially, she's able to describe the contents of the safe. Which convinces the Shrew. In a state of shock, she orders Joni out of her office, still officially in disgrace, and tries to process the information. This fornicating, disrespectful and filthy rich Alfie Silbert is actually her beloved, holy and pristinely pure Avram Silverlight. Not surprisingly, her little Shrew brain can't handle the cognitive dissonance."

They'd now reached the station and were going up the steps that led over the tracks, Rainbottle happily scrambling up them.

"So the Shrew flips out," said Cordelia. "And *lashes* out. In a state of mind that a professional psychotherapist might label 'totally bananas'. "

"Excellent use of technical terminology," said Edwin.

"Thank you. And, after the ashram is closed that night, the Shrew attacks the very books that made her what she is. She tears the Avram Silverlight paperbacks off the shelf, in such a hurry that she scoops up the other books along with them. Possibly she's in a hurry because she has just treated the meeting room like a squat toilet."

"Good lord," murmured Edwin.

"Then, hopefully having first paused to wipe her bottom, she stashes the other books somewhere and takes the precious Avram Silverlight ones to Alfie's house, intending to burn them before his very eyes. Unfortunately for the Shrew, his eyes are elsewhere that night, at a Wet Leg gig, in fact. So she leaves the books hidden in the barbecue in the garage, ready for burning at a later date, and goes away again."

"But she doesn't go away unseen," said Edwin.

They paused on the footbridge to watch a fast train hurtle past underneath them.

"No," said Cordelia, after the train had rattled out of sight— and hearing. "Hank Honeywell is aware of her visit and is also aware of the books in the garage. But he doesn't tell anyone about this because he's planning to use the information as part of a campaign to—I can hardly believe I'm saying this—seduce the Silver Shrew."

"A fatal decision for Hank, as it turns out," said Edwin.

Another train was approaching below them but this one was slowing to a stop.

"Yes," said Cordelia, "though that was still a little while away and a number of significant things would happen in the meantime. For a start, the Shrew disposes of the other paperbacks at the charity shop. And she has a heart-to-heart with Carrie. The Shrew does *not* reveal she's stolen the books or committed an intestinal indiscretion at the ashram. But she does indicate, quite clearly, that she's now willing to listen to Carrie's plan to steal Alfie's money."

"As revenge on him," said Edwin.

Passengers who'd alighted from the train were streaming up the steps and past them, a significant percentage smiling at Rainbottle or making a passing fuss over him. Rainbottle, acknowledging their attention, began to thump his tail in appreciation.

"Very much as revenge on him," said Cordelia. "They both have reasons to hate Alfie. So Carrie and the Shrew dream up a scheme to steal the money he plans to leave to the ashram in his will. In fact, they're going to use it to flee to Morocco together and set up a cooking school, of all things."

"Which explains why the Shrew chose North Africa as her destination when she did make a run for it," said Edwin.

"I imagine so," said Cordelia. "She was still following the old itinerary, although everything else had changed. But before everything changed, while she and Carrie were cooking up their scheme again, no pun intended—they were both blithely ignoring the elephant in the room."

"To get their hands on the money," said Edwin, "Alfie would have to die."

"Exactly right. Unless they wanted to sit around for years waiting for their scheme to come to fruition, and as neither of them were the patient type, they were going to have to hasten Alfie's demise."

"They were planning not just a robbery," said Edwin, "but a murder."

"They were indeed." Cordelia stared at a distant, decorative cloud formation above the railway tracks that stretched towards Richmond. "It's open to debate whether the Shrew was explicitly and consciously signing up for murder at this point, but she'd be explicitly and consciously signing up for it pretty bloody soon. 'Bloody' being the operative word."

"After her encounter with Hank Honeywell on the common."

"That's right," said Cordelia. "But the course of true robbery and murder do not run smooth, to adapt an old quotation."

"It's Shakespeare, actually," said Edwin. "From *A Midsummer Night's Dream*." Edwin knew this sort of stuff.

"Cool," said Cordelia. "Anyway, a complication was about to arise for Carrie and the Shrew. Because as soon as Alfie learned of the robbery it was his turn to flip out. He told the ashram that, if they didn't recover the books, they could forget about inheriting a penny from him. Which put the cat among the pigeons. Is that from Shakespeare?" said Cordelia.

"I have no idea," said Edwin.

"So Howdy and the Shrew had to find the books."

"And that's where you came in." Edwin smiled.

"And that's where I came in. Of course, the Shrew knew where the books were all the time. But she had to pretend she didn't, and to look like she was as desperate to find them as Howdy Doody. And, when the suggestion arose to hire me, she couldn't very well object. She just had to grin and bear it. While no doubt grinding her grinning teeth. But the last thing she expected was for me to find the books, at least not without a lengthy and difficult search. Which meant she could afford to agree to hiring me. And even to paying me an advance. She thought she had plenty of time to work out what to do."

"But then Hank came on the scene."

"Right. Hank invited the Shrew out on the common for a cosy little chat, with added single malt whisky. He may not have been explicitly planning to blackmail the Shrew…"

"But that's what it amounted to," said Edwin.

"Certainly from the Shrew's point of view," said Cordelia. "And though Hank might have had some notion of—yeck—a romantic interlude ensuing, what he got instead was a bottle broken over his head."

"And death by blunt force trauma," said Edwin.

At their feet, Rainbottle whined.

"As we've said before," said Cordelia, "up to this point Hank is more blameworthy than the Shrew. But all that's about to change, because killing Hank seems to unlock something in the Silver Shrew. I'm not saying it was an instant thing, or even that she was especially aware of it at first. For instance, when she left that note in my pigeonhole, asking me to meet her at the abandoned hospital. She said in the note that she wanted to return the books. And I think that, at first, she might actually have intended to give the books to me. After all, I was a useful conduit by which she could return them anonymously. For instance, just by leaving them on that bench where we were supposed to rendezvous."

"Good idea," conceded Edwin.

"But, at some point, her thinking changed," said Cordelia. "After all, she'd already killed Hank. And…"

"In for a penny, in for a pound," said Edwin.

"That's right. She had nothing to lose. But I believe it was more than that. I think she'd begun to get a taste for it. A taste she indulged by trying to kill me with a falling block of concrete—thank you again for saving me, by the way."

"Very much my pleasure," said Edwin.

"Now things start to accelerate," said Cordelia. "And get out of control for the Shrew, because I tell her and Howdy Doody I can guarantee that I'll return the books in a day or two. Rattled by my quiet confidence, the Shrew hastens over to Alfie's garage to look at the books in the barbecue. Only to discover that not only are the books now gone…"

"So is the barbecue," said Edwin. "We really must return that."

"Alfie says no hurry," said Cordelia. "Anyway, the Shrew is now in a very ticklish position. Because she no longer has control of the books. She realises I wasn't bluffing and that I really do have them. And, though I didn't know it at the time, this puts me in a very secure position."

Edwin thought for a moment and then said, "Because, while you have the books, she doesn't dare harm you."

"Right first time," said Cordelia. "It was a brief golden age during which I was completely safe, at least from the Shrew. But it ended as soon as I handed the books over at the ashram. That cleared the way for her to go after me again."

"And why would she want to go after you again?" said Edwin.

"Revenge, chiefly," said Cordelia. "Though, by this time, I don't think she needed an excuse anymore. She was up for obliterating anyone who pissed her off. However, by this time, she also had another complication to deal with."

"Mac at the charity shop with his VHS tape," said Edwin.

Although there was nothing in Edwin's tone of voice to cause it, Rainbottle chose this moment to give a sad and eerie little whine. He rose up suddenly and shook himself, looking at them with beseeching eyes. It was clearly time to resume their walk.

"Poor Mac," said Cordelia as they crossed the footbridge and descended the steps, leaving the station behind and heading onto Barnes Common. "When I told the ashram idiots I'd found the books, I intimated I'd found all of them. So, when the Shrew realised I wasn't bluffing, she knew I must have found the charity shop. Which was potentially bad news for her, since someone might be able to identify her as the person who'd donated the books."

"As indeed we nearly did," said Edwin.

"Not nearly enough. The Shrew scurried over there and, on the basis that the best lies should contain as much truth as possible, told them she worked at the yoga centre, that some books had been stolen and they were trying to identify the culprit, so did the shop have anything like a security camera which might be helpful? And someone—I'm sure it was good old Lipstick Teeth—told her about the VHS set-up and that, in fact, Mac had just taken a tape home with him. They even very helpfully gave Mac's address to the Shrew, so she could get to him before us and feed him some poisoned curry." Cordelia looked at Edwin. "I think, by now, the Shrew was starting to lose it. She was becoming what Dashiell Hammett, long before the Coen brothers, called blood simple. After all, she was taking a ridiculous risk. There was now someone at the charity shop who could identify her and connect her with the murdered Mac."

Edwin shook his head. "You'd like to think so. But I've made some enquiries and, when Mac's body was discovered, the authorities weren't even inclined to treat his death as suspicious." Edwin sounded disappointed. He was, after all, except in his own personal sphere, a firm believer in law and order.

"So Mac is dead," said Cordelia. "Hank Honeywell is dead, and the Shrew has got it in for me. But, meanwhile, there's this conspiracy against Alfie ticking away. With the Shrew and Carrie in league to rob the ashram of his inheritance."

"And hasten his demise to enable that, presumably," said Edwin.

"Absolutely," said Cordelia. "And as soon as I returned the books and Alfie reinstated the ashram in his will, Carrie and the Shrew could roll forward with their plans. Unfortunately for them, Carrie had a lodger with big ears."

"Joni," said Edwin.

"Yes." Cordelia paused for a moment to get her bearings. They were on the tarmac footpath that cut through the common. Cordelia seldom took this route, invariably leaving it to cut through the woods. Now, where had she left it last time?

"And though Joni didn't hear everything," said Cordelia, "she heard enough to want to get in touch with me. But, before she could come to me, the Shrew realised what she was up to and went after her."

"Knocking her off her bike and knocking her on her head," said Edwin.

"Apparently she used the ashram van to do it," said Cordelia. "The Shrew really does love that van. And with Joni out of the way, at least temporarily, I shoot to the top of the Shrew's hit list. And when I'm indiscreet enough to tell Alfie about the party on the houseboat in Richmond, and when he's indiscreet enough to tell Carrie, and Carrie tells the Shrew, the Shrew sees an ideal opportunity to have another go at getting rid of me."

Cordelia realised they'd gone too far along the footpath but, instead of turning around and heading back along it, she decided they might as well strike out into the woods here, and proceeded to do so.

"And is Carrie aware of this?" said Edwin, following her with Rainbottle, who was delighted to be nosing among trees and bushes again.

"Not at all. She just mentions the houseboat party to the Shrew in a general spirit of idle gossip. Carrie's blissfully oblivious of the Shrew's extracurricular activities, so to speak. As far as Carrie's concerned, Hank's death on the common is just a random act of violence by some unknown thug, she has no idea that Mac ever existed and she's unaware of the sundry attempts on my life."

"What about what happened to Joni?" said Edwin.

"Now Carrie does think *that* is deeply suspicious. In fact, she alerts Alfie to how dodgy it is. But she has no reason to suspect the Shrew. As far as Carrie's concerned, the Shrew's only criminal leanings are in relation to their conspiracy against Alfie. In fact, she's being super-careful about the whole bumping-off-Alfie side of things with the Shrew, so she doesn't spook her."

They were walking among the fragrant foliage of the common with the squirrels and birds noisy above them. It was odd to be back here, where Cordelia had so nearly been slain, and for there not to be any outward sign of it. But there wasn't. It was just a beautiful morning in a beautiful place.

"It's actually quite ironic," said Cordelia. "Carrie never suspected she was in cahoots with someone who was, by then, a seasoned killer."

"And it very nearly proved fatal for her," said Edwin.

"That's right. Because when things start to unravel, the Shrew realises a long-term scam involving Alfie's will simply isn't on the cards anymore. Consequently she decides to loot the ashram's funds and take off on her own. Either there isn't enough swag to share with Carrie, or she's become a problem, or the Shrew's just sick of the sight of her. So bye-bye Carrie."

"If not for us," said Edwin.

"If not for us, yes," said Cordelia. "And, while she's at it, the Shrew decides to eliminate a couple of other people she's deeply pissed off with. Alfie and Howdy Doody. With Alfie, the motive is obvious. And, as far as Howdy is concerned, she's probably been nursing homicidal rage against him for years. Hence onto the hit list they go."

"Along with you," said Edwin.

"No," said Cordelia. "I was an afterthought. Once the Shrew had delivered the poisoned curry to Alfie, she hung around keeping an eye on his place. I reckon she planned to wait until he was in his death throes then go in and gloat over him while he 'dropped the body'."

"Good lord," said Edwin. "How sick."

They strolled for a moment in silence.

Then Cordelia said, "But then she saw you and me turn up. We left again and she must have heaved a sigh of relief. But then, when I came racing back on the bike—"

"I really must pick that up," said Edwin.

"Alfie says it's safe and sound," said Cordelia. "You can collect it when we return the barbecue. Anyway, the Shrew sees me race in to warn Alfie and realises the game is up. Now, she'd brought some weapons with her to supplement the poison curry if necessary. And, given a choice between using them on the extremely big and beefy Alfie, who is now on high alert, and using them on unsuspecting little me, she opts for unsuspecting little me."

"Poor Cordelia," said Edwin, and Rainbottle gave a little whine of sympathy.

"And the Shrew followed me to the station and onto the train, which was simple enough because it was busy and the platform was crowded, and she would have found it easy to conceal herself. When we got here and I set off through the common, she just had to follow me at a discreet distance and wait for her opportunity, which she got when I nipped into the woods for a crafty whiz."

Cordelia stopped walking and Edwin and Rainbottle stopped beside her. "Right around here…" she announced, gratified that, despite a certain amount of getting lost and detouring, she'd timed their arrival to perfectly coincide with her narrative.

"And she attacked you," said Edwin.

Rainbottle made an affronted little sound.

"That's right," said Cordelia. She smiled at Edwin. "Luckily for me, a friend had given me a novelty keyring." She checked that the killer dildo was still in her pocket. It had become a reassuring presence.

"I'm so glad it came in useful," said Edwin modestly.

"But, before I had a chance to use it, she chased me all over the place…" Cordelia led Edwin and Rainbottle through the dense, green undergrowth, past trees wrapped with ivy, nettles lashing at them and vines clutching at their ankles. "This is where I found a fallen branch to use as a weapon."

"Very sensible," said Edwin as they paused to look around.

"Unfortunately, it was rotten and fell apart in my hand."

"Bad luck."

"So I resumed running," said Cordelia.

They started to walk again, Edwin and Rainbottle letting Cordelia lead the way. After a moment of puzzled disorientation that involved circling around, she located the spot. "And found another weapon. Here."

They all stopped and inspected the area.

"And this is where you made your stand," said Edwin.

"Rather a grand word for it, but yes," said Cordelia.

"And you threw your club in her face."

"Another grand word. It was more of a tree branch. But yup."

Edwin looked around. Sunlight filtered through the canopy of leaves above them, falling in pale patches on green leaves and tiny white flowers. "And this is where the Shrew lost her own improvised weapon."

"The bola of death." Cordelia was looking around too. In fact, so was Rainbottle. "It must be around here somewhere, but she wasn't able to find it."

"Well, I'm sure we will," said Edwin.

In the end, it was Rainbottle who found it, lying gleaming between the roots of an ancient oak tree.

They left the common and crossed the road, taking care with Rainbottle, as they headed for the ashram. There in the peace garden, Edwin repaired the wind chimes. He was a practical fellow and good with his hands, and it didn't take long. Cordelia was surprised that, once the bola of death had been restored to its proper place, it just looked like one more innocent chrome component hanging with its fellows, tinkling with random fragmentary music in the gentle breeze.

Cordelia and Edwin sat on a bench and enjoyed looking at it, and listening to it. By special dispensation, Rainbottle had been allowed in with them and lay at their feet.

"So that's that," said Edwin.

"Just about," said Cordelia. "They're still trying to see if they can recoup any of the funds the Silver Shrew absconded with. Meanwhile, Alfie's bankrolling this place."

"He's a generous soul," said Edwin, looking around.

Cordelia shrugged. "Well, after all, he bankrolled it in the first place."

"I suppose so."

"And, I suspect as one of Alfie's conditions for his financial support, Joni has finally been renamed Devika and they're letting her teach lessons."

"She's fully recovered?" said Edwin.

"Fairly fully," said Cordelia. "She's doing better than Carrie, who's still a bit of a mess. But Alfie's looking after her. He's also going to cover any legal fees."

"Legal fees?" said Edwin. "Oh, you mean if she's prosecuted for attempting to kill him and steal his money."

"Yes," said Cordelia. The wind chimes jingled with delicate merriment as a current of air stirred through the garden.

"He really is a very forgiving chap."

"He's smoked way too much weed," said Cordelia. "And that just leaves the Shrew, who's languishing in a prison in Tangier or somewhere, waiting to be shipped back here."

"I can't imagine that's too pleasant for her," said Edwin.

The breeze that was playing the wind chimes drifted through the beds of herbs and carried their fragrance to them as they sat on the bench.

"Apparently she's thriving in prison," said Cordelia.

"Really?"

"She's been making herself useful," said Cordelia. "Useful and popular, apparently." Though it was hard to imagine the Silver Shrew being popular.

"Really? How's that?" said Edwin.

"Teaching the inmates yoga."

"Just so long as they don't let her help in the kitchen," said Edwin.

ACKNOWLEDGEMENTS

Many thanks to Ann Karas for reading early drafts and providing valuable advice. And to the usual gang: Rufus Purdy, George Sandison, Nick Landau and Vivian Cheung at Titan, and my stalwart agents Stevie Finegan and John Berlyne. Thanks always to Ben Aaronovitch.

ABOUT THE AUTHOR

Andrew Cartmel is a novelist and playwright. He is the author of the Vinyl Detective series, which was hailed as "marvellously inventive and endlessly fascinating" by *Publishers Weekly*, as well as the Paperback Sleuth series, which features many of the same characters. His work for television includes a legendary stint as script editor on *Doctor Who*. He has also written plays for the London Fringe and toured as a stand-up comedian. He lives in London with too much vinyl and just enough cats. You can find Andrew on Twitter/X at @andrewcartmel and listen to his weekly radio show, Vinyl Detective Radio, via Medway Pride or Reclaimed Radio.

For more fantastic fiction, author events,
exclusive excerpts, competitions, limited editions and more

VISIT OUR WEBSITE
titanbooks.com

LIKE US ON FACEBOOK
facebook.com/titanbooks

FOLLOW US ON TWITTER AND INSTAGRAM
@TitanBooks

EMAIL US
readerfeedback@titanemail.com